WOLVES & MEN

NATASHA WITTMAN

Bee Creative, Inc.

Published by Bee Creative, Inc.
Oklahoma City, Oklahoma

Copyright © 2014 by Natasha Wittman

All Scriptures are taken from the THE WORLD ENGLISH BIBLE: public domain.

Distributed by Lightning Source, Inc.

For ordering information or special discounts for bulk purchases, please contact Lightning Source, Inc., at 1246 Heil Quaker Blvd, La Vergne, TN USA 37086 (615) 213-5815.

Publisher's Cataloging-In-Publication Data
(Prepared by The Donohue Group, Inc.)

Wittman, Natasha.
    Wolves and men / Natasha Wittman. -- First edition.

 pages : illustrations ; cm

Issued also as an ebook.
ISBN: 978-0-9904091-0-6

 1. Witnesses--Psychology--Fiction. 2. Wildlife refuges--Oklahoma--Fiction. 3. Wolves--Oklahoma--Fiction. 4. Forgiveness--Fiction. 5. Suspense fiction. 6. Bildungsromans. I. Title.

PS3623.I886 W65 2014
813/.6

Cover design by Jesse Owen
Interior design and composition by Kristen Verser

Edited by Callie B. Ferguson

Printed in the United States of America

13 14 15 16 10 9 8 7 6 5 4 3 2 1

First Edition

To someone I never knew and will never forget.

I look forward to meeting you, my precious child,

in heaven some day.

ACKNOWLEDGMENTS

Thank you, Father, for every ounce of inspiration, motivation, talent, and any good that comes from this adventure you set me on over three years ago.

My undying gratitude to my parents for your overwhelming emotional and financial support. I am so blessed to be your daughter.

Thank you to the lovely Callie Ferguson of Bee Creative, Inc. Your inspired work on this project has been vastly underpaid but deeply appreciated. I cannot thank you enough for your brilliant editing, suggestions, and guidance throughout the publishing process, and I shudder to think of what this book would be like without you on board.

Special thanks to Dustin Merritt with Protective Solutions, LLC., for your instruction and knowledge on safe gun handling.

My sincere thanks to the teachers who taught, inspired, and encouraged me as a writer and student so many years ago: Roger Colby and Vickie Kuhnley. Your investment in my education continues to be a blessing to this day.

Special thanks to my husband, Micah, for your enduring love, friendship, patience, optimism, encouragement, and invaluable advice throughout this process. Thank you for coffee dates and adventures through the wilderness, for reading untidy first drafts and listening to me whine, grieve, gush, and ruminate all along the way. You are my best friend and the best One and Only a woman could ask for.

"Only people who are capable of loving strongly can also suffer great sorrow, but this same necessity of loving serves to counteract their grief and heals them."

-Leo Tolstoy, Childhood

PROLOGUE

A thin, brown dust filled the air as it swirled up around my ankles and tucked into the creases and seams of my socks where the playground sand hoarded itself. It scratched my eyes and made my hands feel unclean and crude there under the blinding heat of the afternoon sun. I could feel the sun's unwavering stare as I walked with my nine-year-old friends to the far corner of the playground.

It was hot. It was August in Oklahoma.

My black hair stuck against my neck, wiring its way from the ponytail in several different directions across my face, and I used my dirty hands to pull it away. The skinny, yellow-haired boy yelled something at me, but I ignored him. The last time I'd listened to him, he'd started telling everyone that I was his Indian princess and chased me around to kiss me. He'd tackled me, landing in a pebbly pile of sand that scraped my knees. And then he kissed me and ran off, laughing his skinny-boy laugh.

Walking away from the yellow-haired boy, I followed Beulah, Jadyn, and Sarah across the hard earth. We walked through sparse patches of dying weeds, though the tall ones irritated the backs of my legs with green and brown stickers. I wore long, thick, mauve-colored denim shorts and a white and yellow t-shirt that made my skin look an even darker shade of brown, but not the golden tan of some of the other girls with lighter hair. I thought even at the time that my clothes were quite ugly. But I was nine, so it didn't matter.

We sat down at the very corner of the metal chain-link fence, away from the crowds playing London bridge and that game where everyone pretends to marry someone else. Beulah opened up her lunchbox and unwrapped a clear bag of sliced Italian pepperoni. She had family from Italy or something who had given it to her, so it was very special pepperoni. I liked pepperoni, anyway. It was a good day.

What I remember first and most clearly is hearing the sound of shouting and screaming coming from the parking lot.

From our view in the corner of the playground, we were able to see the school's main building and the portables next to it, with the parking lot of cars filling the space between us. A white man with longish brown hair and a black t-shirt was fighting with this woman who had bright red hair and a short skirt. She was beating her fists against his chest as he wrestled to grab her by the wrists. They were both yelling words clearly, though I had never heard half of them before in my life. They were angry.

We all sat there, heads turned and mouths gaping, and I think I'd already started to cry. All of a sudden, he wrenched out a gun from somewhere in his jeans, and a loud, piercing sound erupted through the air. Despite the loudness of the gunshot and the gasps and screams that succeeded it, I distinctly heard the crunching thud of her elbows and knees and chest and head as they hit the gravelly pavement. I imagined that I could see her eyes open from where I was, but that's probably impossible. Nevertheless, I would see her eyes open and that color—that bright, slowly seeping color they call scarlet—for the rest of my life.

The man cursed some more and turned around to see us and what I'm sure were many other kids on the playground, now in shock. I think there was a teacher at the monkey bars, but she must have been as scared as the rest of us because she didn't move. The man opened the side gate and walked angrily right into the playground. He stopped and looked around for a moment until he saw what he was looking for.

I saw the muscles on his neck bulging slightly through his reddish, freckled skin, even from the distance.

A small girl with dark curly hair was cowering on a bench when he grabbed her by the arm and yanked her across the playground back to the parking lot. They were both gone before anyone responded. And he left in his wake a dead mother with her scarlet blood staining the parking lot pavement and over fifty children who were that day what they call "traumatized." It was a day for learning new words.

The four of us sat there holding each other, crying for our parents who were far away at work or home, unable to hear us or hold us or have any idea what we were feeling. I think that's the first time I learned what evil was and what men could do. And it was a lesson I wouldn't soon forget.

The wickedness of men knows no bounds. It does not stop to consider the lives it destroys; does not feel the pain it inflicts; nor hesitates where it devours. Its appetite is destruction, and its darkness infects wherever it wounds. It prowls through night and day, seeking the weak, the innocent, and the pure. Where it finds beauty, it mars; where it sees life, it poisons; and where there is light, darkness will fall.

And so, that was the day that darkness fell over me like a thick, poisonous cloud.

That was the day that changed everything.

Psalm 13:1-2

How long, Yahweh?

Will you forget me forever?

How long will you hide your face from me?

How long shall I take counsel in my soul,

Having sorrow in my heart every day?

How long shall my enemy triumph over me?

CHAPTER ONE

The gate was black wrought iron with pointed arrows lining the top and small, blunted balls at the tips. There were intricate designs in the welding, encompassing the initials W.B., which left those who entered with the impression of a millionaire's self-indulgence or perhaps an English lord's manor. However, it was neither of these things.

The contorted metal had also been meticulously shaped with extravagant loops and unexpected curves that were evocative of feral vines and wayward branches. But those who were familiar with these woods would remark that the dramatic gate design was appropriate. After all, it had been said by more than one guest that there was a certain air of mystery and a kind of wild vivacity to the wooded property known as Willow's Bend.

"I'M GLAD YOU let me drive you up here," my mom said. "But I wish you'd at least brought a bicycle or...something." My mom's black Taurus slowed to a stop at the top of the winding driveway; the forest surrounded us on all sides now. We both paused before unbuckling, facing the small cabin ahead with interest. It was all lit up in the brilliant light of the setting sun, and the abundant windows reflected the light back at us like great slabs of gold. Somehow, though, I still had the impression that the lights were off and the cabin was empty. It seemed to be silently waiting for me.

"I worked it all out, remember? The landlord will give me a ride into town whenever I want." I turned my head to see my mom at the wheel still gazing at the cabin, the sunset casting her thick, sleek, black hair and bronze forearms in the same golden light. Once again, I couldn't help but think of my mother as the wildly beautiful character of Pocahontas. I had seen her that way in my childhood, but the effect of the sunset only exaggerated and magnified that impression now.

Getting out of the car, I fumbled with the white envelope until the key fell out into my hand. I unlocked the door and stepped inside. The scent of cedar greeted me as I took in the warmly decorated walls, wooden barstools, and worn leather couch and rocking chair next to the woven rugs and dark maroon curtains.

A strange mixture of emotions swept over me like a set of waves. The first was relief. But coming up right behind it, and perhaps swelling even bigger and faster, was fear.

It's over, a voice said. For a moment, the memory seemed to echo off the walls of the cabin. It was almost audible. The past had a way of tricking me into thinking it was the present. And I knew the words were only in my mind. Yet for a moment I could almost smell the scent of the newly carpeted auditorium and the buffet of fruit and coffee.

"ONE CANNOT SAY enough about the art of perseverance," I spoke into the microphone. It was the National Honor Society induction ceremony. My senior year of college had just begun when I was invited to give this speech, and due to my cram-packed schedule, I'd spent most of the previous night memorizing it. I was standing in front of a podium and an auditorium filled with college students, a few professors, and a thin crowd of aging parents. The room was filled with an odd mixture of pride and boredom.

"The virtue of self-discipline, the rewards of ambition..." I continued, sticking to my well-memorized script. But my voice cracked, and I was thirsty. My eyes darted around the room. To one side stood a buffet table of fruit, cheese, punch, and coffee. Despite all efforts to the contrary, I couldn't stop myself from glancing at that food. I'd been on a strict diet of energy drinks, smoothies, and caffeine for months now, and this week in particular had left me feeling more exhausted than I could ever remember. *Steady now.* I took a deep breath and managed to say, "Certainly speak for themselves on a night like tonight."

You might say that this speech had become my new anthem. After all, if anyone was mastering the art of pulling herself up by her bootstraps to get work done, then surely it was Charlotte Benson. I spoke on authority. My body was my slave. I could do anything. I reminded myself of these things as I guided my eyes back to the onlooking crowd. But lately, my mind was prone to wander. And what's more, my mouth was prone to water. I swallowed hard.

"The key to success, then, lies in learning..." I managed to speak clearly, though I paused to clutch harder onto the sides of the podium. Even my wrists felt weak as I struggled to keep my balance under the harsh, bright lights of the auditorium. I obviously needed to pull myself together.

"That even when everyone around us is telling us to give up, to quit, or that it's over..." I paused for dramatic effect. "*We. Keep. Going!*"

And then everyone clapped.

Or, at least, I like to think everyone *would have* clapped.

"MS. BENSON?" I opened my eyes to see a mixture of furrowed brows and worried looks forming a circle around me. My eyes rested on one of the professors, Dr. Stanley, who peered down at me over his gold-rimmed spectacles. I cringed as I tried to sit up, but I couldn't. It occurred to me that it was a good thing the room had just been re-carpeted. I was always thinking absurd thoughts at times like these.

Without budging, I moved my eyes toward Dr. Stanley again, as he seemed to be saying something. My vision swam dangerously as I tried to make out his facial features amid the sea of blurry spectators. *Did I really just pass out?* I thought.

"Ms. Benson," Dr. Stanley repeated. This time I heard him. I strained my eyes to meet his intense gaze. "I'm afraid *it's over.*"

It would take me a long time to understand the full meaning of that last statement.

"WHEN YOU'RE FINISHED, do you want to join me on the porch?"

I lifted up my head to peer across the countertop at my mom. I had just started putting my groceries into the fridge, and my arms had already begun throbbing with exhaustion. "Sure, I'll be right out," I replied. I heaved a large glass pitcher onto the countertop, watching my mom's homemade lemonade slosh around against the glass. I wasn't sure how it had survived the bumpy ride through the countryside, but it had.

Here I was still processing Dr. Stanley's words two weeks after my life had succinctly fallen apart. My life had taken a sudden u-turn after passing out at that ceremony, and I hadn't yet decided whether or not I was depressed. Even now I cringed at the memory of that catastrophic experience, and the sense of defeat and mortification swept over me once more.

Although I had vehemently refused to ride in the ambulance the university had called, I couldn't turn down Dr. Stanley's insistence to drive me directly to the hospital. After what I thought was merely a routine checkup to spare the school any legal liability, I was floored to hear the doctor's diagnosis. He informed me that I was malnourished, underweight, and on a fast track toward developing a serious eating disorder. I was stunned to think that just because I'd been losing a little weight everyone treated me like I was neurotic. What was wrong with everyone?

For the days following the diagnosis, I fought hard to convince myself that I was fine and insisted that everyone around me was overreacting. My parents, teachers, and friends all took a part in persuading me to take a sabbatical from school and the café to work through my issues, to "take a breather," as my father put it. But it was my college counselor who informed me that I would be relieved of all of my extracurricular roles and workload whether I left school or not.

Talk about humiliating. I was supposed to graduate in December with honors. I couldn't believe this was happening to me. After all of the hard work and service I'd done for the school and the community, this was the thanks I got. I just couldn't understand it.

In the end, I think it was my pot-smoking coworker who finally got through to me. He called that week to give me a speech about taking proper care of my health. Something about that conversation raised a red flag in my mind. So I began to consider that perhaps it was I, rather than everyone around me, who might be wrong. My parents eagerly encouraged me to move back in with them, but I just couldn't do it. It seemed like it would be too easy to fake it there. If I had to take a break, I decided, I would do it right. The problem was I didn't know *how* to do it right.

Thankfully my old literature teacher from high school heard what happened and told my mom about the Ouachita Writer's Corp, where her nephew, Danny, had a cabin to rent out. My grandparents graciously offered to put up rent for me for as long as I needed, so I agreed to give it a try.

My cabin was in a small, gated wildlife refuge area called Willow's Bend, tucked deep in the heart of Wild Oak Forest, next to the Ouachita Mountains. That's where my mom and I hauled three luggage bags, a blank journal, and a new pair of running shoes, and that's where I'd be making my home indefinitely.

After putting away the last of the groceries, I had to lean against the kitchen island to catch my breath. I was dizzy again. It would seem that my body didn't fully register how weak and tired I was until that very convincing moment on the floor of the auditorium. And since then, I couldn't believe how weak my body felt. The least bit of exertion left me feeling like I'd just run a 5k.

I poured two tall glasses of lemonade before heading outside. I sat down next to my mom on the darkened front porch swing. We listened to the late summer sounds of the cicadas lifting and lowering their chorus in rounds.

"You've got a long journey ahead, you know," my mom said softly.

I handed her a glass. "Are you kidding? I just got here."

"You know what I mean," she replied. "But this is good. This is going to be really good for you. I just know it."

"Well, I hope so. It's not like I have a choice though, is it? I have to deal with things now or keep suffering the consequences." Thinking back, that was pretty much exactly the way my therapist, Dr. Morgan, had put it for me a week ago.

"You will do it. I know you will." However, the tone in her voice revealed uncertainty rather than conviction.

We fell back into silence, letting nature take over around us as the porch swing creaked forward and backward and forward again.

"Do you remember when you were a little girl and I told you that you had a secret name?"

I laughed in spite of the seriousness in her voice. " You told me a lot of things when I was a little girl. Like that time you said I was a princess."

"Well, you're God's princess. That wasn't a lie."

I thought about all the times I begged her to tell me my secret name. I even tried to trick her into it once, using a yo-yo to try to hypnotize her. She obliged me by walking around our house like a zombie but wouldn't give up the information I so desperately wanted.

"Atsila," she said softly. My nostalgic reverie was shattered by that one word.

"Excuse me?"

"Your secret name is Atsila."

I wasn't sure how to feel about it as I processed this new information. The idea of having a secret name as a little girl was incredibly intriguing. Now I wasn't sure how to feel about it or what it was supposed to mean to me anymore.

"Oh, okay," I answered at last, noticing that my mom's eyes were hard and probing. "I was kind of hoping for something more like Tigerlily, to be completely honest."

To my surprise, my mom rolled her eyes before replying. "Atsila means fire. I knew the day you were born that you were fierce and bright like the sun——"

Interrupting her, I sort of snorted into my glass of lemonade. I couldn't help it. I'd never heard anything so ridiculous in my life. "Geez, Mom. That must've been quite a disappointment for you." I laughed but tasted a familiar bitterness on my lips. The swing suddenly stopped moving.

My mom set her glass down on the porch and folded her arms across her chest, the way she did years ago when I was in trouble. "It's not a joke, Charlotte. Atsila." Her voice was stern now. "And you have not been a disappointment. Don't say anything like that ever again. Do you understand me?"

"Mom, I was just——"

"I'm serious. Your heart is fierce, Atsila." I blinked again at the sound of being called something other than my name. "You've spent your life living in fear because of something tragic that happened a long time ago. And as if that wasn't bad enough, you haven't even tried to move on from this new tragedy."

My fingers began to tremble at the mere hint of what had happened nearly two years ago. My mom's voice had been quavering until she stopped and turned away from me with one hand covering her mouth. I thought I detected a tiny gasp, the kind mothers make when they're about to cry. I looked away from her face, away from her warm, flushed cheeks and trembling frown and distorted beauty. Instead I stared steadily out at the sky with its abysmal blackness and dark blues that nearly veiled the subtle outlines of the trees.

And for a moment, instead of trying to understand what my mother—this slowly aging Pocahontas—felt, I grew angry. *Who is she grieving for?* I asked silently. *Who has she lost?* And then I remembered what the answer was.

Me.

Her voice continued, steadier this time. "But you will rise above all of it. I am certain."

I stared hard into the abyss. I was stubborn but feeling myself cracking at the edges. I felt my mom's firm gaze and sensed that her features were whole again. That she had somehow, magically, healed herself in those few seconds of silence. And I marveled at her strength.

Though my eyes were trained on the horizon, on the distance, I felt my mother's eyes just as surely as I had when I was a child, dangling my toes off the edge of the coffee table because I thought I could fly. There seemed to be something in the air between us begging the question: *Will you jump?* But so much time had passed, so much had happened since then. I tilted my head back and drained my glass like whisky.

She began again, "I need you to know that, no matter what happens, this is who you really are. You are strong, brave, and bright like the sun in the sky. Deep down, you are a blazing fire that no one and nothing in this world can put out. I need you to promise me you'll always remember that. Promise me you'll accept that and walk in the truth, no matter what."

Just then, I heard the wind as it sent a breeze through the cedars and maples and their crowded limbs across the lawn. I couldn't see but rather sensed that those leaves were flung upward like damp paper by some careless hand. They sailed invisibly across the darkened grass in great swirls and arcs, clumsy and forgotten. Finally they tumbled down, making their papery scuffling sounds, and settled down onto the night-covered earth. The disappearing sun seemed to sink yet again, just a minuscule movement beneath the horizon, which was probably just my imagination. But in my heart, I felt that it had sunk nonetheless.

"I promise."

Dear Heart,

Why have you gone from me? Why do you return to me in my dreams, only to fade again with the rising of the sun? You know that I would follow you anywhere, if only I could. Each day brings a new devastation, a new disappointment. A new torture to every fiber of my being. A new emptiness. Dear Heart, are you here? Are you somehow with me still?

— R.A.

THE ALARM CLOCK next to my bed read nine thirty. I glared down at it as I recalled that it had been set to go off an hour and a half ago. I was late.

After pulling on my sweats and t-shirt, I had to sit back down on the bed to catch my breath. I was dizzy yet again. I could scarcely wake up without a full ten hours of sleep these days. And after the conversation with my mom the night before, I seemed to be even more exhausted than ever.

I stood up and looked into the full-length mirror on the door. And I frowned. I couldn't get over how much my reflection now differed from photos of myself even just a year ago. For the first time, I knew that I was seeing what everyone else had been so concerned about. My hair was thinner than it had ever been before, long, limp, and brittle. My clothes were visibly too big for me, and my body seemed to lack any sign of feminine curves. My face looked startlingly thin and bony, with a slightly purple tinge beneath my eyes and high cheek bones that protruded against my skin.

I tried to smile at my reflection, but the effort was pathetic and scared me a little. I wondered how I had missed so many glaring signs before... How could I have been so blind? I looked for the answer in my amber brown irises, but all I saw was vacancy between the bones. Perhaps I'd just been too busy to notice.

I sighed before remembering that my new landlord was probably furious with me. Or perhaps he'd just gone home after waiting ten minutes. I stepped into my new pair of running shoes, which I'd bought just before making the drive to Willow's Bend. I told myself they were supposed to symbolize something, though I wasn't sure exactly what. The shoes felt stiff but snug as I traipsed down the short hallway amid its parade of framed pictures of trees and bears against the cedar walls. I passed the kitchen area, which needed remodeling when it came to the linoleum countertops and outdated microwave. But everything smelled like wood. I breathed it in deeply.

Past the kitchen was the dining room with a wide set of floor-to-ceiling windows that formed a rounded nook. Even as I passed by, I could see that the view overlooked the sloping terrain that led to the winding driveway. I walked up to the heavy, oak front door. Peering through the peephole, I wasn't too surprised when I didn't see anyone waiting for me.

Upon opening the door, though, I heard an affectionate voice cooing to my left. "Oh, yes, you are such a good boy, aren't you?" And I saw an athletic twenty-something bent over on the porch bench as he scratched the furry, white belly of a panting collie. Two other dogs barked higher pitched yips when they saw me, and the stranger immediately stopped and looked up as well.

"Charlotte?" he asked, standing up quickly and walking toward me with a lopsided grin. He wore a dark green cap, well worn at the edges and a little dirty. His shoes were of the hiking variety and somehow went well with his khaki shorts and gray polo. Something about the way he moved reminded me of the dogs and their enthusiastic greeting.

"Uh, yes," I answered, timidly, fending off one of the dogs who had jumped up to put his or her muddy paws all over my t-shirt.

"I'm Danny. It's nice to meet you. I hope you don't mind, I went ahead and fed 'em for you." He indicated the three canines who were stumbling over one another to sniff me. For a moment, I wondered if Danny was about to start sniffing too. But before I could answer him, he continued in his fast-paced manner, "I meant to warn you about the alarm clock. It occurred to me 'round nine fifteen when I was sittin' out here alone that maybe that's why you weren't out here yet." He laughed amiably.

"Well, I'm so sorry I made you wait," I answered. "I feel terrible." *Or at least I would, if I was awake,* I thought.

He waved a hand in dismissal, saying, "Don't worry 'bout it. I should have included that in the note I left you. Did you have any trouble gettin' in?"

I remembered the envelope of information he'd left in the mailbox at the edge of the long driveway. "No, everything was fine."

"So you have the key then? And the code on the lock box didn't give you any trouble? I once had a tenant who broke through the back window just to get in. Didn't think twice about it, just started prying it apart. Helluva lot of work gettin' it fixed. Course, I prob'ly should of expected that sort of thing from a man who writes mystery novels for a living." He muttered this part quietly, perhaps more to himself than to me, before perking right back up. "You know, some people have trouble with the kitchen sink too, but if you give the faucet a good hard thump, it'll loosen right up." I had no idea what he was talking about. But I just nodded anyway as I silently wondered if he was always this intense.

"Yeah, hey, would you mind if we had some coffee?" I offered.

"I'd love that. You know, I haven't had any yet this mornin'." My eyebrows were raised high as I let him pass me through the doorway to the kitchen, and I tried not to cough on his musky cologne.

"Listen," he began again. "If you still have that map I left you, we can decide how long of a tour you want since there's so much ground to cover."

I agreed and left the room to search for the map I'd grabbed the night before. A few minutes later, I came back down the hallway yawning.

I looked eagerly around the kitchen as I smelled the distinct and ever-welcome scent of coffee. My eyes rested on a light steam emitting from an antique-looking metallic contraption.

"I started the coffee. Hope you don't mind," Danny said.

"Great, but what is *that*?" I asked, pointing the map in my hand toward the contraption.

"It's a percolator. You know, a coffeemaker? All the cabins we lease have one." I walked up to the tall, shining piece of metal with a spout projecting out of one side and a glass lid perched on top. I could see something sloshing around inside as it made its guttural *bok-pe-cock* sounds, like there was a hungry chicken down in there.

"Oh, and uh, before I forget," he said, pulling a folded-up newspaper out of his back pocket and tossing it onto the counter next to the phone, "I drop off a complimentary paper for all my tenants once a week. Some writers say it helps when the writer's block sets in, and I have a deal with the paper."

"The wildlife refuge has a paper?" I asked skeptically.

He chuckled before responding, "It's the county newspaper. Their office is just a few miles outside the refuge, and they sometimes cover Willow's Bend's news. Not that anything happens 'round here, quite frankly."

I opened one of the cedar cabinet doors and retrieved a simple, sleek, ebony mug. I held it thoughtfully in my hand as I walked up to the windows, inhaling the ever-present cedar aroma, and took in the picturesque scene: Tall sycamores towered above, intermingling on the property with firs and cedar and pine. A thick fog hovered amid the tree trunks so that I could just make out the timber that lined the winding driveway.

I heard a *tap, tap, tap*, and my eyes instantly located a woodpecker hammering into the white and gray trunk of a birch. A red hummingbird feeder was dangling at the top right-hand corner of the window.

"I think your coffee's ready, Ma'am," Danny said, with a jovial tone, calling my attention away from the landscape. I was surprised to see that he was wearing a gentle smile.

"Great," I answered. He picked up the percolator and reached out his hand. "So do you know much about the other tenants?" I asked, handing my mug to him. His hands were nice, I noticed, with a foray of freckles trekking down to his wrists. A series of colorful threaded bracelets stretched across the width of his forearm.

"Yeah, but none of them are half as mysterious as you are." He poured my coffee and held the steaming mug out to me. I stood there wide-eyed for a moment before accepting the mug. He cleared his throat and looked away before continuing. His words came out slower this time. "I think you're the only one here who didn't exactly come just because you wanted to. You had a pretty impressive track record though, I have to admit. Before things went south, I mean."

"Listen, Danny, I—." My eyes fell to the floor, mortified. One thing I had hoped to leave behind on this trip was my reputation. "I really don't—"

"Don't wanna talk about it?" I looked back up to see a pained expression in his dark brown eyes. "I'm sorry," he continued. "It's not my place..." But his words trailed off toward the end.

"You know, this thing is useless out here, right?" He'd turned around and walked back to the countertop where I'd left my cell phone. "You can't get service out here. Have to use the good ol' land line." He hitched his thumb toward the bright red corded phone that was attached to the kitchen wall beneath a floral calendar.

"Oh I, uh, didn't know that." I sipped some of the hot coffee as I tried to figure out how I could have missed this particular detail. I wasn't even certain I would have agreed to stay in a cabin alone if I'd known I couldn't use my cell.

"There's a list of contacts in the first drawer by the phone," Danny said, perhaps sensing my unease. "The police department, the ranger's station, poison control, and most importantly, my number." He winked, causing me to laugh out loud, unexpectedly. "But I'll be checking in from time to time, making sure rent gets paid and, you know, you're alive and everything."

"Good to know," I muttered before blowing on the hot coffee.

We spent the next fifteen minutes in the dining room as I sipped from my mug and Danny hummed "Blue Eyes Crying in the Rain," sounding uncannily like Willie Nelson. When he wasn't humming, he was talking animatedly about our tour. We briefly went over the map together, which revealed that Willow's Bend was remarkably larger than I had imagined. Since I had no plans to explore the many other sections of Wild Oak, I decided to keep the tour within the gated refuge after all.

Eventually we climbed into Danny's Tacoma and started out down the sloping driveway with the windows rolled down, listening to the crunch of the gravel, sticks, and bright auburn leaves beneath the tires. Every now and then, Danny would mutter something like, "I knew we'd never meet again," and, "only memories remain."

Danny later switched his melody to "Bonaparte's Retreat," which reminded me of my grandpa and some old riffs he'd play on his harmonica. As Danny broke in and out of song, I admitted to myself that he was actually kind of charming, even given the slight southern drawl and cologne and everything.

We drove out south toward the main entrance, back the way I'd come in the night before. While Willow's Bend had several entrances into the refuge, the main entrance led out closer to the bigger town nearby and the interstate.

"You heard any history on this place?" Danny asked, sending me a sidelong glance. He'd raised his voice as the sound of the wind picked up around us. I shook my head, my hair whipping violently in front of my face all the while. "Well, the entire refuge used to belong to a wealthy family about a hundred years ago. There used to be a mansion in the northeastern corner, where the family threw these unbelievable parties. I mean, the works."

"Is it still here—the mansion?" I interrupted. I loved old houses. There was something incredibly poetic about old mansions. Maybe it was all that nostalgia that seemed to emanate from those historical structures.

"Unfortunately, the house caught on fire nearly fifty years ago. Terrible tragedy..." Danny shook his head at the windshield. "The house was burned to the ground. No survivors."

There was a moment of reverent silence hanging thick in the air as Danny followed the road's snaking path. We hit a bump in the road that made me instinctively reach out to the handle above my window. Danny continued, "What's strange is that the property was inherited by the gardener, who in turn sold nearly everything to the state. Of course, he did have the mansion rebuilt from the ground up, but uh...nothing's really being done with it these days. And it's not exactly open for exhibition."

"Can we go there first anyway?" I asked. I had a sudden urge to be on the same ground as such an intriguing part of history. "Maybe the owner will let us look around?"

Danny laughed unexpectedly. "I'm afraid that's not possible. The guy's one of those very private types. He wouldn't want us snooping around." His face grew very serious again. "Especially me."

"Why you?"

He hesitated, casting a nervous glance my way, but finally answered, "I guess you could say we used to be pretty close. But uh, somethin' happened, and he decided I wasn't worth talking to anymore. Decided most people weren't, actually."

"That's a shame," I muttered. A few minutes passed by as I slowly gave up on visiting the historical mansion on our tour.

"Of course, if you're really that desperate, you could always sign up for shooting lessons," Danny said. "I figure he'd probably speak to you if you were paying him to lecture you about shotguns and pistols, since that's his job and everything."

"Ah. No, thank you." I looked out the window, avoiding Danny's gaze.

"Hey, I have an idea," Danny said.

I turned back to see him smile at me before he wheeled the truck around at a crossroad and we headed in a different direction. I tried to keep tabs of where we were on the map as he drove.

We ended up at the eastern side of the property overlooking the Otter River. Danny pulled the truck up to the side of the road right next to a large stone bridge.

"The site of the mansion is a quarter mile the other way, but I reckon this is the best view in Willow's Bend."

As we walked across the bridge, a flock of geese ascended the surface of the water in the distance, fanning the air as their long black necks gave way to a peek of white at the jawline, reminding me of Catholic priests. "This is incredible," I muttered breathlessly.

We leaned against the railing on the bridge and looked down between the two sides of the river with its wide curves and bends as it meandered toward the southwest. The late morning sunlight gave the river a nostalgic glow as it hit the water with its innumerable ripples and prismatic reflections. By the water's edge, wide cypress trunks sprawled out in numerous clusters, with their thick-banded multicolored rings hinting at high waters and floods in years past.

Around the bend I could just make out something emerging on the water. As it came nearer into view, I saw that it was a long, thin boat of men, rowing in perfect synchronization with their tall, broad backs sailing swiftly toward us. I heard a deep voice call out orders as they went, the sound of it intermingling with the cawing of geese and trilling of the waterfowl.

"You do not have to be good," Danny said softly. He had moved in close beside me, and the nearness of his voice startled me. But his eyes were trained on the distance. I recognized the lines of Mary Oliver's poem "Wild Geese." His voice carried over the water delicately, then trailed off, as though he wasn't certain if he should continue. Then he picked it back up again, reciting the rest of the first stanza of the poem.

While I loved Oliver's writing style, I had always thought there was something conflicting in her words. Danny's voice was imbued with such conviction and an almost reverent devotion as he spoke of cruel repentance and easy love... I can't explain why, but it sounded profoundly sad to me in the midst of such pristine and almost religious beauty.

"Tell me about despair, yours, and I will tell you about mine," I answered, continuing the poem. But I stopped there, training my eyes on his until he finally looked back at me and smirked.

But he didn't tell me of his despair. He kind of laughed instead, taking a measured step away from me. And the sound of his laughter was empty. Then he said, "There's nothing like talking philosophy on a bridge with a poet. It's a beautiful poem, don't you think?" For a moment I couldn't believe this was the same landlord I'd met an hour ago—the same youthful, chatty guy who imitated Willie Nelson so well.

"It is beautiful. But not all that glitters is gold," I answered, remembering the Thomas Gray poem about the cat drowning in the bowl of goldfish. I'd recited the poem in high school, and the image had always stayed with me.

"Oh, admit it. Isn't that what you came here for? To walk on your knees through Willow's Bend? Well, you aren't the first. Some of 'em may never leave." He turned his back to the rowing crew now, letting his gaze land somewhere toward the top of that historic hill that loomed up over us, shrouded in trees and mystery.

That's when I saw a glimpse of a house's white balcony between the treetops. And for a moment, I thought I saw someone back away from the railing. But whatever it was, it was gone before I could be certain of anything.

The rowers were nearing our bridge, with that deep voice calling out orders all along the way. And the geese had made their way back again, with their sleek necks and graceful faces cloaked in sable. A loon waded closer to the bridge, nibbling at its tawny feathers in the back.

"No," I finally answered. "I came to love what I love. What my soul loves." Even as I spoke the words I wasn't entirely certain what they meant. And what's more, I was surprised by them. But once they were out there, I knew that they were true. This is what I'd come for. Healing, rest, the rediscovery of a certain rightness that I couldn't quite put my finger on... that evasive, ethereal concept of home. *Sehnsucht*, perhaps. *My soul's true home. To love what my soul loves.* Something like that.

"You know, most women just swoon," Danny muttered before drifting away from the rail. The rowers had stopped rowing and leaned back as they glided beneath our bridge and the shadows fell off their grinning faces one by one. Their voices broke into song, singing verses of "Danny Boy" as they drifted by. I heard myself laugh out loud as Danny scowled down at them.

As we walked back across the bridge, Danny resumed his former nonchalance, saying, "We see a lot of the OCU rowing team, not to mention people comin' on break to canoe and kayak... By the way, I have a tandem in case you're ever interested." I saw that a playful grin had returned to his lips.

"Thanks," I answered, evasively. "You know, I never would have guessed that you'd studied poetry."

"Oh, I never *have* studied poetry," he replied. "Just women."

I shot him a disdainful look. But I wasn't sure I believed him. "Listen, are you sure we can't walk back toward the house? You could stay in the truck if he hates you that much."

"Like I said, the place isn't open for visitors," he answered. I thought he sounded a bit evasive though. "Besides, poets are supposed to go on long walks, and you can see it for yourself if it means that—"

He was interrupted with a series of gunshots that erupted through the air. I hit the ground immediately.

And stayed there.

Danny reached a hand down toward me, but before I could accept it, another shot rang out in the distance, causing me to recoil.

"Are you okay?" he asked. But he was laughing as he said it.

"No!" I answered hotly. I finally took hold of his hand and stood up, looking around for where the noise was coming from. It must have been a ways off, but it was unnerving nonetheless.

"It's up the hill," he said. "The shooting range is on the north end, over that hill."

"Can't you make them stop?" I asked angrily. I winced as another shot was fired. The sound wasn't terribly loud, but I couldn't help shuddering every time I heard it. It was an annoying reflex.

Danny laughed again. "Don't worry. You're safe down here. Come on, let's get out of here."

As we climbed back into Danny's truck, I couldn't keep my eyes from glaring up at the hill. Danny turned the truck around, and we headed back west, the way we came.

"Charlotte, you're shaking," Danny muttered. I glanced down at my hands to see that he was right. "Something tells me you're not a huge fan of the second amendment."

"I guess you could say that," I replied. But I had never organized my feelings into any political theories. Gunshots brought back vivid memories and long-buried fears. It had been a prominent goal in my life to avoid them.

The trees formed a canopy around us, completely obscuring any lingering view of the mansion. I breathed a heavy sigh as the sound of gunshots died out in the distance. I felt safe at last.

"Are you okay?" Danny was glancing at me again as he drove. I nodded back. "Just stay clear of that part of the woods, and you'll be fine."

And that's when I lost all interest in the history of the old Willow Mansion.

CHAPTER TWO

"I went to the woods because I wished to live deliberately, to front only the essential facts of life, and see if I could not learn what it had to teach, and not, when I came to die, discover that I had not lived."

—*Henry David Thoreau*

It was five o'clock in the morning when I put on a cup of coffee. The sun wouldn't be rising for at least two more hours, but here I was listening to the percolator and the light rain that hit the dining room windows. I laid the blank journal out on the table and turned to the first page. The blue ink painted the page in what I intended to be a bold, confident scrawl. I dated the entry at the top and then began writing below.

Had another one of those dreams. The face underwater with the light shining through and lighting it up in fractured lines and glowing prisms. It was a boy, maybe. Probably. A face I've never seen before. Not sure why he's following me or what this means. It wasn't Gavin, at least not Gavin when I met him. Could it have been Gavin as a little boy? Today I intend to be better, to go places, to do things, and leave these dreams behind.

I signed my name at the bottom and closed the journal with a sense of accomplishment. I poured my cup of coffee and ate my breakfast. Then I just sat there staring out the window and listening to the soft melody of rain *pat-patting* against the windows ahead of me. I took in that sound and the beauty of the rich reds, browns, and evergreens that stood before me like a very large, very elaborate painting created just for my enjoyment. And I suddenly had a good feeling about this whole refuge thing. I had a good feeling about Willow's Bend.

During our tour, I agreed to only wander the countryside with one of those gorgeous collies around. Although I wasn't afraid of the woods, Danny reminded me of the unpredictability of wildlife in the refuge. After all, in addition to healthy populations of coyote, deer, prairie dogs, and buffalo, it was also common to run into snakes and tarantulas in the woods of Willow's Bend. However, Danny insisted that the dogs kept the wilderness safe. They could handle anything, he said.

At my cabin, there were two collies and a border collie. One of the collies was named Charles, with a bulky tan and white coat, and the other was Hamlet, who looked similar. I was told that Charles was Hamlet's big brother. The border collie was slightly smaller than the two and was black, white, and tan. Her name was Cleo. They were all beautiful and friendly, though Charles and Cleo were more protective, and Hamlet was a bit rambunctious. I was thankful to have all three of them around.

After all, it wasn't as easy as I thought it would be, being alone in the quiet with my thoughts. I felt like a stark naked firefighter walking into a house of flames. I felt unprepared, inadequate, and afraid. So I clung to their company.

Eventually though, I did start to get the hang of things. I began by making every effort to get back into shape. I took walks every day. Then I stretched them into longer, faster walks with the dogs, down the winding driveway and past the others converging off the main gravel road. My goal was to take up running again. But in those first couple of weeks, I had to think smaller. I ate healthy meals and got plenty of rest, and pretty soon I was already able to see some improvement in my appearance. I was finally beginning to recognize myself.

One morning I was down at the creek, pulling my hooded sweatshirt off as the air warmed up around me. The weather had been back and forth since I'd been there, and though it had cooled off through the night, it would be hot again by noon. I'd jogged for the first time that morning and already found gravity to be a fickle friend. I sat on the edge of the creek to catch my breath, looking down between the two slopes and observing the quiet monotony of the green-brown water and moss and tiny spiders sailing across the surface.

Charles and Hamlet wandered up to me with a bit of mud on the whites of their coats and soil on their noses, exhaling in that jovial way dogs have with excited little puffs of pungent breath and bluish-pink tongues lapping out. I wrapped an arm around Hamlet, who was sitting down on his haunches closest to me, and smoothed my hand up and down his tufted fur, which was still damp from the morning dew. I tugged at a sticker caught in his fur and looked into those golden brown eyes of his. One puffy tan eyebrow seemed to cock this way, then that as his head turned from side to side, puffing all along.

"They were wrong, you know," I said while trying to catch his meandering gaze. "I had everything under control." I let myself fall back onto the ground, with the sticks and leaves poking at my spine through my cotton shirt, and silently wondered if it did any good at all to lie to myself.

I looked up through the underbellies of the birches and cypresses surrounding the creek. "Charles, do you think I'm crazy?"

Before I had time to imagine his reassuring answer, I was startled by a sound just a few yards away. I sat up and jerked around to see a man with a long gray beard and heavy layers of brown clothing appear through the bushes and branches. I wondered how long he'd been there, as he seemed to be frowning straight at me through that tangled beard of his. He slowly turned away from me.

I thought I heard him mumble something as he went, but all I could make out was "highfalutin," as he chuckled, coughed, and wheezed his way back up the hill and out of view. Whatever it was, he was probably right. I pulled at the twigs and dead leaves from my hair as I looked after him.

I got up and walked back up the road and across the rocky terrain in the direction of my cabin. Quickening my pace, I began to jog. My muscles felt stubborn and lethargic as I moved. I pushed myself along in a constant state of frustration that I couldn't run faster. I finally settled into a slower pace and aimed for endurance and stamina instead. It was a bizarre sensation, this running without fear. This so-called jogging. This slower, sometimes excruciatingly slower pace. I felt sweat begin to trickle down my back just as a merciful breeze rushed through the fiery-colored trees, sending out ripples of relief against my neck and shoulders amid the hum of stirring insects.

I began to feel a rhythm in my pace at last and kind of let myself ride it out like a current, ignoring the increasing burning sensation in my calves and thighs. I forced my breathing into slower, steadier cadences and focused all my energy on orchestrating my body to do this single thing well: keep moving.

I veered off to the right at the last second when I came to a fork in the road. Feeling somehow stronger than I had five minutes ago, I decided on a detour to prolong my workout.

Before I knew it, I rounded a corner, finding myself running parallel with the river. I heard voices in the distance above the water's rushing melody. I passed through a copse of trees to see a group of people, swimsuit clad, standing at the edge of the bank next to several kayaks that were propped halfway in the water. There were six college-age girls and two guys talking animatedly. The girls erupted into laughter at something one of the guys said. I kept running.

"Charlotte, wait up!" I recognized that familiar, southern dialect.

I slowed down and gradually came to a stop, taking the chance to catch my breath. Danny ran up beside me.

"Hey, I thought that was you."

I looked up and wiped a sheen of sweat from my forehead with the back of my forearm. I kept breathing hard and waited for him to start talking, as I knew he would.

"Well, you're lookin' better already," he continued. "I was a little afraid you weren't gonna eat. And then you'd just blow away in that great Oklahoma wind of ours."

"It's always a definite possibility," I admitted between breaths. And this was true. Especially during tornado season. "But thanks." I smiled as I stood up straighter and looked back at the girls stumbling into kayaks. I squinted at the can in the grasp of the girl closest to us.

"Geez, don't you have a rule against that? Kayaking under the influence?"

"I'm sure we do," Danny admitted. "It's a weekend job."

I threw him a doubtful look for a few seconds, punctuated only by my labored breathing.

"Well, more of a hobby, actually." Danny chuckled awkwardly, shifting his weight where he stood and reaching one arm out to lean against a tree trunk. "You see, my buddy Sean needed help. There's a huge bus of cheerleaders that came down, and he just needed someone to—"

"You don't have to explain it to me," I cut in. "Philosophy on the bridge, remember? Wild geese. I get it."

Danny looked down at his feet, smirking.

"Danny, dude, are ya comin' or what?" Sean yelled toward us. The girls were splashing around in the water and screaming at the chill as they fumbled with faded neon life jackets and bikini strings.

I slowly turned and started to jog back the way I'd come, leaving that scene with all its tired clichés behind.

"Mind if I join you a ways?" I was startled to see that Danny was following me.

"Just try to keep up."

Half an hour later, we were sitting on the steps of my cabin's front porch, trying to catch our breath. I had made it my ambition to run hard and fast enough to keep him from talking along the way. I had nearly succeeded.

"So, uh, why didn't you go with them?" I asked at last. "It's a wild bird's dream, isn't it?"

He laughed. "You're never gonna let me forget that, are you?" I shook my head before he continued. "Well, let's see... There you were, joggin' so gracefully down the straight and narrow path..."

We both laughed.

"And I said to myself..." he paused. His gaze grew serious for a moment. But then he shrugged. "Well, I don't remember what it was, but it was damn philosophical. And deep."

"Hmmm..." I breathed into the buzzing forest before us. I looked beside me to where he sat with his hands clasped in front of his chest, forearms balanced against his knees, gazing downward at the wooden steps. "I don't know..." I continued. "Perhaps you felt like changing directions?"

At this, he laughed. "You know, you remind me of someone I used to know." But his voice was weighted with sadness.

"Oh really?" I muttered as I watched the shadows dance in the light on the grains of wood. A red wasp swooped down in front of us, causing me to lean one way and then another, but it mercifully left us alone.

Danny turned to me with an intense look on his face. "Charlotte, life is so short. It's just so damn short." I remember that there was a great deal of pain swimming in his dark brown eyes. And it was all too familiar.

"Yeah, yeah it is," I agreed. But in my mind, I was thinking about how it so often felt terribly, terribly long.

I GLANCED OUT the dining room window as I tied my shoes with cold fingers and prepared for a long walk. A cold front had blown down through the countryside, and so the air felt as though all the moisture had evaporated from the world. My hands had taken on that red and purple tone that occurs in colder weather, the skin there feeling stretched and stiff as I tugged on shoelaces in the golden morning light. The early October sky was clear and bright, so I was counting on warmer weather throughout the day.

I stepped out the door, casting one last glance around the tiny cabin. It seemed bare and slightly drooping as I walked away from the heavy curtains and plantation shutters, the silent planks of wood, and flannel throws. On one living room wall had been hung a collage of shabby woodland pictures, which, ironically, managed to echo nothing of the majestic beauty that surrounded the cabin.

Closing the creaking door behind me, I faced the crisp wind and soon felt the crunch of gravel as my shoes hit the ground. Charles and Cleo followed closely behind, trotting through crunchy leaves, though at times running into my legs to be petted and playing games with one another along the way.

I fingered the map in my pocket as I walked, but I was in the mood to wander. At some point, I decided that I would make my goal the Corner Store, several miles out, to pick up a few things. I headed south and east, veering off from my road to a narrower path that I knew would intersect with the main road later on.

As I walked, I watched and listened to the quiet awakening of the world around and above me. The yellowbellied larks and tame robins with umber-colored breast; the scurrying of hares; and even the occasional spotted fawn, making its graceful leaps, cocking head to the left, ever cautious in its gait—they all contributed to the symphony. As the morning wore on, I took in the humming of the mosquitoes still lingering in the air—seemingly caught up in the not quite warm, not yet cold ambiguity of autumn.

The woods were full of vibrant hues dangling from limbs and being cast off into the brush below. The brilliant scarlets and vermilions intermingled with the rusty and chestnut browns, and also with the bright gamboge and cadmiums, to form a thick churning of crunching leaves. The trees' rustling in the wind, losing their russet-tinged leaves, made me think of hands falling off a clock. Something on the fringes of change and new life and transformation. I breathed in the rhythm, the busyness of nature running its course, and decided that I too must choose to transform.

I drank in the melody of the season as I walked, remembering a psalm about a tree planted by the water. The crispness of the air pierced my heart with a sense of awakening, a certain expectation and excitement I hadn't felt in such a long time. I took in another deep breath and another as I walked, finding a kind of euphoria in the beauty around me and discovering a new appreciation for solitude. But eventually I found myself in the presence of human society again.

I heard laughter as my path intersected with Splinterwood, and I knew that I was almost to my destination. Directly in front of me was the bridge that crossed over the river, where the Kayak Shack and Fishing Hut stood on either side of the water, hugging the edge of the road in an impossible tug-of-war. Taking a step up to the raised curb, I balanced along its breadth just as two vehicles drove by. The dogs, somehow knowing better than to follow my lead too closely, made a wide detour to trot straight into the shallows of the river. I watched them as I balanced, stepping gingerly with my hands shoved deep in my pockets while they splashed in their own route.

There were two narrow walkways, one on either side of the bridge, where a few fishermen sat balancing their poles or digging around in tackle boxes for lures and line. The wind brushed up against their foreheads, sweeping their hair from place to place as it pleased. The water rushed below my feet in places soft and gentle, like the smoothness of the skipping stones beneath.

Watching the dogs in their playful tread, I decided that maybe I was better off letting them lead after all. After a moment's hesitation, I made a u-turn, stepping off the curb and around the side of the road to the water's edge. I slipped my feet out of my socks and shoes and rolled my capris above my kneecaps. I cheerfully chased after the dogs for a moment until I registered how freezing cold the water was. A few yards away from me, a huddle of three skinny kids jumped around in utter delight, splashing one another as their white-blond hair blew in all directions. I quickly passed them, leaving their childhood thrills behind.

Just as I stepped out onto dry land, I was frozen in place by the sound of a piercing scream. It was high pitched, the sound of a child. The cries were interrupted by gulps of water and the laughter of people who seemed to think it was a joke. I scanned the area near the bridge, where I could just make out the frantic hand flailing above the water's surface. A few yards away were the other children, their parents out of sight.

I dropped my shoes and ran back into the water's shallow depths, quickly finding that it was getting much deeper the closer I got to the bridge and that hand. In the few seconds it took me to get there, though, the hand got lost from my view. I plunged beneath the surface where I had seen it and opened my eyes beneath the water.

I felt my body physically jerk back in response to what I saw and resisted the urge to gasp. The young boy's bright blue eyes were wide open and frantic. Yet his youthful face was cast in the curious lights and shadows of the river as though made immortal and pristine beneath the surface of the water. Then his eyes met mine, and the former portrait of peace vanished. Now all I could see in those eyes was panic.

I quickly recovered and grabbed him around his ribs. As his head broke the surface of the water, he gasped for air. But my sense of victory was fleeting. I watched in utter disbelief as his body heaved back down below the surface again, pulling me down partially with him. I took a deep breath and dove down to where he was again, this time finding that a piece of rope was binding him to a large pile of brush at the bottom of the river. Mercifully, I found that I could push the rope down beneath his heel. As soon as it slipped down far enough, I made one last all-out attempt to get him above the surface and stay there.

He must have been decent at holding his breath, because he was still conscious, just gagging and coughing when I pulled him back to shore.

A woman ran up to us in a panic. "AUGUST!" she screamed. I moved away from him to let her take over, then watched her pull him in for a desperate hug. "My baby," she said into his ear.

A crowd of locals huddled around August, the kids already beginning to tell the story of what they saw happen. Somehow, though, I managed to retrieve my shoes and disappear without being noticed. It's not exactly that I didn't want any praise. It was that image of the drowning boy in the water. Something about his face...or maybe the innocence in his eyes, or...a memory. He seemed so familiar, though I couldn't remember why. Whatever it was, the whole thing left me feeling completely unnerved. It was as though I'd just been jerked back into one of my recurring dreams, but this time with my eyes wide open.

Thankfully the dogs followed me without my calling to them, and I continued walking until I came to a bend in the road. I stepped off the path, where I could see numerous picnic tables scattered throughout the woods. I sat down at one of them, hoping that nobody would notice me as they drove past. I put my head down on my arms, and to my complete confusion, I began sobbing.

It was a delayed reaction, and not what I expected when I walked away from the boy and his hysterical mother. It must have been a combination of several things. For one thing, I'd never attempted to save a life before, and it was a whole lot scarier than I could have imagined. The boy, August, could have been dead when I pulled him out of the water. He could have needed CPR, something I didn't know how to administer. And then there was the fact that I distinctly recognized a boy I'd never met before. Something about seeing that face underwater was vividly familiar, and perhaps that was the most startling thing of all.

After a while, I pulled myself together, realizing that I was still soaking wet and beginning to get cold. I had come all this way to go to the Corner Store, and there was no point in walking all the way back home empty handed. Cleo came up to me where I sat at the table and let me pet her for a while. Then I finally stood back up and began walking again on the path toward the store.

I continued on as the sopping wet dogs shook and shivered gleefully behind. But I walked uncomfortably, dripping water with every step and hoping the store would have a towel I could use. Here the road began to turn dusty with that familiar red dust of the Midwest, though it was also sandy, reminding me of something sacred I couldn't quite put my finger on. Black-eyed Susans watched me from the thick of the brush, craning their skinny necks in the wind for a better view and intermingling with a backdrop of browning heath asters stirring in their yellow-dotted clusters.

Soon, I was back on gravel and standing outside the Corner Store, whose signs boasted, "All Your Wilderness Essentials," but appeared to be little more than a gas station. It was also just a stone's throw away from the ranger station, with its taupe-colored tin exterior.

The Corner Store parking lot was nearly empty, with only two oversized trucks, one with obscene stickers, the other with an ugly camper shell on top. There was also a smaller truck carrying kayaks and other gear in the truck bed. This smaller one caught my eye only because it had an Irish setter sitting in the front seat happily watching for birds and fogging up the driver's window. The dog caught sight of Charles and Cleo and began barking like mad behind the glass. I cast a glance to the store window and saw the darkened silhouettes of two people at the cash register turned to look at me. I hoped neither of them was the owner of the dog.

I smiled at the canine before turning back toward the tacky posters covering the Corner Store's windows and doors. Charles and Cleo sat down obediently beside the doorway as though to say, "We'll be right here, but don't take too long. And let us know if things start to get ugly." If I'm not mistaken, this was the exact moment that it dawned on me that there might actually be a such thing as spending too much time alone.

As soon as I stepped inside the store, conspicuously chiming one of those annoying bells in the process, I heard a woman's voice at the cash register. It was rather deep and husky, as though she'd been smoking cigarettes for most of her life. And yet, it was the kind of voice that reassured me from time to time, *Yes, I am in the heart of Oklahoma.* I couldn't help but overhear her conversation, as her voice seemed to fill up the entire building.

"So I was just wondering if your dog's been actin' funny, 'cause Lucky's never done that before." She paused and then continued, "Well, if not, then maybe I'd better get him checked..."

It was odd to see that she wasn't on the phone but talking to a silent customer right in front of her. I chuckled to myself as I walked toward the back of the store but took no further notice of her monologue as I shopped.

I picked up a package of granola, a can of bug repellant, chocolate, a bath towel, and ChapStick, and then headed back toward the register. Wilderness essentials, indeed.

The woman was still talking to the man when I made my way to the register, apparently unaware that his receipt was sticking up just behind her elbow, waiting to be torn off and handed to the customer. I went to stand in line behind him, judging that it was going to be a while.

I only saw the man from behind, but he was fairly tall in stature. He wore a thin plaid shirt rolled up to tan elbows, denim-washed khakis, and he had thick, dark hair. I also noticed that he smelled vaguely of pipe tobacco and cinnamon, and so I was reminded of my dad's pipe smoking by the lake as I waited.

"James told me about what happened to her, by the way," the woman said between dramatic jaw movements around her gum. Still, the man made no visible acknowledgments of what she said. And apparently that was okay. "Funny, I never took you for a drinkin' man. Do you think it was meant to be, though? Like they say in church? I mean, sure it was. Still, I don't know how you're makin' it. I just can't imagine the guilt..."

At this, I barely caught the impression that he'd started to open his mouth but decided not to speak after all.

Just then a man I hadn't even known was in the store appeared inches away from my right elbow. He threw me a crooked smile and a nod, saying briskly, "You new 'round here?"

I looked up at him in utter dismay, mostly because he scared the living daylights out of me. But also because he looked exactly like the kind of person my mom always told me not to talk to as a child. And maybe not to talk to him as an adult, either.

His face was mostly red, but reflected a slight tan outlining sporty sunglasses, presumably the ones on his head. He was inches taller than the other man in the store and a good ten years older, with lighter, close-cropped hair. He had one front tooth sticking out more prominently than the others. I tried hard not to recoil from him. It wasn't that he was horrible looking, but there was something off about the proportions of his face and the angular way he carried his body that made me uneasy.

"Yes," I said, nodding and attempting in one word to convey the message that this was the end of our conversation. I turned back toward the front of the line.

"You're pretty wet," he observed.

"Mmm," I replied without turning around. I rubbed my arms up and down to abate the chills.

To my surprise, the woman was staring at us now. "Oh, hi there, James! Speakin' of the devil..."

At this, the man in front made a gesture to clear his throat, which effectively got the woman's attention. She made a big show of apologizing. "I am so sorry, hon. Here's your receipt. Now you take care," she said. She ripped off the receipt she had been holding hostage and begrudgingly handed it over.

With a slight nod, he accepted the thin little paper. He picked up his dog food and headed toward the exit. I stepped forward quickly, hoping against hope that she'd let me go easier than he but somehow knowing I was entirely at her mercy.

Before the previous customer made it to the door, the devil behind me made him stop. "Hey, buddy, long time no see," said James. "We should grab a drink some time." His voice was pointedly loud and seemed to reverberate off the shabby walls.

With one hand on the door and clutching the gigantic bag of dog food beneath his other arm, the stranger's head started to turn, as though out of reflex. I barely made out the edge of what looked like a raw cinnamon stick clinched in the side of his mouth.

"Ya know, like old times?" James continued.

With that, the stranger pushed the door open and left without saying a word. That cacophonous bell left its chime in his wake, along with a jarring slam of the door as it closed.

"Well, hi there, hon," the woman said with a great deal of effort around that golf ball-sized wad of pink in her mouth.

I hate being called "hon." But even more than that, I hate being called "hon" by a forty-year-old woman chewing pungent watermelon gum while intentionally withholding receipts from her customers. I was stepping up to bat already annoyed.

"Hello," I answered. I pushed my purchases across the counter, already feeling pessimistic about the situation.

"You sure are wet, hon," she said.

I merely smiled and looked away.

"So, you been to Sacred Hill yet?" she asked. I thought about how to answer this. The scanner beeped as she waited.

Danny had kindly warned me of this tourist trap on the outskirts of Willow's Bend. For all the grandeur of the name, to call it a disappointment was an understatement, he'd said. I recalled vividly his expression as he informed me that, "Yes, if by 'sacred' they mean 'tacky,' and by 'hill' they mean 'gift shop,' then by all means, it is one helluva sacred hill. But I'd rather visit that pet cemetery on the side of the road, if I had to pick."

"No," I answered. "But I've heard about it."

"Well, be sure and grab a free coupon on your way out," she said.

"Hiya, Tammy," said the man standing right behind me. He sidled up beside me, much too close for comfort. "You hear about them government officials 'round here?"

Tammy actually stopped chewing her gum and looked up at him excitedly. "You know, one of 'em came in here earlier today?"

"Yer kiddin' me. In here? Wha'd they say?"

I stood awkwardly between the two, sort of grabbing at the bag that now had all my stuff in it, and staring at my receipt right behind Tammy. On the wall behind her was displayed a cheap, thin brown frame with a gigantic, wide-lens photo in bright colors. It was a panoramic view of a field of flowers with a small label at the bottom of the frame that read, "Firewheel Valley." Looking at those furry, round centers and fat red petals that turned a stark yellow as they fanned outward, I realized that I'd always heard them called Indian Blankets. I was thinking of bulls' eyes, though, when I accidentally started tuning back into the conversation.

"They didn' say much, but I'm sure you're right—'bout what you said."

"Yer kiddin' me," James reiterated.

"No, they said they's come to check out the coyotes, but they brought this huge truck, an' me and Billy think they're doin' some kind of *experiment* 'round here. With *wolves*," she added.

James let out a whistle of disbelief and a long, drawn-out expletive.

"Excuse me, did you say wolves?" I asked. Granted, I wasn't that interested, but I felt that I needed a foot in the door to the conversation if I was ever going to leave. And precisely how clumsy that foot would be, I wasn't too concerned.

"Yeah, you know somethin' about it?" Tammy inquired.

"Oh, well, not exactly. But I'm definitely against it. If anyone asks." I shrugged. She looked at me with a combination of confusion and annoyance that told me nobody was asking. "Say, could you do me a favor? Could I just grab my receipt, if you don't mind?"

The woman rolled her eyes at me while yanking the receipt off the jagged metal of the machine and slamming it down onto the counter.

"If things get any weirder, I'm headin' out of here," Tammy told James behind my back.

As I walked away from the register, I noticed a rack of pamphlets and maps—one of which read, "Is Willow's Bend Haunted?" Another read, "Sasquatch Among Us." And so everything was beginning to come together. This entire community was nuts. Just for kicks, I grabbed a Sacred Hills coupon on my way to the door.

The two of them continued their conversation as I snuck out of the building, feeling a bit elated to get back to the company of Charles and Cleo. Their driver seat friend had disappeared from the parking lot along with the truck, and they seemed as ready to go as I was.

CHAPTER THREE

My eyes flew open but only registered darkness for a few seconds. I blinked until I recognized the contents of the cabin bedroom. The alarm clock read that it was just past three. I heard the distant sounds of locusts and bullfrogs from outside my window as I sat up. I tried to catch my breath, remembering the dream I'd just had.

I realized then that when I came here, I was counting on leaving that part of my past outside the ornate Willow's Bend refuge gates. But perhaps it wasn't that kind of refuge after all. I'd had this same dream off and on for months now but always figured it had something to do with Gavin. I'd never actually believed it was a real person out there in the world. But now I knew who he was. He was August.

August. His mother's voice was ringing in my head during my dream, and it continued to call out even now. August, the hottest part of the year. August, the beginning of the new school year.

I jumped out of bed in one panicked motion. I had come here to face my ghosts, but I certainly wasn't about to face them all at once. I turned on the lights, looking around as though I actually expected to see the ghosts scatter from the room. But I was all alone. I took out the journal and began to write out the dream, my thoughts, some kind of interpretation...I just kept writing, hoping some kind of meaning would come to me. But in the end, I only knew that it all came down to that one word, *August*. The boy underwater.

I SMACKED MY lips before washing down the peanut butter with icy-cold water. The glass left a pooling ring of water on the linoleum as I tilted it toward me. From where I sat cross-legged on the countertop in my kitchen, I could see the dogs through the windows running their joyful circles in the front yard. I had gone on a jog at the crack of dawn, but I was already considering a second as I finished an early lunch.

The truth is, I was feeling nervous, and I wasn't really sure why. At first, I told myself that it was because Danny hadn't called or stopped by in a few days. But deep down, I knew that that wasn't it. I felt the water go down as I thought about Danny. At first glance, he wasn't the kind of person I would typically go out of my way to befriend. His openness about chasing women and his incessantly flirtatious way of speaking were features in other men that typically drove me away with a single glance of pity and scorn. But something about Danny was different.

There was a genuine kindness in his eyes and gestures that made the forced façade of shallowness fall apart in a second. I saw right through it. And maybe I did pity him a little. But I also liked him. And I felt that I could trust him. So during the first month that I settled into Willow's Bend, Danny and I had inexplicably become good friends. What did we have in common? What drew me to him? What drew him to me? There was no rhyme or reason to it; it just happened. It was as though an invisible wind had blown us together and held us there. Or perhaps that was just another mystery of Willow's Bend.

In the end, I genuinely liked Danny, but there was nothing romantic between us, and I knew it. Danny knew it. Heck, even *Charles* knew it. But as I sat there, taking my last bite into a pale, sweet banana, that's exactly what I was trying to tell myself.

And I was scared. I sensed that I was standing on the verge of truth—the truth about myself that I'd been ignoring for two years now. And while I couldn't quite wrap my mind around it, I knew it had something to do with giving up on life. It was about having taken the easy way out for two years and knowing that I couldn't do that for the rest of my life. *I could still call Danny, though.* I reached my hand out and touched the red phone against the wall. *Coward.* I recoiled, scowling at myself for being so weak.

I chucked the banana peel. With every ounce of resolve I had left, I walked to the front door and slipped on my running shoes, grabbing my music and headphones from off the table. I took off out the door, calling Cleo to come with me.

I jogged down the winding driveway, feeling the presence of the fiery sweet gums, maples, and other trees and what they meant to me, exhaling life back into my lungs one breath at a time. They meant something deeply organic and real and unashamed. I listened to a Joni Mitchell album a roommate had given me back in freshman year, letting the melodies compel me over the gravel and red dirt beat by beat. All that stuff about blood and holy wine always got to me. Something about it rang true and felt, very, very good.

Eventually I came to a sharp curve in the road and did a double take to my left. Something through the brush was dazzling, reflecting a glistening light. I could just make out through the thick veil of trees that there was a small, inconspicuous body of water that, even from the distance, stood placid and clear. I yanked off my headphones and made my way through the trees. The sunlight filtered through, clean and unpolluted in thick streams of light, illuminating the insects buzzing in the air. The edges of the land fell steeply into the depth of the water, yet I could still make out the smooth, mossy gray of the pebbles and tangled grass at its bottom, as well as the thick, gray bands of tree roots that curved up and plummeted back down into the riverbed.

I sat down at the edge and let my hand run up and down the trunk of an oak tree as I examined its rugged bark. I stared wistfully at the blue-gray lichen with the narrow, tubular thallus sticking out and tilting its small, vacant cups up toward the light. I was thinking of the grandeur of a piece of bark, and I was mesmerized. I was suddenly captivated by life and its hidden beauty, its unexpected rhythm.

I laid back against a large, warm rock and just soaked in the beauty of the sunlight, the peaceful view of the water. I let the warmth of the sun soak into my skin and felt that I had become a part of its rays. The light was in me. *Can I let that resonate? Can I let it pour out of me and reflect that there is more than just pain and torment in this life?* I considered that perhaps I could.

And I found peace.

To commemorate this first glimpse of true healing and relief, I felt the need to do something spectacular. I heard Paul Newman's voice in my head as the line came to me, "Get out of character, lady. Get way out." It was from the film *The Long, Hot Summer.* And so I basked in the Clara Varner of it all, suddenly feeling stronger and more clever than before.

I looked down at the water and seriously considered—for the first time in my life—swimming in the nude. It was such a profound moment, and to not do it seemed like kind of a letdown. I had come all this way, and I was certain that this was the spectacular thing I needed. On the other hand, swimming naked in a river comes with an awful lot of variables. The truth is, it's more romantic in theory than actuality. I thought of Prince Andrey Bolkonsky from *War and Peace*, one of my all-time favorite characters in literature.

It was wartime when Bolkonsky and his regiment stopped in at Bald Hills estate in the Russian countryside. I remembered that it was unbearably, unquenchably hot, dry, and dusty, and that Smolensk had just been abandoned to Napoleon. Everyone around "our prince," as his regiment called him, was stripping off their clothes and diving into muddy green waters in the miserable heat of summer.

What would he do? I asked myself.

I glanced back at the road behind me before taking off my shoes and clothes.

I TRUDGED UP the hill toward my cabin, with my feet just barely damp in my tennis shoes and my clothes sun-dried and smelling both sweet and mossy. The afternoon had left me exhausted, sore, and a little lightheaded.

Overhead the sky was gray, with a herd of clouds drifting slowly toward the west, creating giant shadows that seemed to hover over me like silent monsters as I walked. I stopped at the top of the steps when I realized that it had begun to drizzle. And so it was one of those oddly beautiful days more typical of the spring than the fall, when the sun shines brightly in the distance but the rain falls anyway, evidently undaunted by that incandescent orb of fire. I was enchanted by it.

I looked around. Cleo sat on her hind legs and scratched behind her ear with great fervor. There was no one else. Charles and Hamlet had disappeared. I stepped back out from the shelter of the cabin's eaves and back down onto Mother Earth, kicking off my shoes and stepping into the thick, unkempt blades of grass. I lay down in the middle of the yard, with the tangled Bermuda on my back as I had loved to do as a child. And I laughed. It was a quiet laugh, at first—a self-conscious laugh—but it seemed to replace the need to cry. And so I let myself laugh harder and louder, feeling the sudden outthrust of my ribcage and the shudder of my shoulders with every movement.

I turned over onto my belly as my body calmed down. And slowly I began to ask myself what this great outpouring meant. I asked myself too why men carried guns in school parking lots, why fathers killed mothers, why love at first sight existed—and more than that, how it could exist, only to be crushed into nothingness by tragedy. I knew then that I had been living a life of fear and anxiety and chaos. But what was the alternative? *Who am I? Who is Atsila?*

I felt a stubborn stream of tears run down my cheeks even in the midst of the rain. But when I closed my eyes, they felt more like two gentle and compassionate fingertips running down the curves of my face and dropping off at my chin.

As the water continued to fall, I fell asleep in the grass with the soft blades cushioning my skin and the sky steadily darkening around me.

Dear Heart,

How long must a man suffer before he is allowed to die? How could your words possibly comfort me when you yourself are gone? What a pathetic exchange, an inadequate replacement for the person I love most. How could you not know that I would have wanted to be there? Did we misunderstand each other so thoroughly that you really believed me to be that weak? Perhaps I am the monster that you assumed me to be, since I have behaved monstrously in your absence. But then I am not myself away from you. And so I sometimes think that you must have taken me away with you after all.

—R.A.

I WOKE UP to the sound of thunder. Lifting up my face, I could feel that it was now indented with vertical and oblique impressions from the grass. A storm had blown through while I slept, and though the rain was mild, the lightning and thunder were fierce.

I hastily jumped up, tripping over the wet, grassy mounds in the yard and the wooden steps of the front porch until I found Cleo, pawing anxiously and whimpering against the front door. I let us both in, glancing around in the process to see that Charles and Hamlet were still gone. I turned on the emergency weather radio just in case of an unexpected tornado and listened to the mechanical speech emitting from the speakers. After glancing down at Cleo, who was whining and moaning, I stooped to get down on the floor with her and hold her.

"I know the feeling," I said to my frightened companion, brushing her fur down with my hand.

Later that evening I started up the percolator, and as the storm pounded out its raging threats, I was reminded of one of my favorite Elizabeth Bishop poems, "Electrical Storm." There was a certain excitement to it, a tangibility within the lines that always stayed with me long after reading. I fought the same urge as the poem's feline Tobias, to run and jump into my bed, hiding in the covers until it was all over.

Although I didn't share Cleo's phobia of storms, I knew the terror that she felt. And so, for the moment, I had Cleo, and she had me.

We stayed up through the night with the cabin lights on, listening to the radio and the clattering and scraping of tree limbs against the roof and windows. We listened to the heavier pelts of raindrops and the roaring wind between the vivid flashes and pealing thunder. The storm grew louder and stronger, then more quiet and calm, and then back again with more strength than before. It reminded me of the crashing and retreating of waves on a shore. As the storm raged on, I dug out a dog-eared paperback of poetry and read poem after familiar poem until I fell asleep next to Cleo on the couch.

The next morning, I awoke much later than usual with a splitting headache. From where I had fallen asleep on the couch, I could hear dogs howling and barking in the distance again, a common background noise since I'd first come to Willow's Bend. But this was the first time I'd noticed the sounds so early in the day.

I could barely see anything for the blinding light that poured in through the curtains. Rubbing my tired eyes, I stayed there on the couch for a while until I finally persuaded myself to get up. Cleo was whimpering at the door again, this time probably to relieve herself outside. I dragged myself to the front door to let her out, then to the shower, where I took twice as long as usual to wash and scrub. It was one of those days when I absolutely dreaded having to pull back that curtain and dry off. But I did. And I even got dressed and fried an egg. No small victory.

I later stood out on the front porch in my sweats and an old sorority t-shirt, pouring a gigantic bag of dog food into one of three metal bowls. Hamlet's and Charles's were still full from the day before. *Where are they?* I wondered. I made a mental note to let Danny know the next time I saw him. As I refilled the bowls with water, I was surprised that Cleo hadn't come up the steps expectantly.

Walking down the front steps, I scanned between the trees for Cleo. I called out her name and the names of the other two as well as I walked along the cabin walls. Finally I saw Cleo's small form on the back side of the house, apparently sleeping.

"Cleo? Old girl, what are you doing here?" I asked her. She slowly stood up, breathing out her usual enthusiastic greeting and followed me back around to the porch. I sat down on the bench next to her, watching her begin to eat her food. She sniffed at her water but didn't drink any of it.

"Cleo, dear, you should drink your water," I said, dotingly as usual. I moved it closer to her, but she backed away. "Hmm, well somebody's being stubborn today, aren't we?"

But she sat down next to me and let me pet her, so I decided to let her do what she wanted. As I pet the top of her fur down to the middle of her back, feeling the soft, thick strands on my palms and between my fingertips, I acknowledged how beautiful she was.

"My beautiful Cleo," I cooed down to her. "My stubborn, beautiful—" I stopped mid-sentence when I saw a flash of red. There on the edge of her nose, smeared up toward her left eye, was what looked like dried blood. At first glance, I'd assumed it was mud, but looking closely now, it was too red. I gently lifted her jaw up toward me to get a better look. There was more of the dark red on her jaw as well. "Cleo," I finished, frowning at her.

I felt and heard the low rumblings of her growl. Startled, I dropped my hand, and moved away. Her head never turned toward me, but she stopped growling once there was space between us. As she walked slowly down the steps and disappeared around the corner of the cabin again, I saw that she had barely touched her food. Cleo had never growled at me before. What was going on?

I heard the phone ring and reluctantly went inside to answer the call.

"Good morning, Char," my mother sang through the landline. "I'm glad to hear you're still *alive*." I grimaced as I realized that I'd forgotten to call her in the last few days. It was unusual for me to not check in with her every so often. Having seen her daughter survive more than one emotional meltdown, it was understandable for her to notice more than a few days without phone calls.

"Good morning, Mama. And, uh, thanks."

She updated me on the recent escapades of my brothers. I couldn't help but chuckle weakly. It was good to hear her voice.

"I've been worried about you," she continued. "Are you okay?"

I answered her questions, quickly acquiring a positive note in my voice to reassure her. As we talked, I wrapped the thick, spiraling red cord around my fingers, then around my hand. Then I made knots from the top to the bottom.

After a while, I spoke to my father, who had a surprising piece of news for me.

"So, your mother and I..." he began, pausing dramatically, "are going to California for a couple weeks."

Complete and utter silence on my end.

"Char, hon? Did you hear—"

"Dad!" I gasped. I ran my hand against my forehead, pushing my dark hair back up and out of my face.

"I know," he said, chuckling on the other end. His voice had grown slightly raspy over the years, but I could still hear afresh in my mind his passionate stories of our relatives in California. It was the last place on earth I would expect him to visit for vacation.

"Your mama wants to see the ocean," my father continued. "You know, to take long walks on the beach and hunt crabs and whatnot. And, believe it or not, we've got a wealthy distant relative who's decided he misses me. God only knows what took him so long. Oh well. We'll be staying with him in Redding for a few days too."

"When do you leave?"

"We're actually packing right now. Kind of spur of the moment, I know. But your mom saw that Meryl Streep movie last week and seems to think that we aren't spontaneous enough."

Just then, I heard a knock on the front door. I could just make out the top of someone's head through the fanning windows.

"Dad, I should go," I said.

"Oh, hey, Charlotte, one more thing," my dad said hastily. "I just wanted to let you know that they're having some trouble out there with the population of the coyotes. I don't know if you heard anything about it."

"Of course I did, Dad. I'm here."

"Oh, really, you did?" he asked.

I saw Danny's figure appear through the large windows in the dining room. He cupped his eyes as he leaned into the glass until he must have seen me. He stood up straight again and waved before shoving his hands into his pockets and disappearing again.

I glanced down at last week's paper on the countertop. The headline read, "Willow's Bend Coyote Population Explodes, Researchers Say." The front page story of the week before was about a pole that had fallen over at a grocery store in town. It was no wonder this coyote thing was big news.

"Yeah, but I don't think it's a big deal at all," I answered him. "Danny told me that the coyotes tend to stay on the far west side of the property, and they rarely ever venture anywhere near the cabins he leases. You know how the media is, always trying to make something out of nothing. I only go walking with Cleo anyway. And I haven't seen anything weird at all since I've been here." Obviously, I was making an exception for the good folks at the Corner Store.

"Hm. Well, just be extra alert for me, okay, hon? I don't wanna have to worry about you. And don't wander off too far."

I agreed and reassured him. Before I could get off the phone, he added that I needed to write down a new number to reach them in case I needed anything while they were gone. My parents were particularly old fashioned when it came to technology, so I had grown used to leaving messages on the home phone. I scribbled the new number down on the back of an old receipt before we finally said our goodbyes.

After hanging up, I rushed to the front door to let Danny inside. He greeted me with his usual smile and waved the newest paper at me as he walked through the door. During the last few weeks, I had found the weekly paper on my doorstep with no signs of the person who left it there. This morning his complexion was a little more tan since I'd last seen him, with the charming appearance of freckles on his slightly rounded face. He looked nice.

"So, how's everything been going?" he asked casually. But something in his tone lacked its usual buoyancy.

"Good," I answered. Then I decided to be honest. "I was beginning to wonder if I'd ever see you again."

"Yeah, sorry about that. I wanted to come earlier, believe me. But there's been some, uh, trouble." His eyes certainly reflected that much. That's when I realized that the newspaper he'd brought me was already slightly crumpled, as though it had been read several times on the way over.

"Is something wrong?" I asked.

"Actually, yes," he answered, following my gaze.

He laid the paper out on the table and pointed at the cover story headline, which read, "Vacationing Couple Gone Missing in Willow's Bend."

"I just happened to run into the park ranger on my way out of town. He said that after that paper was printed, they recovered the bodies. They must have gone hiking because the ranger found them near one of the trails at the edge of the property. Looked like some kind of animal attack." As he spoke, the morning light picked up shades of bronze and red in his hair, though there was nothing of that brightness in his expression.

"I'm sorry," I muttered. "That's so sad."

"Yeah, but, uh..." He shook his head before continuing, as though he were trying to sort through the conflicting thoughts in his mind. "The ranger, well, I've known him for a long time, and he always gives me the inside scoop. I knew when he was tellin' me what happened that somethin' wasn't right. He seemed really disturbed, and I can't explain it, but I know that there was somethin' he wasn't tellin' me."

"Like what?"

"I—I don't know. Maybe I'm wrong." He shrugged off the last sentence like he wanted to change the subject.

I didn't know what to say, but just by looking at Danny's demeanor, I felt chills race down my back. I looked down at the paper and skimmed the story from top to bottom. My eyes drifted to a headline in smaller print, that read, "Land Owner Protests Lack of Coyote Population Control." More coyote rubbish.

"You know, the dogs have been actin' really strange," Danny began again, as though he'd glanced at the same headline. I looked up in time to see him roll up one of his sleeves, indicating a bandage on his arm. "I was checkin' in on a tenant just yesterday, and their dog bit me. I think it was an accident—I was tryin' to get a tennis ball from him. But the whole thing was still a little weird." His tone became more playful as he put up his hands and said, "Don't worry. I've had all my shots."

I laughed at his crooked grin. "That's definitely good to know." He unrolled his sleeve to cover up the bandage again.

"Now that you mention it, though, you should probably look at Cleo." As I explained her strange behavior, as well as the disappearance of the other two, the effect it had on Danny was more than I expected.

"I don't think you should go out alone at all for a while, Charlotte," he said, holding the front door open for me before stepping out onto the front porch. "Without the dogs to protect you, it just seems too dangerous. At least until we can figure out what's going on."

"Yeah, you're probably right," I conceded.

But by the time we'd made our way around the cabin, Cleo was already gone.

Danny called the dogs' names for a while before putting his hands on his hips and shaking his head dejectedly. "This is wrong, Charlotte. Somethin' is wrong. They've never done this before."

"Well..." I began, scratching my head as I looked off into the distance. "Maybe they just went on...you know, an incredible journey." It was a feeble attempt at humor, only to mask the nervousness in my voice.

Danny looked at me and smiled. "Right," he said. "Whatever they're doin', I'm sure they can take care of themselves." His words lacked conviction as his eyes continued to scour the wooded view before us. "Do you feel that?" he asked.

"Feel what?"

"In the air." I lifted up my chin and gazed into the horizon, waiting for Danny to continue. The sky was clear and brilliantly blue above, but off to the west, I spied the faintest outline of storm clouds. They hovered dark and ominous behind the trees, as though waiting for us to look the other way before making their descent upon the refuge. "Another storm system must be rolling in."

And I did feel it. That static electric something. It was as though the entire woods around us was holding its breath. The trees stood still and patient, as though watching and waiting with us. It was a feeling of expectancy, or like time had just stopped. I'd felt something like it a handful of times in my life during tornado season but never at this time of year.

"You know," Danny began. "I kind of just feel the need to get out, if you know what I mean. Somethin' about livin' inside these gates can drive a person nuts if you're not careful. Anyway, I wondered if you'd be interested in takin' a day off from journaling or...whatever it is you do around here all by yourself."

I laughed but decided not to admit that I hadn't been accomplishing much at all since I'd come to the refuge. "Actually, I'm starting to feel the need to get out myself," I answered instead. "And I could use a few things from the store." I walked back through the door to retrieve a small piece of paper from the kitchen.

"You're not hungry, are you?" I heard Danny call out. "We could grab a pizza or somethin' while we're out. I know a great place."

I met him back on the porch and gladly agreed.

"Great," he said. "You're gonna love the food there. They even have live music on Fridays."

I followed Danny out to his truck, thankful to have something to do rather than stay at the cabin alone and worry about Cleo. Besides, ever since Danny showed up, I was feeling more and more on edge.

The truck doors slammed shut and the engine started before Danny spoke again. "Guess what? If you play your cards right, you'll even get to see that light pole that fell down last week." I smiled back at him. I had to appreciate his resilient sense of humor.

As the truck sped on down the winding drive toward those ornate gates on the edge of Willow's Bend, I grew more and more relieved at the prospect of getting out to a restaurant and listening to the busyness of bartenders and waitresses and quirky patrons. My world had become incredibly small, after all. Come to think of it, I was even starting to miss Tammy and James. If that wasn't a red flag, then I didn't know what was.

Danny hummed "Rainy Day Blues" as the road took a bend, and we passed an old abandoned animal shelter, which I hadn't noticed on my way to the Corner Store a few weeks back. Danny told me during our tour that it was shut down for lack of funding a few years ago, and I could see that the shrubbery inside its fencing already looked haggard and neglected from the road's view. The proprietors were considering using the facility for an additional wildlife museum, perhaps an annex, though for now it was empty and unused. At the sight of the old shelter, I remembered Danny's guided tour and tried to place everything in my mind as we drove along.

I recalled that much of the refuge had become overgrown property and woodlands. In the southwest corner of the grounds, several miles beyond anything I'd explored on my walks, there was a range of small mountains and hills. A lot of groups went rock climbing and hiking, though Danny insisted he would go with me anytime.

And on the southeastern side was the Otter Lake, which I'd only seen the northern tip of on my first day in Willow's Bend. The locals had grown accustomed to using the name as a pun as much as humanly possible (i.e., "Not that lake—the Otter one," or, "You really Otter go," etc.). Its other claim to fame was that it was where a young Sasquatch had been spotted three years ago. He was taking a dip, I suppose. Or maybe picking up an al fresco fish dinner. One could hardly blame him. I imagined there wasn't a whole lot going on around Otter Lake these days, what with the weather growing colder. But folks were always on the lookout. I have to admit, I was sort of rooting for Bigfoot. That's just the kind of person I am.

After the road took another curve, we drove slowly across that familiar bridge with its shacks and walkway. I recognized the Fishing Hut, covered with signs about fishing and tubing, though some of the signs were askew or had fallen to the ground, and there was neon yellow paper littering the ground.

Last night's storm seemed to have cast leaves and limbs into the water as well, as there were no apparent customers around, but the clean streams of sunlight made it look peaceful anyway. We continued to drive in silence as my mind wandered from contemplation to contemplation on its own meandering path. It dawned on me that my tour guide was being uncannily silent. It was easy for me to be so introspective after spending so much time alone. But I didn't expect Danny to be lost in his own thoughts.

"Danny, you don't seem like yourself today. Are you sure you're okay?" As I looked at his face, his eyes reflected fear. He furrowed his brow and turned to look at me. A tender smile broke out over his features as he spoke, like an afterthought.

"I'm sorry, Charlotte. I guess I'm just kind of anxious to get outta here. You know, if this investigation doesn't get wrapped up by sunset, I almost think maybe you should pack up your bags and spend a few nights away from this place."

"Are you really that concerned? Surely the ranger would have said something if he thought there was any reason to be afraid."

"You would think so. But I know him, and I got the feeling that he doesn't want people to panic."

I felt my grip on the piece of paper in my hand tighten and tried to force myself to relax my muscles. "Well, then we should definitely not panic. Besides, my parents are on their way to California right now, and I don't have anywhere nearby to stay."

We fell back into an uneasy silence as I tried to think of where I would go if I needed to spend a few nights outside the refuge. The truck slowed briefly to ease over a fallen branch in the road, just as I noticed a small brown sign indicating a cemetery down the intersecting path.

"Where are you going to stay?" I asked abruptly, trying to sound nonchalant.

Danny threw me an incredulous glance. "Me? It would take a lot more to convince me to pack up my bags than that."

"But you said—"

"Listen, I'm one of the few residents in Willow's Bend who was born and bred here. This is my home, and I could never give it up. You know what I mean?"

I turned my head away, leaving his question unanswered only because I didn't know what he meant. My family had moved a couple of times in my life, and I'd never known such a deep-rooted sense of place. Instead, I stared out the window at the flecks of grass encroaching onto the gravel road and listened to the hum of the engine as we turned the last bend and the wrought iron gate came into view at last. But the gate, with its extravagant loops and snaking curves, was inexplicably closed.

CHAPTER FOUR

"What the—" Danny filled in some colorful blanks as we pulled up to the towering black gates. "What is this?"

We could see through the metal and vines that there were police cars with lights flashing and men in military gear standing on guard on the other side of the gate.

Danny pulled his Tacoma up several feet away from the gate and stepped out of the truck. I hesitated, then finally pulled myself together and got out of the truck to join Danny. He had his hands on his hips while speaking vehemently to the camouflaged men until he threw his arms up, exasperated.

"I don't know what you're talking about!" he shouted. But they didn't seem to hear him. From where we stood, I could see that not only was the gate being guarded but there were also soldiers patrolling down a long stretch of the periphery.

"Sir, please step away from the gate. We have orders to shoot if you approach any closer," the guard spoke with gun aimed.

Another voice from a soldier with a megaphone blared from farther away. "STEP AWAY NOW. COME ANY CLOSER, AND WE WILL SHOOT." Adrenaline in this place was escalating quickly as Danny stood there irate, red-faced, and shaking. My heart raced at the sight of so many guns. I didn't know what was going on, but I knew that I couldn't let Danny get shot. I pulled him by the crook of his arm. He reluctantly followed my lead back to the truck, though he shouted explicitly at the men on the outside of the gates the entire way.

"We are not sick, you idiotic—what do you think we have, small pox?" We slowly made our way back to the truck before Danny turned around again. "Do we look sick to you?" He left them with that one last thought to chew on before climbing angrily back into the truck and slamming the door.

"Charlotte, this is madness." Danny put his head down as he fumbled with his seatbelt, muttering under his breath. "They said that all of Willow's Bend is being held in quarantine because of some fatal disease that's spreading." He started up the truck and skillfully turned the vehicle around on the narrow gravel road.

"What do you mean *quarantine*? When are they going to let us out?" I had never been quarantined before, but it didn't sound like a sabbatical. Danny drove slowly, reluctantly, as though he hadn't completely made up his mind yet that he couldn't take out two police cars and four military personnel.

"I don't know," Danny answered. "I guess when they assess whatever disease they think we have. Have you been feeling sick at all? Weak?"

"No, nothing. Like I said, I went jogging yesterday. And I feel better than ever." He hit the gas, and we sped up the winding terrain.

"I haven't noticed anything either. This is nuts," he said. The truck lurched forward as I groped nervously with my seatbelt. I couldn't stand to be in a vehicle with someone who drove angry. And Danny drove furiously. He was still flushed red from shouting at the gate.

"It must be pretty serious, whatever it is. Don't you think?" I asked, trying to calm myself down more than anything else. "To make securing the grounds such a huge deal?"

"Yeah, you're right," he said. "From the look of things, they're covering all of Willow's Bend. Whatever this thing is, I hope we outlast it."

We headed back to my cabin in agitated silence. From the passenger seat, I heard the growing *thump-thumps* of helicopter blades as a chopper flew overhead. We watched it disappear in the distance. As Danny drove back the way we'd come, I noticed that the scenery looked pointedly different than it had before. Perhaps we just hadn't noticed earlier, but the woods around us seemed to emanate a certain...*eeriness.* You might say that it was too peaceful, maybe like a cemetery. The natural rhythm, like breathing, which had enveloped me on my walks just days ago, was gone. Where was everyone? There were a few birds and a squirrel along our route, but even they seemed hushed and still in a way I'd never seen wild animals behave before.

There was a flash of color in front of us before the truck slammed into something heavy. My seatbelt caught me as I lurched forward in my seat. Danny and I were both silent as we waited to see a deer raise its head up over the hood of the truck. But it wasn't a deer. And it didn't get back up.

I felt the hum of the engine cease and heard the sonorous beeping as Danny pulled out the keys. Then there was silence. Danny slowly unbuckled and pushed his creaking door open before getting out of the truck. I watched his reaction as he rounded the hood of the truck. He covered his mouth, stifling a horrified yell, and reeled backward away from the vehicle. My stomach lurched.

"Danny, what is it?" I couldn't move. I knew then that the brave thing to do was to get out of the vehicle and help him cope with...whatever was out there. Instead, I remained petrified beneath my seatbelt, feeling the color drain out of my face as I waited.

Danny ran his hand dramatically through his gold-brown hair and turned his head away.

"Charlotte, stay in the car." His voice sounded all wrong.

I tried to stare at my hands, scrutinizing the cuticles and rough edges on my nails while I knew he was removing the body I did not want to see. Despite my efforts, I heard the sound of a body being dragged across the gravel road into the grass. Glancing up at the rearview mirror, I saw Danny's hunched form a few yards away from the truck. I heard the sound of his vomit, his gagging and coughing and sniffing.

A helicopter flew overhead. I looked up instinctively but was shocked to see a shower of neon yellow sheets of paper gliding down to our road. The papers swirled, caught up in a gentle wind stream, and glided this way and that like wounded canaries. One of them landed on the windshield, directly in front of me, catching one corner between the glass and the windshield wiper blade. I rolled down my window and reached around the windshield. I peeled the paper off the glass and sat back against my seat to read.

I read the words on the paper twice. It appeared to be some kind of official notice. I heard Danny shut the driver's door with a thud. Then I read the flyer out loud to him:

ATTENTION Residents and Visitors of Willow's Bend Wildlife Refuge:

You are hereby notified of a United States federally authorized quarantine administered by the Centers for Disease Control and Prevention (CDC) and enforced by the United States Army. All persons currently within the property limits of Willow's Bend Wildlife Refuge have been identified as possible carriers of an aggressive communicable disease. At this time, the disease remains undetermined by name but is considered a highly contagious, untreatable, and potentially lethal condition.

It is no longer within your legal rights to leave the aforementioned area. You are furthermore recommended to maintain an appropriate distance from the property fencing, which will remain heavily guarded during quarantine. These restrictions will be physically enforced as necessary by military personnel. NOTE: DO NOT attempt to leave Willow's Bend.

You are encouraged to seek shelter near a telephone and await further contact and assistance.

Thank you for your cooperation during this difficult time,

CHARLES ASHKENASI
Senior Director
Centers for Disease Control and Prevention

I looked up from the notice to see that Danny was holding his arms extended completely straight on either side of the steering wheel. It was as though he was trying hard to steer us, though the vehicle remained where it was. His chest rose and fell slowly, dramatically, as I wondered if he'd heard anything I'd said. He finally turned the ignition and began to drive again. From the view of the side mirror, I caught a glimpse of a human body stained crimson, lifeless and limp next to the road. That's when it hit me.

"Danny, you can't just drive away!" I shouted in one swift breath, feeling my chest collapse in anguish at what had just happened. He ignored me. "Danny, I'm serious! You have to go back! We have to call—"

"Charlotte, shut up!" His hand banged hard against the steering wheel. "Please! Just—"

"What—what are you doing?"

He merely cursed. I felt tears sting my eyes, but none fell as I turned around in my seat. As horrified at the scene as I was, I couldn't live with myself if we had just killed someone and ran. *I couldn't.* But I also couldn't jump out of Danny's speeding truck.

"I—I just need to think, okay?" he practically shouted. Something in his tone told me it wasn't a request.

BACK AT MY CABIN, Danny paced back and forth across the hardwood floor as I went through the house and checked every door and window to make triple certain that they were securely closed and locked. I was reviving an old compulsion, but it seemed appropriate now in a way that it never had before. My mind wandered back to the vacant body that I knew was still there in a heap on the side of Splinterwood Road. *Why would any sane adult throw themselves in front of a truck like that? Isn't that what happened?*

Yet we didn't call the cops. Accident or suicide, that was a crime itself, I knew.

"Danny, what are we going to do?" My voice was quiet at the memory of his harsh tone.

He stood looking out the window, deep in thought and significantly calmer than before. But he answered at last, "I just don't think there's any point in calling the cops right now. We know where they are: on the other side of the gate. Besides," he said, turning his head slowly to look back at me. "The body. It wasn't normal. I think it must have had whatever's out there—the virus or whatever." But his tone changed abruptly. "Charlotte, what are you doing?" he demanded.

I had moved to the landline in the kitchen, but Danny's tone caused me to hesitate with my hand on the receiver. "I'm calling my dad." At my words, he stood there wearing a pensive expression. I waited, uncertain why I was seeking permission from Danny to do something.

"Okay, go ahead. Just...don't say anything about the body yet, okay? I'm still working out what to do."

I had some things to say about that, but I wanted to take advantage of the chance to talk to my parents first. I dialed their home phone and waited.

The phone went to a voicemail account, just as I remembered that they were gone. I reached inside my pants pocket for the new number, but it wasn't there. I hung up the phone, thoroughly checking all my pockets before scanning the cabin floor. I groaned in frustration, wondering how I could be so careless. Of course I could call one of my brothers or my grandparents to get the number, but I didn't want to scare them, and I just couldn't manage nonchalance at a time like this.

I collapsed on the couch, letting my head rest on my palms.

"I just can't believe this is happening," I said, turning back to Danny. "Only last week the biggest piece of news was about those wolves."

"Coyotes," Danny interrupted.

"What?"

"There are no wolves in Willow's Bend. Just coyotes and dogs."

"Either way," I began, though I could have sworn I'd read something about wolves in Willow's Bend recently. "You would think this was the stuff of major news headlines, wouldn't you? How could we not know about the infection until now?"

"Yeah, I guess it must've happened pretty quickly—I don't know. Hey, I'm gonna call around, see if I can find out anything."

As Danny went to the phone, I stood up and started taking things out of the fridge to make sandwiches. Despite my growing anxiety, I was hungry. More than that, I was growing desperate to do something that felt normal.

"Danny, where'd you get that?" I asked, between bites into my turkey and cheese sandwich. He was holding the phone to one ear with his shoulder, waiting for someone to pick up. But in his other hand, he held a long metal bar.

"Oh, this?" Danny asked, holding the bar up. "Found it in the utility room. Just in case." As I stared at the crude weapon in his hands, I couldn't help but feel that there was something sinister in the whole thing. It seemed barbaric.

As I finished my sandwich, Danny made calls to the ranger's station, a local bar, the Corner Store, a distant relative, and a few of his tenants. The line at the ranger's station was busy, and nobody answered at the bar. The Corner Store had an automated message saying they were closed. His relative didn't answer either. Two of the tenants didn't answer, but the third did.

"Hello? Tammy, are you okay? No, this is Danny!" I couldn't hear what was being said on the other line, but it was clear that something was wrong. "Tammy, what do you mean? Who's there?" I was gripped in anticipation, waiting for Danny's next response when I distinctly heard someone screaming from the receiver.

"Tammy! Tammy? Hello? Is anyone there?" An excruciatingly long moment passed. "Who's out there?"

He hung up with a frightened look in his eyes, staring at the red phone as though it was responsible for whatever happened to Tammy.

"Danny, what's wrong? What happened?"

"I think she's dead. I think she...she must have picked up the phone to call for help, and I answered." Danny sat down on a barstool in silence, face completely drained of its former healthy glow. I felt the color leave my own face as it sank in. We had answered an emergency call for help; we who were becoming incredibly more aware of our own helpless state by the hour.

He walked back to the window and peered through the blinds again as he spoke. "There was a lot of noise, glass breaking, dogs barking, and...well, you heard."

Yes, I had heard.

"Are you, um..." I began. "Going to eat something?"

"I don't know how you can eat at a time like this, Charlotte," he said, still looking away. "Besides, I haven't had much of an appetite lately."

"Okay, I'm just trying to stay calm," I replied as I put the rest of the sandwich stuff back in the fridge.

"Her cabin is just down the road."

"What?" I let the fridge door shut with a thud and turned to face Danny.

"Tammy's." As we stared at one another across the room for a long moment, the fear in his eyes mirrored my own. But there was something else.

"Danny, your eyes..." I began, walking slowly toward him. "What color would you say they are?"

"Brown, why? What's wrong?"

"They're brown. They just seem...I don't know, lighter than I remembered." They had changed to a shade of tan that I'd never seen before in anyone's eyes.

He walked away to face the mirror hanging in the living room. He stood there examining his eyes for a long time while the sun sank beneath the horizon and the wolves howled a constant, haunting chorus in the distance.

DANNY AND I moved to the hallway between the bedroom and the kitchen and stayed there, sitting against the wall in the centermost part of the cabin as though we'd been told that a tornado was about to tear across Willow's Bend. We turned on the emergency weather radio, which gave the same weather report over and over again. Storms were coming, but we already knew that. What the radio did not tell us was what was going on in the woods surrounding us, how serious the infection was, and how to tell if we were in fact already infected.

I don't know how I got any sleep that night, with the wolves howling in the distance, but I woke up with my head slumped against Danny's shoulder.

I sat there for a while, blinking away the last moments of an obscure dream, before I heard the sound.

Knock, knock, knock.

Danny must have heard it at the same time because a moment later, he jumped to his feet and headed to the door. The first hint of sunlight slipped through the windows from the back of the house, following Danny's path.

"Danny, wait!" I said. He had just reached the door.

He turned back to face me, revealing dark circles beneath his eyes that told me he hadn't gotten any sleep last night. "It's okay, I'm just seeing who it is." He leaned into the peephole on the door and examined the scene. "That's weird. I don't see anyone—"

Next to where Danny stood, glass suddenly shattered and flew across the foyer in a small explosion. Danny turned and covered his face but not before getting showered with glass.

There was a pause.

"Clemens, is that you?" a familiar voice asked. I remained frozen where I was. Although the voice was familiar, it did nothing to comfort me about who was outside the door.

Danny's hands remained covered over his face, muffling the sound of an expletive. But then he recovered. "James?" He unlocked the door and opened it with a jerk, revealing the same man I'd met at the Corner Store a few weeks ago.

This time he carried a huge shotgun and wore a red bandana on his head and somehow managed to look even less approachable than before. He carried an old brown leather backpack across one shoulder.

"Sorry 'bout that, kid. Thought the place was abandoned."

"You didn't see my truck?" Danny asked. He closed and locked the door behind James.

"You didn't hear me knock?" James retorted. Then his eyes found mine. A slow smile crept across his face. "Well, well, well. I do believe we've met before, only I didn't catch yer name."

"James, this is Charlotte," Danny said. "Charlotte, James has been on the refuge about as long as I have."

James crossed the distance between us, though I fought the urge to recoil. He reached out his hand. "Pleasure's all mine."

I stared down at his hand but couldn't bring myself to shake it. "I'm sorry... Isn't there an infection going around?"

Danny laughed then said, "Good thinking."

But James merely dropped the smile from his lips and turned away.

Danny began quizzing James. "So what's it like out there? How bad is it?"

"Actually, kid, I didn't come to swap stories. I gotta lady friend waitin' on me at the cabin. Just came by for supplies."

Danny's features fell. James seemed to notice his expression. "Well, I'll tell ya. I've seen only a few so far. The humans, I mean. The dogs are a different story. They've taken over the refuge. It all belongs to them now, so it's best to stay outta their way." James walked over to the living room and collapsed onto the love seat, kicking his feet up onto the leather sofa's arm and reclining with his arms behind his head. For someone who just came in from the woods, he seemed incredibly relaxed to me. His backpack and shotgun remained on the floor next to the couch. "Personally, I think it'll all blow over in a few days. The feds will have to release us—not that I'm goin' anywhere anytime soon. We natives go down with the ship. Ain't that right, Clemens?" He tilted his head up toward Danny.

Danny threw me a nervous glance. "Yeah, of course. So you think Charlotte can leave in a few days?"

"Sure, sure," he said, speaking slowly. "Wouldn't worry too much, kid."

James's nonchalant presence just wasn't adding up for me. "Well, if it isn't that bad, then why did you risk leaving your cabin to come look for supplies?" I asked.

To my surprise, James laughed before replying. "Don't worry yer pretty little head, Miss Charlotte. This whole thing caught us at a bad time. Ran out of food and cigs. But come to think of it..." he slid his legs back down onto the floor and stood up. "Someone is waitin' on me back home. So if you don't mind, I'll just get what we need and skedaddle."

With that, he walked straight to the kitchen and began opening the cabinet doors.

"Um, excuse me?" I said. I threw Danny a look of disbelief.

"Yeah, uh, James, listen. We don't have a ton of supplies either." But James was already emptying my cabinets of the cereal and granola bars I'd had stored there and shoving them into his backpack.

"Don't worry so much, kid," he said without turning around. "We'll be cleared outta here in a jiff anyway."

"Well, if it's not going to be that long," Danny began. He stuck an arm out to block James from pulling out more groceries. "Maybe you could just take the bare minimum?"

James moved from the cabinets to the fridge and began pulling out my groceries one by one, dropping them into his backpack. "Sure thing, kid, just the bare minimum. Swear it on my mother's grave."

"James." Danny moved to stand right behind him. "You're not taking everything."

In another second, James had completely cleaned out my fridge of everything but a few condiments. He closed the buckle on the backpack and turned to face Danny. What I saw in James's eyes was unsettling. I had seen it before through the chain-link fence on a playground. It was something I couldn't quite define, but it gave me the unmistakable impression that he was willing to do anything to get what he wanted.

"You're not telling us everything, are you?" I said. I was surprised to hear the words come from my own mouth, but I was desperate to do something to keep James from hurting Danny. "It's bad out there, isn't it?"

James briefly looked at me but then stared back across at Danny dangerously. "Boy," he said slowly. "You oughta get those eyes looked at. Somethin' ain't right, if you know what I mean."

Danny took a step back to let James pass. He seemed to be stunned by his words.

"Do you have an emergency aid kit around here?" James asked. I couldn't believe this entire situation. When I didn't reply, James took a few steps toward me. "Look, sweetheart. You ain't gonna need it, anyway. Believe me." Another moment of disbelief passed. "Probably in the bathroom, right?"

I nodded vacantly. I was still processing what he'd just said about not needing first aid. Did he only mean that we were getting out soon? Somehow I knew that his meaning was more sinister than that.

While James helped himself to our emergency supplies, I looked incredulously at Danny.

"Danny, we can't let him do this. What if this thing lasts more than a few days? What if it's worse than he's telling us? It doesn't make any sense!"

But Danny was staring off into space. When he finally spoke, he didn't look at me, but kept looking straight ahead. "Charlotte, I think I might be—"

"Well, I think that about does it," James interrupted. He walked back into the room carrying a very full backpack this time and a smug smile.

"How can you be such a coward?" I asked James. It was impulsive, but I said it quietly. At first I didn't think he heard me, because he continued to approach the front door. But then he stopped and spun around on his feet.

I remember seeing James's irate features, which suddenly glowed brilliantly in the morning light. I had found myself in a room with a dark angel, it seemed. As he walked toward me,

I realized that he was incredible and terrible at the same time, like an elaborate and skillful portrayal of a perfect storm. Like a painting I'd seen by Thomas Moran at the Philbrook Museum. I remember that moment as though I'd gazed at it thoughtfully at length, like a painting hanging on a wall. I remember too the explicit word he used under his breath.

What I do not remember is him pulling back his arm to punch me in the face.

The collision sent my body to the floor.

"James, no!" Danny shouted.

It took me a moment to open my good eye enough to see what was happening. A scream escaped my lips even before I could cover my mouth with my hand. James held the shotgun up just inches away from Danny's forehead.

"Are you gonna stop me, boy?" he asked. "Are you?"

"N-no," Danny answered.

With that, James lowered the shotgun and turned back around. He flung open the front door and walked confidently into the open yard.

Danny helped me up and began looking over my injured eye. But I had already forgotten about my eye and was trying to recover from the sight of that pointed shotgun.

"Close call, eh?" Danny said with a half smile.

But before I could answer, we heard the sound of three consecutive shots being fired not far away. I nearly collapsed back onto the floor again. The front door continued to hover open, as James hadn't bothered to close it behind him. It drifted farther open, as though inviting us to take a closer look outside.

And suddenly it was quiet again. There were no birds stirring or singing in the yard. There was no sign of wind in the trees. Everything was perfectly still. It must have been around nine o'clock, so the view was already illuminated by the morning light, revealing the dewy grass that glistened and sparkled in the distance. I heard Danny's voice again.

"What's that?" he said to himself. He pushed open the front door and walked out onto the porch. I took a few measured steps back toward the kitchen, though I could still see him plainly through the dining room windows. I watched him as he paused and stood peering into the woods, as though he saw something. I had stopped breathing.

Danny slowly approached something at the edge of the woods and knelt down. I could just make out the misshapen body of a dog. The colors of the coat were the same as Cleo's, though it was difficult to tell around the scarlet and brick red of blood. I started forward without thinking. I wanted to know for sure if Cleo was dead. *Cleo,* I thought. *Oh, Cleo.* Even in my uncertainty, my chest ached with sorrow.

But then Danny stood up. He reached out a cautious hand and seemed to be talking to someone farther out. The fog was still hovering and obscuring whoever was out there, and I could only see as far as Danny's figure. He shifted his weight back, paused again, and slowly took a few cautious steps backward toward the porch, still speaking into the fog.

For the briefest moment, I was certain that we had found Bigfoot.

CHAPTER FIVE

A large man emerged from the woods. He was covered in bruises, cuts, and dried blood. His clothes were torn, and he seemed to be limping on one leg. But soon he was moving toward Danny with a dangerous intensity.

"Danny!" A scream escaped my lips as Danny came closer, the man right behind him. Danny managed to make it into the cabin before the man touched him, slamming the front door closed.

Once he was inside, the man turned and walked toward the shattered glass from the foyer windows. I was petrified. I couldn't move and only watched as the gigantic stranger stepped clumsily through the shards, sending more glass into the living room as he pursued Danny.

Danny had already crossed the room to retrieve the metal bar by the couch. And as the stranger crunched across the glass on the floor, I saw that Danny was getting ready to fight.

The two men stood in the living room clenching their fists in the same manic fashion. A tremble shook my body as I watched them facing one another, showing the same bizarre compulsions at the same time. Danny crouched down with the metal bar and banged it against the hardwood floor several times, as though inviting the stranger to fight. Was it courage? Or insanity?

"Come on..." He growled at the other man. I couldn't believe my eyes. He was challenging a man almost three times his size. The larger man picked up a heavy chair and heaved it against the wall, barely missing Danny. He roared like a wild animal, and the sheer volume of his voice caused me to stumble backward toward the back door. As I backed into the knob, I heard Danny roar back in the same barbaric way. My heart pounded painfully in my chest as I gasped for each breath, struggling against a panic attack.

My vision fogged, crowded out by my breath and pounding heartbeat. From around the corner emerged Danny's attacker. With my back pressed up against the door, I clutched for the knob, attempting to unlock it without turning away from the scene before me. The man was tall, with dark hair and a mustache. His hand dripped fresh blood, and drool was slowly seeping from the sides of his mouth.

"Danny!" I shouted. But he came up behind the man and slammed the metal bar against his skull. The giant shuddered and collapsed a few feet away from me. I watched Danny stare down at that enormous, haggard body. His features were contorted into fury as he continued to breathe heavily.

As I watched him, I instinctively remained near the back door, eyeing Danny cautiously and trying to steady my breath. I couldn't believe Danny's sudden talent for violence, and it left me completely unsettled. Neither of us said a word. I couldn't keep my eyes off Danny's altered form. I realized then that he must have taken a blow from his attacker, after all, because one side of his face was visibly bruised.

The sound of the metal bar dropping to the floor met my ears.

"Charlotte, are you okay?" Danny asked. But before I could answer, we were interrupted once more.

A snarling figure stepped into the room, this one shorter than the last, but stocky, muscled, and bald. Danny immediately turned and charged at him, but the man deflected the attack and shoved Danny away with an audible crunching sound before Danny's body collided with the wall and fell lifelessly to the floor. My stomach turned instinctively. Somehow I knew that the crunching sound was Danny's neck breaking.

And somehow I knew that Danny was dead. I watched his crumpled form for only a second before his attacker noticed me from across the room.

I looked up in time to see the man's vivid yellow eyes lock on mine. His sleeves and most of his shirt had been ripped off, leaving his pale arms exposed and the muscles rippling beneath the surface. A long thin line of drool made its way down the front of his shirt. I had plenty of time to observe him as I found myself rooted to the floor, caught like a deer in the headlights.

Just as he began making his way toward me, the unbelievable happened. It was a purple and crimson blur in my vision, which my frantic mind couldn't even make sense of until later. Danny's first attacker had stirred and then jumped up, intercepting the shorter man before he could close in on me. His movement was unbelievably fast, throwing his entire body at the man unlike anything I'd ever seen.

My fingers came back to life to turn the handle on the knob, and I fled without ever looking back.

I didn't have Danny's truck keys with me, but even if I had, I doubt I would have had the sense to get inside the vehicle. I didn't stop to think. Instead I dove into the woods, crashing into leaves and tripping over fallen branches in my path. I was already in the thick of the woods when I realized that I had no idea where I was going. But wherever it was, I was getting there in record time.

THEY'RE DEAD, I thought. My vision blurred in the cool wind, but I could still make out the bodies in the not-so-distant bushes lying against tree trunks, sprawled out in the damp morning grass. *Who are they?* I thought. *Residents? Vacationers? Writers?* I didn't slow down long enough to take a close look. But I did notice that they were not moving and that the dewy green of grass was intermingled with red blood.

And then there were the live ones. Or *were* they alive? They were moving and breathing but not much else. Men stumbled through the woods around me as my feet crunched against leaves and mulch while I ran. Some looked lost and dazed, as though they were sleep-walking. I was startled to come across one old man who was cursing himself at the top of his lungs. Others were also visibly angry, violently hitting their chests, slamming fists into the earth, or wildly tearing up bushes and the spindly branches of young redbuds. Some screamed. Others roared.

Two young men were in the middle of a death match when I rounded a covering of bushes to avoid their attention. They were pulling hair, biting arms and ears, and bleeding like mad. It was the sight of these two that made me stop beneath the covering of a small copse of trees. I sank low to the ground as I caught my breath, but I was trying not to hyperventilate. I'd never witnessed so much raw violence, so much fury and chaos.

Then I heard more screams. These were from women. Or children. But I was certain that they were not screams of anger but of terror, of pain. The sound was bone chilling. And it compelled me to start running again. Yet even as I ran, I knew that the rising and falling of those screams would follow me across all of Willow's Bend, maybe for the rest of my life.

I was amazed to still be alive and running when I crossed a road into more woods. I was also amazed that no one had overtaken me by now. I ran on, unwilling to stop for anything. I had no idea where I was or where I was going, even though the last of the fog had lifted and no longer obscured my vision. I couldn't tell what time of day it was; the sky was completely overcast now, hiding the sun from view. I only knew that there was still danger all around and that I couldn't stop if I had any desire to live.

I unexpectedly came across a man who was hovering over a dead animal. He turned on me with a snarling face and creamy yellow eyes that reminded me of Danny's. Without hesitating, I did the only thing I could, which was to keep on running, and preferably run faster. And it worked.

I noticed that the woods were thinning out now, and soon I found myself in a wide expanse of grass and tall weeds that came to a steep slope leading into a valley. I stopped. This time I was convinced that I was reaching my physical limit.

Surprisingly I didn't see anyone chasing me at the moment, though I knew that danger had to be lurking nearby.

I bent over with my hands on my knees to catch my breath. I coughed. How long had I been running? How far had I come? I had no idea. The distance might have been only a few miles, or it might have been ten. A long list of things I was so certain of only twenty-four hours ago now seemed void and null. Even my perception of time and space was unreliable as I struggled to breathe and calm down. I was exhausted, and my surroundings were unrecognizable.

From where I stood just a few yards away from that steep slope, I could see the storm brewing ahead of me, just beyond the valley. I tried hard not to think about the people I'd left behind, the humans who had been contorted into violent animals. I tried not to despair that I hadn't passed any cabins or buildings in my desperate route away from my attackers, or that my complete lack of direction led me to this great expanse of earth with no shelter in sight.

I stood there for another moment longer, feeling the storm's cool breath on my neck, making my skin tingle and my bones feel more alive than before. I shook off the distinct impression that I was being watched. Perhaps by the storm itself.

Just then a very small, distant part of my brain registered that Danny was dead. Before I had only time to feel that sinking, numbing sensation, but no time to let the actual logic of it enter in. And here, now, I could only afford a tiny part of myself to acknowledge the truth. I would never see Danny again. I had to accept that. I was all alone. And I had nowhere to go.

I was tempted to let my emotions overtake me. To give up, to break down. I imagined myself standing up straight at the precipice and screaming at the top of my lungs. Screaming at the threatening storm, screaming at the infected men. Screaming at the very one who came to steal, kill, and destroy.

Instead, I suppressed the urge. There was still a larger part of myself that had the will to go on.

I began coughing, struggling to catch my breath. I heard barking in the woods behind me. I stood up, straining to hear. I had never paid much attention to the nearly incessant barking before—it was just something I accepted about Willow's Bend. But as I listened now, I knew that something was off in the sound. It wasn't normal. And the sound was growing louder. *They're coming for me.*

It was time to run again. But where? I took a few steps to the left, then the right. The barking grew louder, closer, leaving me no time to make a decision. My legs began moving down the slope. My calves flexed in unfamiliar ways as I rushed down at a steep angle, struggling to keep my balance. The terrain began to even out a little, allowing my arms to pump energy in a familiar rhythm. And down I went.

I was still running at an angle when the fear caught up with me. It occurred to me, amid the barking and yelping of the pack, that I was about to die. I couldn't outrun them. I wasn't going to make it. This was it. This was the end of Charlotte Benson. And so I panicked.

As my feet pounded the hillside, I trained my eyes on the covering of woods ahead of me, irrationally believing them to hold some kind of shelter from the wild.

I sped toward the towering trees, with their austere branches and auburn leaves seeming to beckon me in my descent. My vision blurred in the wind, though I could still just make out the shocks of red and yellow from the firewheels in my path before I crushed them beneath my feet.

There was the sound of my breath, my feet hitting the ground, and the wind blowing the grass in a perpetual cacophony as I ran through the valley. There was the wind roiling leaves across the field and the thunder rumbling in the distance before me. But then it was all drowned out by the howling. The hellish sound of the beasts nearly brought me to my knees. I caught a glimpse behind me as I turned my head. One dog, then another, and more appeared over the top of the hill I had just descended. Rugged, large heads lifted red-stained noses to the sky as they sounded their feral alarm, weaving the lower notes around the yips and whines of the others.

My shins pulsed with pain as my feet pounded one after the other toward the copse of trees ahead of me. I forced myself to look ahead to keep from tripping over the rocky terrain. The tall grass and thin, white dandelion heads hid treacherous rocks and soft ground covering mole holes, but I had no time to consider them. I hit them instead, jarring the weight on my joints and ignoring every possible hindrance to keep moving forward.

As I finally entered the thick of the woods, I peered harder into their depth. But I didn't see the refuge I'd set my hopes on. I was soon surrounded by dense trees and tall brush with no sign of help or shelter. My right foot hit something hard in an overgrowth of dandelions, and I rolled my ankle as I fell to the ground. The sharp pain only momentarily blinded me from my need to move on. I attempted to right myself when I heard a gasp of pain that was not from my lips.

I looked around to find, of all things, a small boy clutching his shoulder. He groaned on the ground. "Ahhh!" I realized that I must have stepped on him when I twisted my ankle.

"Where did you come from?" I asked, astonished. I'd begun to think I was the only sane, living human in all of Willow's Bend. And I certainly had not expected to find a small child. This one looked to be about five years old and was covered in dirt and filth.

I couldn't believe my eyes. Beneath all the dirt was the boy I had saved in the river a few weeks ago. It was August. For a moment, I was frozen where I was. Yet the wolflike dogs barked wildly as they approached, forcing me to accept this new reality. "We have to move, now!" I urged him. "Let's go! They're coming!" I grabbed him by the arm and tried to pull him along.

"I can't! They won't let me in!" he said, panting and looking around, refusing to move. He had light blond hair and clear blue eyes just visible beneath the smudges of dirt.

"What? Who won't let you in?" I stopped, entirely at a loss. We needed to move, but I wasn't leaving him.

"The shelter, on the other side of the fence. But they won't let boys in anymore. They won't risk it—I tried!"

"Look. We have to move. They will kill you. Do you understand?" I urged him forward as he finally began to run.

I forced myself to ignore the stabs of pain in my ankle. We had only been running for a minute or two when I saw the corner of a metal fence. It was tall—way too tall to climb over. We certainly were not climbing it, and neither was anything else. We turned the corner and ran alongside the fence for the longest minute of my life before we saw the other corner.

We heard a loud gunshot right behind us, and without thinking, I threw myself over the boy, simultaneously screaming panicked bloody murder. We heard a canine yelping not far behind as we struggled to start moving again. Judging by the loudness of the gunshot, I knew that either the dogs were closing in on us or someone else was trying to kill us.

We turned the corner at last and ran up to the large, mechanical gate. The boy and I began banging on the fence, shaking it to make noise while yelling for help. I looked up at the large white building that rose up from the middle of the fence line. It was the same building I'd seen from the road, but it looked much more austere and sinister up close. It was enormous, with only a narrow walkway and an overgrown hedge of bushes lining the inside of the fence, their fanning leaves pushing out through the holes in the fence.

We heard more mysterious shots fired behind us, which sent my heartbeat hammering at unhealthy speeds. Another dog yelped. A door at the front of the building opened before us as a tall woman emerged.

"Hey! Let us in!" I shouted. She carried a gun as she walked toward us. Before the woman reached the gate, she stopped to get a better look at myself and the boy. In one swift motion, without either hesitating or blinking an eye, she pointed the gun at him, holding it with two hands for a clean shot. I lunged in front of him, realizing at last the truth in what he'd said: Anything male was a threat.

"Are you insane?" she asked. But she reluctantly lowered the gun. "I could have killed you!"

"Me? You're trying to murder a child! The dogs will be here any second! Please! Let us in!"

"The last boy we had compassion on became rabid and killed about three of our friends and family." Her voice broke slightly as she spoke. "I'll let you in, but that thing needs to get as far away from this place as possible. You have no idea what they're capable of." She spoke directly at the boy when she said, "Isn't that right, August? We told you not to come back, didn't we?" Then she looked back at me. "You don't know how dangerous they are. After what we've witnessed, we're practically *hunting* them."

Tears welled up in my eyes as I looked down at August, the boy underwater. I had no idea what she was talking about, but she made it clear that she wasn't letting him inside. Our eyes met, and I knew he was reading my mind. His blue eyes were big and slightly wild looking as he backed away from me and took off running. The woman remained at the gate with the gun pointed away from me, but she wasn't putting it away altogether either.

"Give me a—a weapon, anything." As I spoke, my eyes fell on the gun in her hand. But I didn't have the courage to ask for it.

She looked through the fence at me, startled. "Are you out of your mind? I'm letting you in here!"

"A weapon—a knife. Anything! Now!" I shouted, panicking.

"I can't! We can't spare them!" She backed away from the gate as she realized I definitely wasn't coming in.

"Fine!" I shouted, starting to back away from the fence.

"I'm sorry, I can't give you anything. I just can't afford to." She looked at me darkly as she warned, "Listen, I'll do you this one favor and that's it. I'll give you this advice: There is no room for compassion in Willow's Bend. Not anymore. Trust no one!" She'd had to shout that last piece because I heard the dogs' barking growing closer again and had started to run.

And so I'd turned away for the last time from the only refuge I'd hoped for and followed the direction of that mysterious child from my dreams.

I ran past the oaks and elms as they blended into the sprawling timber and realized that August had disappeared entirely during those few seconds I had let him out of my sight. Shots rang out every minute or so, causing me to scream and whimper out loud, and another dog yelped and went silent. And every time, I wondered which one of us had been shot. I came back to my senses, realizing that the pack was thinning out. *This is a good thing, right?* I ran anyway, fearful, angry, confused; all this not being made any easier by the occasional stabs of pain in my ankle.

Overhead, the clouds had gathered into a heavier blanket, rumbling and rolling out and back into itself like a tide, gathering strength for one massive wave. Rain hit my face in large drops and began to soften the earth beneath my feet. It seeped down at the nape of my neck and cooled the warmest parts of my skin.

The sound of the dogs had stopped altogether. So had the gunshots. And for one long, delusional moment, I imagined that I was one of the pack. I forgot that they had been chasing me, and I ran on with the terror that I was being hunted by someone who knew how to use the very weapon I'd feared all my life. Yes, he was no longer hunting the dogs—he was coming for *me*. The man from my childhood nightmares, the man with the gun was hunting me down at last.

The sky darkened everything around me, causing me to slow down just to keep from tripping. I found myself turning from left to right with nearly every step, sweeping every inch of woods in view. Where had the boy gone?

I thought of calling out his name, but I didn't want to attract attention from the wrong person or animal. Besides, after seeing the woman try to shoot him, he might decide I was one of them and run farther away before I could catch up. As I surveyed the darkening scene around me, I felt yet another chill run down my spine. One thing I was certain of in these woods: We were not alone.

I continued a desperate tread, wiping the water from my eyes with every heaving breath. I panted into a mode that left the realm of physical exhaustion and reeked of emotional hysteria. I inhaled air with every breath as though it were my last and tried to calm down, as I realized it wasn't just rainwater brimming in my eyelids.

I took a signal from my body for the first time since I had left that hill and searched for a resting place. I examined my surroundings again. There was nothing but wet trees; deep brown, red, and ochre leaves crunching beneath my tread; and a growing darkness above. There was no longer any sign of where I had come from or who I was chasing...or what was chasing me. I collapsed against a leaning, fallen oak tree. *Probably struck by lightning,* I mused.

I hit my head back against the rugged, mossy bark in mental frustration. *What now?* I'd lost the child. I was stranded in the woods with rabid animals and murderous humans. Meanwhile, through the rainfall, I could just make out the distant sounds of helicopter blades. But something told me that nobody was coming to save me.

After a while, I couldn't tell if having stopped was making it easier to think or more difficult. It was true that my body was no longer in panic mode. And I was actually able to see clearly around me and breathe calmly. The pain I had been ignoring was mostly dull and numb, my limbs and fingers quickly growing colder in the rain and wind. I knew that I wasn't getting back up again anytime soon. I clutched my knees against my chest and tried to situate my right leg in the most comfortable position possible. It throbbed anyway.

I turned my mind back to the boy. What was he doing out here all alone? Had he been driven from his home as well? Where was his mother? During my escape from the cabin, I'd come across more than a few madmen who seemed ready to kill everything in sight. Hadn't the boy met any predators before I found him? I recalled how filthy he was, as though he'd been in the woods for a long time. How had the child survived for so long? He didn't even seem very concerned when I urged him forward. I had to *convince* him. Why didn't he run as soon as he heard the pack approaching? Who was shooting that gun? I had to find August. I had to get answers. I had to get up. I had to...

I had to rest for just a moment longer.

The rain continued to pour from the sky, past the branches; heavier and heavier, it weighed me down. Down my hair, my face, my clothes, my arms... Like a beautiful sonnet, I was hypnotized by its constancy. It rocked me gently, deep beneath my bones. Underneath my flesh I was drenched, like the rough-hewn bark scraping against my back.

I allowed my heavy eyelids to close with the feeling that I may never be able to open them again. And as soon as I did,

I began to feel myself drifting away from consciousness, away from Willow's Bend and the danger of the woods. I slowly let go of that last faint grasp on my surroundings and the reality around me. And it felt good.

Suddenly I was back in that familiar place, standing in my nana's living room, with the street lamps lighting the driveway past the silently stirring curtains. This time I was there alone. There were no crowds shifting and talking and laughing around me. I was waiting for it to happen, the very event that led me to Willow's Bend in the first place.

Instead, he walked into the house as though nothing had ever happened, as though no tragedy had occurred on the car-lined streets.

"Gavin," I said. "How did you get here?"

He was alive, unbroken, and smiling that charming smile. "What are you talking about, Charlotte?" he asked. Then, the sound of his voice altered into something deeper, older, and more urgent. "I'm looking for August. Where is he?"

The sound of an F-150 pickup that roared its engine over the hill ended the dream, as it always did. And I somehow knew that I was back in the woods. Yet I couldn't bring myself to open my eyes. Although I'd had dreams like this one for so long, I was still shocked every time I visited that scene, every time I saw his face and heard his voice all over again. Even as the dream ended, I knew that it was only a dream. And I was disappointed because I had hoped that coming to Willow's Bend would end these dreams for good. And yet, even here in the middle of these plagued and tormented woods, the dream had found me once again.

Where is August? The voice whispered between the trees, but I knew it was only my subconscious. It wasn't Gavin. And it wasn't real.

Where is the boy? the imaginary voice urged louder. It was so urgent, I almost opened my eyes to look around. But I couldn't move.

"He's probably dead," I muttered to myself. After all, so many people were.

"He cannot be dead."

The voice of my subconscious thundered like the storm above. My subconscious grabbed me by the arms and began to shake me. My subconscious slapped me across the face.

My eyes flew open at last to see not my subconscious at all...but something much less believable. Looking sternly into my eyes, only a few inches from my face, was the sopping presence of a pair of murky green eyes, a tan face dripping with rain, and slightly wild-looking dark hair. It was, of all things, a man.

And slung across his shoulder was a gun.

CHAPTER SIX

As my mind registered the eyes that appeared just inches in front of my face, I gasped. The man who had slapped me took a step back, looking slightly unnerved through the liquid veil of rainfall.

"You're the one who was shooting," I said, though my voice broke, sounding thick and raspy with exhaustion and dehydration. "You were hunting me!"

A glance at the shotgun slung on his back compelled me to try to get up and run. After all, it was suddenly quite clear that I was about to get shot. As my stiff and weary body moved to try to stand, my shoes got caught in muddy clumps of grass and sticks. The pain of my ankle caused me to fall back down to the earth. Trembling, I tried to pull myself up against the fallen tree trunk.

But the man's reaction stopped me as I glimpsed his widened eyes. "Stop, please!" he said. His arm was extended to me through the veil of rainfall. "It's okay. I won't hurt you."

I stared down at his outstretched hand, palm facing down so that I could see the tendons and muscles flexed beneath the tan skin of his lower arm. But they weren't twitching or flexing like those of the men who attacked Danny. I decided that this man might possibly be sane. And then, just before I looked away, I caught a glimpse of something on his skin. On the top of his forearm, there were slightly raised, pink lines curling out from his rolled-up sleeve toward his wrist. Scars, maybe. I blinked, not even certain of what I'd seen.

"Please," he insisted. I'm not sure why—perhaps it was the gun, perhaps it was the sight of those peculiar scars, or the fact that I knew I couldn't outrun him even if I'd wanted to—but I obeyed. I continued to stare at the gun, fairly certain that it could go off at any moment. One pull of the trigger and my life was over.

I used the trunk of the tree to slowly pull myself to stand and felt the heaviness of the soaking wet clothes and my tired body. I was still wearing my hooded sweatshirt and the now incredibly uncomfortable jeans made stiff from the rain and mud. A groan escaped my clenched teeth as a sharp, piercing pain shot through my foot.

"Are you okay?" the man inquired.

"Yes," I answered dully. But I was thinking how absurd a question like that was after everything I'd been through that day.

"I'm assuming you know about the quarantine," he said, removing from a pocket that familiar neon yellow notice. His copy was folded, creased, and dirty.

"Yes," I repeated as I struggled to sit on the fallen tree trunk. "Who are you?"

"My name—" But he stopped abruptly. His eyes darted around sporadically and then stopped for a moment, as if he was listening for something and heard it. Seconds passed as I observed how perfectly still he was. There was no sign of breathing, no indication of thought running through his mind beneath the now relaxed contours of his forehead. There was only the constant rain, which made me wonder what good it was to try to hear anything else at all. As I tried listening, I could only make out the sound of raindrops colliding with everything in their path, the air shaking the branches above my head and disheveling my damp hair in the wind's unpredictable course.

I could feel my hair stuck to my skin across my forehead and weighed down to my neck beneath my sweatshirt. I felt disgusting and miserable, even as I wondered whether I should be running for my life away from this deadly stranger. Regardless of whether he was a threat, there were plenty others nearby who wouldn't hesitate to kill me. But I remained where I was.

I took in his soaking wet form while I waited. Despite the mud and torn clothes, he was significantly cleaner and certainly more lucid than the deranged men I had passed in the woods. His demeanor was calm, collected, and stern. Where had he come from? Why was there no sign of fear etched in his features? Questions filled the thick, rain-scented air between us during the silence.

"Okay," he uttered with some authority. I exhaled as I realized that I had been holding my breath. However, he maintained an almost menacing look of intensity in his features, mouth subtly pulling downward at the edges and jaw made rigid, as though still watching, still listening.

He looked warily in my direction before he added, "I thought I heard something, but I think we're safe. And I think the storm is going to get much worse."

I looked up at the underbellies of the trees and their sprawling skeletal branches that seemed to be reaching out to touch something invisible in the air. The storm had withdrawn before it even began. Yet the thick layers of cloud continued to brew ominously over the treetops.

The man tilted his face straight up to the rainfall and the canopy of branches and swirling darkness above. He seemed to be embracing the falling water, the cool air, all of it. While I was just beginning to shiver, there was something about his posture that seemed to be saying, *Yes, let's have some more.*

His eyes were closed when he spoke again. "What's your name?" I didn't respond right away, trying to decide whether I should admire or laugh out loud at his queer but peaceful stance, so perfectly in tune with what was going on around him.

I recognized the fleeting traces of a smile as he slowly looked back at me again, reminding me to speak. "My name is Charlotte Benson." I touched my face again, remembering the sting he'd left there. But if I was being perfectly honest, I was more embarrassed than anything else. "You didn't tell me your name."

"I'm sorry if I hurt you, Charlotte. My name is Roden. Adams." He spoke solemnly. "I tried to wake you for some time, but it wasn't working. Do you know where the boy went?"

"I...I don't know," I began, suddenly remembering August, the white rabbit of a child who I'd began to think I'd imagined. He was real. And alone, and helpless in these woods. I began to stammer, overwhelmed and scared at the thought that I'd lost him. "I—I tried to follow him. They wouldn't let him in the shelter."

"I know. Because he's dangerous," he said as he looked down at a pair of gloves in his hands. "Like me."

He looked away into the woods surrounding us as I watched him, puzzled by his words.

"I saw you from a distance, running," he continued. He eyed me suspiciously now, brow furrowed and gaze careful. "I don't know how you made it as far as you did. But never mind that," he continued after a vacant pause. "We need to find August now. We don't want to be caught in the storm when it hits hard—and it will. When we find the boy, I know where to go, but please, right now just *try to remember*."

I looked away from him as I tried to think. Everything that had happened that day was a confused blur. The images of Danny, the men, the woman at the shelter, August... I was having trouble putting them on any kind of timeline. I was just too exhausted.

"Honestly, I have no idea," I admitted, feeling the rough bark press into my palms where I sat. "I lost him at the shelter. I only know that he was headed this direction from there, but after that..." I shook my head. "He could have gone anywhere."

Roden approached my fallen tree and sat down next to me. He rested his head in his hands, gloves off. I noticed a brown leather backpack across his shoulders next to the gun over a long-sleeved plaid shirt and torn denim. But I couldn't take my eyes off the gun.

"Wait a second," I said. "Did the boy, August, know that you were protecting him?"

He looked up, puzzled. "I don't know...I guess he had to know someone was protecting him."

"And...had you been there for long, in that area?" I asked. I figured that if I had realized that someone was protecting me out there, then I would eventually return to that spot. It was a simple theory, but it was the only one I could come up with.

Roden stood up. "He could be back there now," he muttered. He was suddenly alert and already moving in that direction.

I followed him as quickly as I could in my condition, though I couldn't help wincing with every few steps. He slowed considerably when he realized he was losing me.

Every few minutes of running was punctuated with a sudden stop. Roden quickly shushed me and held out one hand to my shoulder. I turned to see him turn to stone again for moments that felt interminable with tension. He sometimes went down to one knee and observed something I couldn't see on the ground or listened to something I couldn't hear through the trees and the wind. But what was invisible to me was obviously crucial to him. I had no idea what he was listening for or how he could hear over my laborious panting. *Coyotes*, I supposed. *Or footsteps, maybe?* Whatever it was, it was lost on me.

"Let's go," he said.

And off we went, each time it seemed with a new wind and more urgency than before. Every now and then I would hear the sound of howling or barking in the distance. "It's okay. They're nowhere nearby," Roden assured me. "At the moment." This last part was mumbled as he turned his head away from me, and I had the distinct impression I wasn't supposed to notice.

As we continued on our way, my mind disobediently trespassed into darker corners. I began to think of Danny. And when I did, I felt sick to my stomach. I could not begin to make sense of Danny's behavior in the last twenty-four hours. I recalled what happened in only brief glimpses and a feeling in my gut that made me want to break down and sob in the middle of the woods. I recalled blood, wounds, and bruises. I saw a flash of yellow eyes, reddened skin, and a look of innocent fear in his features. What it all added up to, I couldn't decide. That's when I remembered that he was dead.

We were moving past two towering cedars when Roden abruptly veered to the left, waving for me to follow. I hesitated, uncertain, surprised by the sudden change of direction.

"Wait a second. Where are we——" I began.

"Shh," he urged. He stopped and pulled me to the ground, listening again.

"Why did we——" I began again. He covered my mouth with his hand while holding a finger up to his closed lips with his other hand. Slowly, he moved his hand to turn my chin to the right. From that angle, my eyes rested on the hazy, large silhouette in the distance. It was another man, in such ragged clothing he was nearly naked as he stomped through the leaves. And I knew that he was one of *them*. I watched him disappear from view.

"We're changing directions because," Roden began in a quiet, but sharp whisper that I could barely hear above my still pounding heartbeat. But his eyes continued to scan the horizon even as he spoke. "If they see me near the shelter, they'll start shooting." My eyes widened at this claim. "Trust me——" he insisted. "It's already happened once. Besides, the same goes for August, and he knows it. We're more likely to see him on our way if we go around a safe distance. Let's go." He made a motion with his hand, and I followed his lead.

I was just thinking that he made a lot of sense about going around the shelter, when he stopped again so suddenly I nearly ran into him.

"What am I thinking?" he asked, slinging the shotgun farther back on his shoulder. "You need to go back to the shelter, *now.*"

"What? No, I'm helping you find the boy."

"Charlotte," he continued. "That's very nice of you, but it's not going to happen. I can keep protecting him just as I have for days now before you showed up and complicated things." His whisper was sharp and commanding. "The best thing for you to do is to go back to the shelter—*right now.*"

I stood there, conflicted once again. My mind told me that what he was saying was reasonable. I didn't owe this boy anything. And who knew how many other lost people, children included, could be out in these woods right now? Was I going to rescue them all? No. I wasn't even sure I was capable of protecting myself. The right thing to do was to find shelter on my own or with the other women.

Suddenly I was gripped by a flashback. I was underwater, staring into that youthful, tranquil face. It was August. And then it wasn't August. It was Gavin. And I was about to lose him again. But this time, I had a chance to save him.

"I'm sorry, but I can't."

"What do you mean, you can't?" Roden asked, clearly taken aback. His voice sounded mostly surprised and only somewhat angry.

"The traditional meaning," I spat back at him. "I'm incapable."

"But that's ridiculous. Listen," he began as he grabbed me firmly by the shoulders and peered fiercely into my eyes. "You don't seem to understand. August could kill you." I looked doubtfully back at him. "*I* could kill you. There's an infection spreading rampantly. You have no idea how much danger you're in out here."

"Look, I can't explain it," I said. I felt the inadequacy in my words but refused to look away as I spoke. "But I know what I need. I need to help you find August. I need to do something to make sure he's going to be okay."

He stepped back at the end of my response and seemed to be assessing something. The green-hazel eyes lingered for a moment on what I was sure was still a slightly purple hue around my eye. But then he continued searching my eyes. What did he see? Did he see the image in my mind of leaving Danny on the floor of my cabin? Was he watching me cower in the confines of a playground when I was nine? Aren't these the events that defined me? As far as I knew, there was nothing else to see there.

Finally, though, he broke his gaze and turned away from me, leaving me to wonder whether he was satisfied or revolted by what he'd seen. The seconds ticked by as Roden looked around in the opposite direction, surveying our surroundings.

"Okay. It's your fate," he said. "But if you have any reason to believe that I or August have been infected, no matter how lucid we may seem, you have to promise me you will run for your life back to the shelter for good. Because once that happens, there's nothing you can do to save us." And as though it were just occurring to him, he added, "We may not know each other, but I don't think I can stand seeing another person get infected or killed."

I considered this as I remembered the way that man snarled and knocked over heavy furniture in his rage-driven pursuit to kill me. He must have had this mysterious infection. And what of Danny? It wasn't just that I'd left him alone that bothered me. It was the way he changed before my eyes. I shook my head. I couldn't process it. Not now.

"We're wasting time," I said, hoping to sound about a thousand times braver than I felt.

That storm Roden had promised seemed to be brewing just behind us. I listened to the soft, rolling thunder in the distance, reminding me of water just simmering on the stovetop. And I knew we had to hurry.

We continued on a wide curve around the shelter. With all of Roden's caution and vigilance along the way, the journey took much longer than I'd expected. I kept moving just behind him, stumbling up and down the rugged terrain, below and around and over the monotony of tree limbs and soggy, blackened leaves along the way.

We eventually arrived at the edge of the clearing where I had first trampled on the boy, but he was nowhere to be found. What was worse was that the storm was threatening to overtake us, and the sun was setting. It was getting darker every second, causing the distant firewheels' scarlet patches to glow ominously beneath the canopy of clouds. We were out of time.

Roden was scouring the weeds and brush to my left as I approached a scattered pile of those bright flyers on the ground. I thought I saw a shoe sticking out from beneath the pile.

"August?" I cried tentatively, thinking that perhaps he was hiding in the weeds again. I was beginning to get a little spooked in the dark shadows of the trees and tall grass, with the reverberating thunder at my back and flashes of lightning playing with my vision. The object didn't move. So I moved in closer, mumbling, "Hey, Roden, come over here." I picked up a long stick from the ground and used it to prod the object.

There was no denying it. It was a shoe...*with a foot in it*. I moved some of the weeds with my hands to get a better look. It was the body of an old man. I leaned in closer, despite the growing sense of terror at what I was seeing. It wasn't just a dead body—it was distorted. A blood and foam-stained mouth and shattered glasses. Blood was drying on his shoulder where his shirt had been torn, and thick clots of blood stained his fingernails and palms, as though he'd been digging into them himself.

"Roden!" I staggered away from the corpse.

Everything happened so quickly I didn't have time to respond.

Out of the darkness, a man lunged toward me from behind a large oak tree. He was short and stocky, carrying the same trademark as the corpse I'd just found: a blood and foam-stained mouth. He seemed to be groaning as he lunged at me with a jagged, broken glass bottle in his hand raised menacingly above our heads.

He was just inches away from my face but stopped. Just as quickly as he'd appeared, the body violently shuddered and slumped backward to the ground before reaching me.

I stared down at the body, bewildered to see Roden removing the submerged blade from the man's back and beginning to carefully, methodically wipe off the blood. I was stunned. I continued to watch, unable to look away from the slow, gentle movement of a blue bandana against the red-drenched metal blade. There was something sinister in the placidity of this man's movement, as though it were neither his first nor second time to do this. And I was still sickened by the sight of Roden wiping the blood off that blade when he pulled out his gun and shot the already still body in the chest.

I cowered to the ground at the sound of the shot, futilely covering my ears. I'd never been that close to a gunshot in my life. My ears rang loudly, and for a moment, I was a nine-year-old child again.

In my mind, there was the fence. There was the blood. There were children, afraid, screaming, and crying. I hadn't relived that day so vividly in years, but here it came in a rush of buried memories.

"Are you okay?" I became aware that Roden was kneeling on the earth close to me. I looked up to see his eyebrows furrowed with concern.

I shuddered at first, at the man with the gun who was not afraid of blood. But then I was so stunned by this unexpected concern for me that I couldn't come up with an answer.

"Charlotte?" he urged.

"I'm...I'm fine."

"Are you sure? Are you hurt?" He persisted, pulling my hands away from my ears and looking me over.

"No, I'm fine," I insisted, instinctively pulling my hands away from his and back to my ribs protectively. *Away from the shooter. Away from the killer.* As I wiped my eyes and waited for the ringing in my ears to stop, I silently wondered if I was wrong to be afraid of this man who just saved my life.

Just then, I caught a glimpse of something behind Roden. I couldn't believe my eyes. The boy was standing next to an elm.

"August?" I gasped.

He raised his head farther and stepped forward in the rain. I stood up and began moving toward him, saying, "We've been looking everywhere for you!"

But something was wrong.

Roden stood up and turned around slowly to face August and immediately froze where he stood. Looking back at August, I saw that he too was completely still. Both were staring at one another, mirroring the same look of fear.

In the next moment, both sprang into action.

It was like watching a cat pounce on a helpless mouse. Roden bounded toward the child and picked him up off the ground in one swift motion. August screamed where he was held immovably in Roden's arms. The boy shook and fought for his life as the man placed one hand across his mouth to stifle the sounds of his struggle.

"What are you doing to him?" I nearly screamed. As I watched, tears began to seep down August's reddened face, but he continued to fight for his life.

"Shh! I'm trying to keep him quiet," Roden answered. "Help me calm him down."

Something wasn't adding up. "Why is he so afraid of you?" I demanded.

It was difficult to see through the rain and the darkness around us, but I sensed a certain dread rise up within me as I waited for his answer. I heard the large, fat raindrops spatter against the leaves and the mulch and our tired, sopping heads as I waited. And I noticed that August had momentarily stopped struggling, as though he were waiting too. I heard the thunder roll out in the distance and watched the lightning strike jaggedly, as though the thin yellow lines had been cut mercilessly into the black sky with a box knife. And then I heard Roden's voice. "Because he watched me kill his father."

Psalm 13:3-4

Behold, and answer me, Yahweh, my God.

Give light to my eyes, lest I sleep in death;

Lest my enemy say, "I have prevailed against him";

Lest my adversaries rejoice when I fall.

CHAPTER SEVEN

"What?" I gasped. "What are you—" But I stopped. I was speechless. Had I really been so naive? After all, what did I really know about the man with the gun? *Nothing.* Then I remembered: The newspaper article about the mysterious murders in Willow's Bend. I felt my pulse quicken as I frantically stuttered out the words, "You're the murderer, aren't you? This, this whole time, you're the one—"

"What are you talking about?" He scowled at me through the rain. "There is no murderer except the infected—and they're also the victims. *I am not a murderer.*" I watched that small child begin writhing anew in his stoic arms.

"I had no choice," he continued. "His father was infected. Look, I'll tell you more about it later. Right now, we need to get somewhere safe."

"This is insane," I said, overwhelmed. I wasn't sure what to believe. The seconds ticked by as I slowly shook my head, trying to come to some reasonable conclusion. Meanwhile, the rain poured down harder all around us.

However, I admitted to myself that this story about August's infected father was at the very least plausible. And I was convinced that Roden had been shooting down our enemies just hours earlier. Didn't he just save my life, after all? Yes, I had to trust him. At least for the moment. I had no choice. And I had to persuade August to trust us both.

I walked up closer to the two of them. "August, hey, look at me." He opened his eyes, but his expression was hostile. I stepped closer to him and wiped his blond hair from his eyes, finding in them something strangely familiar. "Hey, my name is Charlotte, and I'm going to do everything I can to take care of you, okay?" The hostile look remained. "It is very dangerous out here, and Roden and I want to take you somewhere safe. But you have to trust us and come with us, okay?"

The boy blinked back at me. Yet, he had stopped fighting.

Slowly Roden let the boy down to the ground as I added, "I'm going to hold your hand, and we're going to follow Roden..."

"We're going to my house, okay?" Roden finished. At this the boy turned, taking my hand and looking warily back at Roden, who was extending that hand of his again, asking for trust. "I'm not going to hurt you, I promise. I just want to keep you safe."

They looked back at one another for several seconds before either one of them moved a muscle. How Roden could even ask for the boy's trust after every confusing and tragic thing that had happened, I didn't know. The boy merely nodded as I watched water drip down his trembling cold chin, and we began the journey to find shelter. After some time, I was surprised to see that August had taken Roden's hand after all.

Roden urged us up through uneven terrain, mud sloshing up our pant legs with every step. Lightning struck nearby trees as we tripped through the thickets and thorny branches that tore at our clothes and skin. The thunder erupted all around us, making it even more difficult to balance in the flashes of light and overwhelming darkness. It took all of my energy just to keep moving forward, and so I didn't even attempt to watch for predators. I left that entirely to the man with the gun.

We hiked through the trees, climbing ever upward against a steep hill, sometimes slipping and nearly falling in the slick mud and wet grass. More than once, the boy and I nearly fell to the ground, and so I had to reach out to Roden's arm to keep us upright. Mostly, though, I pulled hard on long, thorny patches of weeds just to keep our weak bodies moving forward and upward. My palms stung in the rain where they were cut and bled from the razor-edged grass.

Once, August nearly tumbled backward down the hill, but Roden quickly picked the boy up and hoisted him onto his back. And so we tripped on, stumbling through the darkness and the onslaught of rain that steadily soaked us through.

A few agonizing minutes later, my sore ankle hit an unseen mud hole. I slipped and fell all the way to the ground with a cry of pain. I knew that I couldn't keep going. I'd been moving all day long, with no food or water since that sandwich the evening before, and freezing cold in the October wind and soaked clothes. Trembling, I lifted up my head and wiped the mud off my face with an already muddy sleeve. In the darkness, I could just make out that Roden and the boy hadn't noticed I was no longer right next to them. I lay my head back down, having emptied myself of every last bit of effort. I simply could not move. I knew that I *had* to move, and yet I simply *couldn't*. There was nothing left.

"Charlotte?" I heard his voice shouting through the rain from far away, already slightly hoarse since I'd met him just hours earlier. It must have been the weather. "Charlotte!" His voice grew nearer until he stood right above me. "Hey, you have to get up, okay?"

I barely lifted my head up in the middle of the weeds and mud. It was all I could manage in response.

But he didn't stop. "Charlotte, you have to get up! Come on, right now!" He continued a long stream of shouts just a few feet away from me. I couldn't move. "Get up! Do you hear me? *Get up!*" His voice insisted, but I still could not move. He simply didn't understand that I was incapable of going on. There is a point of total exhaustion—a point of no return. Why didn't he get that? "Charlotte, come on! Get up! It's just a little farther, you can make it! But you have to get up *now*!"

I had to tell him I was dying. I'm not sure why, but it seemed crucial that I communicate this to him. His yelling was futile, after all. And he was risking the boy's life by waiting around for someone who wasn't going to make it.

My legs moved around, clumsily, painfully. My arms moved and pushed off the ground until I was sitting, panting, and trying not to cry from sheer effort. Roden kept yelling. *Why does he keep yelling like that?* I wondered. I had to tell him to stop yelling so I could die peacefully. But instead, my arms and legs pushed off until I was standing. And I stumbled toward him. And I *kept* stumbling toward him.

The terrain was finally beginning to even out when I caught a glimpse of an enormous structure at the top of the hill. At the time, I still had no idea where we were within Willow's Bend. My sense of direction had been lost long ago. As my legs propelled me forward and we approached the structure, I made out that it was some type of mansion, with tall pillars and bright red French doors. There was a dim light on peering out at us through the darkness. The mansion itself was set between two weeping willows. But I made that dim light from inside the house my focal point. And I somehow climbed that hill one step at a time, with Roden's help.

We made our way up the large, wet stone steps until we were finally beneath the shelter of the porch's eaves. I watched as Roden carefully set the boy down on the dry, cold stone before reaching into a pocket and pulling out a ring with keys on it. As he did this, I fought the temptation to collapse right there in front of the door. Roden unlocked one door and pushed it open, pausing to listen for the sound of intruders. Then he stooped down again and picked up the boy.

"Go on," he said, nodding for me to go in first. I turned away from his dripping chin before taking a few timid steps forward into the darkness. Behind me, Roden closed the door again and locked it. I heard the flick of a switch and watched the darkness before me give way to light.

I found myself standing in an elaborate foyer before a grand staircase, wanting to take in the beautiful sight. But all I could think about was water and someplace to lay my head.

"This way," Roden said softly as he passed me to the side of the steps and beneath a tall arch into another room.

I followed him, feeling completely bewildered and wondering if I was in some kind of a twisted dream. This would be just like one of my dreams—nothing made sense.

After making our way down hallways and sharp turns, we arrived at a large room, perhaps what people used to call a sitting room. There was a large, extravagant fireplace with a matching set of furniture placed surrounding it. Roden gently laid the child down on the couch and pulled a blanket down from the couch's side to cover him. I watched Roden tuck it in around the child's body with those torn and ruined clothes. And I watched him pause to retrieve a russet leaf from the boy's wet hair.

"Stay here—I'll be right back," Roden said before disappearing down a hallway.

I stood over the boy, watching his flushed, puffed-out cheeks and slow breathing in his sleep. Mud was spattered across the side of his face near where the top of the blanket had been pulled up to his chin. He was shivering in his sleep. I remembered the first time I saw his bright cerulean eyes beneath the blanketed sky amid the grass and the weeds. It was like something out of a dream. It could not be real. He could not be real. But somehow, we had survived.

I heard a thud behind me. Roden was unloading an armful of firewood. I watched him prodding logs around in the fireplace, crouched down in those torn and fraying clothes as I rubbed my frozen hands together and breathed into them. When Roden turned toward me, most of his features were darkened while the dim light from another room illuminated the jagged cut across his face. The effect was frightening.

"Do you think we can get him cleaned up?" he asked.

I looked back down at the boy again. He desperately needed to be cleaned up. And yet... "I don't know. I think he might have a fever or something."

Roden wiped back his thick dark hair with a muddy forearm before answering. "Well, let's do what we can and just go from there."

I HELPED RODEN set August back down on the couch, now fairly cleaned up and already asleep again. Although he seemed feverish, we were hoping he just needed rest, and so we decided to wait things out for the time being. He was wearing one of Roden's T-shirts; it was much too big for him, but it would have to do. Meanwhile, his own pathetic clothes, along with that blanket, were in a pile to be washed, or more than likely, to be thrown away.

My gaze had drifted to the fireplace when I realized that Roden had left the room again. Now that he'd disappeared, I noticed the sounds of the raging storm outside once more. I gathered that we were near the heart of the house, for there were no windows rattling nearby. Yet the sound of thunder lost none of its menacing nature as it traveled through the labyrinthine mansion to where I stood, still damp and shivering. Rather, it almost had an echoing effect, like shouting into a tunnel. I turned my head back toward the boy as the thunder momentarily softened and waned, giving way to the raucous downpour of the rain on the eaves.

I turned to see Roden shoving a huge couch from another room into this one. He swung one edge of the couch around to face the fireplace, next to where August was, and then stood up straight again, turning toward me.

"I thought you might want to stay close to the boy tonight," he said through panting breaths, wiping his brow with his forearm. "We can figure out a better situation in the morning. I'll stay here with him while you get cleaned up, if you like."

I hobbled my way down a hallway with black, dimly lit sconces toward the bathroom. It was the same bathroom in which we'd tediously wiped the mud from August's delicate form. I paused to look at myself in the mirror, but the sight was nearly unrecognizable. A few minutes later, I climbed into the claw-foot tub where the wide shower head was spewing its clean, hot water and decided that I was never going to get out again.

I watched the mud, dried blood, and red dirt reluctantly release their hold, slip down my skin, and swish into the drain. The hues swirled and melded into ambiguous shades before they slowly disappeared. I watched my palm where it stung with the water's spray and traced the thin red lines with my finger. Those thin red lines kept forming again and again, feeling like recurring paper cuts. I picked up a washcloth, rubbing it hard with a bar of soap, until it was white with suds. Then I began washing very gently, first over the scrapes and bruises on my legs, then my swollen ankle, which was slightly lifted to keep the weight off it.

But as I watched the parade of bubbles on my kneecaps and calves, I heard a voice in the back of my mind whisper, "You do not have to be good." And I heard the geese rise up into the air in the distance on that fine September morning. The steam of the shower became the lifting fog upon the river with its chorusing row team and cawing game. And I recalled the way his hands were in his pockets when he stood outside my window and the way the sunlight danced in his hair as he pet Cleo and Charles and Hamlet as though they were his family.

I pressed the fabric hard against my arms, knowing that it would flush red. Back and forth I shoved it against my shoulder, grating it against my collarbone. But still I heard our panting breaths from the day we jogged and collapsed on the front porch steps of that shabby, claustrophobic cabin. And I heard him tell me I reminded him of someone he used to know.

The cloth stung and burned where I tried to wash away the memories, but they came to me in torrents anyway. I saw Danny's bruised and altered face when he killed the man who was attacking me. And I saw that frightened look in his eyes just before they filled up with renewed hatred for me. I dropped the cloth in the tub and watched as it began to clog up the drain. My skin burned, leaving me feeling raw yet unsatisfied. And then I fell to my knees and cried until I hit empty.

BY THE TIME I'd gotten out of the shower and put on the clean clothes Roden had left out for me, I couldn't decide if my reflection looked better or worse than before. My features were cleaner, but my skin was red and my eyes puffed up from crying. I could still make out that purple arc from James's

109

right hook next to a few other scrapes and cuts from when I fell in the woods.

When I got back to the sitting room, Roden stood up, saying that he was going to shower. I sat down on the floor against August's couch, wrapping a warm blanket around my shoulders, and stared vacantly into the fireplace. Before me the fire sent out dazzling sparks and a soothing crackle that felt intoxicating to my weary bones. The heat it gave off reached my skin welcomingly, overwhelming my mind, body, and soul with the simple sensation of comfort. How good it was! And in my weariness, I vaguely wondered if there was a happier woman in the world than I.

I drifted in and out of sleep, feeling the weight of my head tilt downward again and again. But I struggled to remain upright and still. I was not ready to sleep, not yet ready to give in. As nonsensical as it may sound, I was too tired to sleep.

When I heard quiet footfalls across the hardwood floor, I turned to see Roden walking into the room with a tray of tall glasses and a cup of hot tea. I stared. He looked strikingly different now that he was cleaned up, dried off, and in decent clothes. He even wore glasses with thin silver rims that reminded me of a professor I once knew. Once again I had that uncomfortable impression that I was in a bizarre dream.

"I thought you might like some tea," he said. He placed the tray on the floor in front of me before sitting down against August's couch right next to me. "And water, of course. You must be pretty thirsty."

"Thank you," I said. I picked up the small, cobalt blue teacup and held it in both hands up to my lips, inhaling the humid warmth rich with the scent of chamomile. But then I set it back down and started drinking water. Water had never tasted so good. I drank it quickly, greedily gulping down the liquid that my body literally ached for.

"I was in a tree when I saw you," Roden said. His voice was quiet, cautious in a way that it hadn't been out in the woods. I turned my head slightly to see him resting his arms against his knees, grasping a half-emptied glass of water in two large hands that were covered in cuts and scrapes. I wondered if he too had traced the thin red lines in the shower. "I watched you appear at the top of that hill. And at first I thought you were one of them. But the way you were running..." He turned to look at me as he continued, "You were running fast. Faster than I could believe. And you were running straight for August...I wondered how you knew."

"I didn't know," I said. "About August, about anyone. I thought I was alone, running toward...nothing." I shuddered at the memory of that feeling. Having just seen Danny the way I had. And having run longer and harder than I'd thought possible. Having only been conscious of the canines behind me.

"Where did you come from?" Roden asked. "If you don't mind."

"I don't even know how I got there, really. I mean, I came from a cabin on the other side of Willow's Bend. I was renting a small cabin." I wasn't sure if I was making sense anymore, I was so tired. And these facts seemed so distant, as though they were a part of another lifetime or someone else's life.

"By yourself?" he prompted.

"No. Well—yes. I was staying there alone. But I wasn't alone when..." How could I put it into words? My mind scrambled for anything that would do. "The men came. Well, no. That's not right. My friend and I went out for pizza...the dogs had disappeared, but we'd gone out for pizza when the gate was closed. And so we drove back..." *Why do I keep mentioning pizza?* I knew I was too tired to communicate. And yet I was aware of a certain desperation to get the story out and to have it shared with another human being. So I pressed on. "We stayed at my cabin. We were scared. There was something wrong with his eyes..." What did that have to do with the story? I didn't know, but there it was. "The next morning...this morning...we were robbed. And then he went out looking for Cleo—"

"Did you say Cleo?" he interrupted.

"Yes, my dog, Cleo. A man came and chased him back inside. They started fighting, but another man showed up..." I shook my head at the flames that danced before my eyes. "That's where it all gets confusing. I honestly don't understand what happened. But my friend...didn't make it."

"Was your friend..." Roden began, but hesitated. "Was he your landlord?"

I looked up at him, astonished. "Yes, how did you know?"

"Danny and I," he began, but seemed to change his mind about something. "I've known him for a long time."

"I'm so sorry," I said. "But Danny is dead." And I would have cried had I not been so tired and still so dehydrated from all of my former tears. Roden let out a heavy sigh, almost causing me to regret telling him the news.

"I'm very sorry to hear that," he said, his voice thick with sorrow. "I'm sorry to hear that he's dead. I'm sorry to hear what the two of you had to go through—it must have been a nightmare." I wasn't sure if he was still speaking to me or merely to himself. "And I'm sorry because we hadn't spoken in over a year." I could see that there were tears swimming in those pensive green eyes.

Despite all this, I acknowledged that my burden had been lifted. Even if it was only by the smallest amount, I felt the relief wash over me. He really was sorry. And he knew Danny, probably much better than I did. And he too had lost him.

As I sipped the warm chamomile, I was grateful to be in this mysterious house with these two strangers—one lying asleep, completely vulnerable, and the other having just saved our lives and given us shelter. And yet I didn't know that I could trust Roden, really. I still didn't know him at all.

I looked down at my tea cup, watching that pillowy bag of leaves against the thin, white enamel in the firelight.

"How did you find August?" I asked. I longed to stay awake long enough to know. I needed to know who had saved my life.

He cleared his throat before speaking. "My dog, Altus, started acting strange three days ago. I knew he had some type of rabies, but it was too late to save him. I had to shoot him." There was a kind of reverent pause before he continued. "I'd suspected interbreeding for a while now. The overpopulation of the coyotes, the change in paw prints, the depopulation of the deer... Everything pointed to the fact that someone was breeding wolves with the coyote population on the refuge. And I knew that came with risks. But I had no idea that this could happen...this..." His voice faltered.

In the silence I heard the soft sounds of the boy's breathing just behind us. Rhythmic and peaceful. His puffs of breath stirred at the back of my drying hair.

"So you think that's what the infection is about?" I asked.

"It's the only way I can make sense of it. The interbreeding, the rabies, the behavior of the people I saw in the woods."

I remained silent, waiting for him to continue.

"Then I found the notice about the quarantine. But I had no idea that the disease was turning people rabid, destroying their minds. I was out looking for answers when I heard sounds coming from a cabin. When I got there, I saw August's father attacking his mother. That's when I learned what the disease really did."

I shivered, finishing off the tea and setting it down before pulling my blanket up closer around my chin.

"It strips them of their humanity, Charlotte. They might as well be wild, rabid wolves to do the things I've seen. August's father killed his mother before I could save her. I found August hiding beneath the kitchen sink, but he ran from me. And I followed, keeping a safe distance so that I could protect him." A curious laugh escaped his lips. "I didn't even think it would work. I just kept trying, kept following, kept shooting. Along the way we saw so many people out of their minds. So much inhumane violence..." He turned his head toward me, letting the light from the fire reflect off the glasses so that I couldn't read his eyes. "Well, you know."

"Yes," was all I could manage, trying not to shudder. I vaguely acknowledged that in hearing his dreadful story, I'd somehow inched closer to him across the floor. But he didn't seem to notice, and I was too tired to care.

"I followed the boy to the shelter. He's smart, you know," he said, nodding toward the couch behind us. "But Jess, the woman they put in charge there, wouldn't let him in. I couldn't believe it. She's always been very kind, and to think she actually threatened him...but then I think that this is the kind of thing that changes people, you know?"

I thought of that. *The kind of thing that changes people.* How many times had I changed? How had I been shaped by the atrocities and tragedies of life? My vision began to swim with exhaustion. I forced my eyes wide open.

"So Jess thinks it only affects males, and maybe she's right. I didn't see any infected women along the way. When she was yelling at August, a girl must have spotted me through the trees. She started shooting at me." His hand went up to the nasty cut across his cheekbone. "I tripped and hit a rock trying to get away. The girl didn't know what she was doing with that gun, or I'd be dead right now. But I somehow escaped, and eventually caught sight of the boy again."

I battled the luring unconsciousness of sleep, uncertain if I'd missed something in his story.

"Anyway, for some reason, the boy went back to the edge of the woods and laid down in the dandelions. I don't know why...it's almost funny. And so I was in that tree for a long time, until you showed up."

"And complicated things," I heard myself say. But I realized my eyes had fallen closed and jerked them open again.

"Yeah," he admitted. "But I'm really glad you did. I mean it."

I managed to meet his gaze for a moment, uncertain.

"I know what I said out there," he said. "But I was wrong. He never would have trusted me if it wasn't for you."

I let my eyes close this time. I'm not sure why. Maybe just because it felt so good to give in a little. Just for a moment. And maybe another moment too.

"Now I know that he needed you," I heard a voice say amid the flames and the rhythmic breathing. "Now I know that *we* needed you."

My mind desperately tried to cling onto that last little phrase as I slipped down, down, down into obscurity. And I continued to hear his voice in some distant cadences for a long time throughout my dreams.

CHAPTER EIGHT

The first thing I registered was the word *momma*. I shook my head where it lay, shaking off some ephemeral impressions of a dream. When I blinked there in the darkness, I recalled a sunlit image of my mother standing up and walking away from me.

Then I heard another sound. I started to turn around. My neck and limbs felt stiff where I sat leaning back against the couch and against Roden. His head was tilted back with his arms sprawled out wide across the length of the couch. But even through the darkness I could see the stiff places in his flannel shirt where my head must have fallen in my sleep.

"Daddy—no!" I heard from behind me. I quickly stood up and found August's writhing figure twisted in the sheets and blankets. His hair was wild, leaving me to wonder how long this had been going on. When he wasn't moving, he was shivering uncontrollably. "Momma!" he nearly shouted in a gut-wrenching cry of panic and desperation.

I fought back tears as I watched him. But I knew that there was nothing I could do.

He screamed, "Noooooo!"

Roden jumped up from where he was on the floor as the child cried and continued to plead with his dead parents.

"What the hell? What's wrong?" Roden said. Before I could answer him, he started trying to wake the child up. "August, hey, hey, wake up!" He began to nudge him, but the boy kept thrashing and crying, completely oblivious that we were even in the room.

"Why won't he wake up?" Roden asked, sounding furious. But I could hear the same panicked desperation in his voice that I was struggling with in my silence.

"It's a night terror," I answered. "There's nothing we can do. He'll wake up on his own, and he most likely won't remember any of this." Even though I believed my explanation to be true, it didn't alleviate the agony I felt as I watched the boy continue to writhe.

"How do you know?" Roden asked. I couldn't read his expression in the darkness, but he sounded skeptical.

"My parents told me," I answered. "Because I used to have them."

We both stared down helplessly at the child for some time, unable to look away. I wrapped my arms around my ribcage as I wondered at this new torture to my soul. Why couldn't I help him? I couldn't fathom how my parents made it through my childhood, having to witness this sort of thing. Roden's arm bumped against my shoulder, causing me to glance up at him. He ran his hands through his hair before saying, "How long can this go on?"

"I don't know," I answered, but I was cut off with another piercing scream for August's momma. And then there was more crying. Then he stopped, shuddered there against the blankets, and appeared to be waking up at last.

"August, sweetie?" I began, moving toward him. I gently nudged at his pillow as I wiped the damp hair from his eyes. "It's just me—Char. Everything's going to be okay."

He didn't answer, but he didn't seem to mind when I sat down on the couch and moved his pillow onto my lap. He lay his head back down on the pillow and shivered beneath the blankets. Roden sat back down against the couch in front of us where he had been before. I stared for a while into the darkened fireplace where the last embers had long since faded.

And so I somehow fell back to sleep again, this time with the feverish child snoring quietly in my lap.

UPON WAKING the second time, all of my senses were slow to return. It was morning. My body throbbed with sore muscles and bruised bones. My ears took in a strangely familiar sound of *pok-be-cock* as I tried to remember where I was. I took in the fireplace, the blue-gray walls and high ceiling, the sleeping boy curled up against me. And so I remembered the mansion, the journey, the nightmare.

I also remembered that I had just dreamed of being on a beautiful sunlit farm, talking to William Carlos Williams about using that red wheelbarrow of his to move the chickens to the other side of the farm. I smiled at the recollection. But the sound I had been hearing wasn't a chicken, I realized. I inhaled deeply the aroma of coffee.

My eyes took in the sitting room around me, which had somehow brightened with the dawn, despite the fact that there were no windows in the room. To my right there were two open doors; behind me the hallway that led to the bathroom I'd used and the foyer. And before me, on either side of the fireplace, were two more hallways that led to rooms I hadn't seen. Something about the daylight made the grandeur of the room more vivid, more vibrant, without taking away the air of mystery.

The stonework in the fireplace appeared more intricate, more artistic and awe-inspiring; its elegant curves evocative of something very much alive. The hardwood floors, though visibly covered in dust and the mud we'd tracked in, gave off a deeper, richer hue. I stood up, stretching my arms and my back. And as I did, I was struck with the memory of that late-night conversation. It's remarkable the way something can feel so comfortable and natural in the firelight and then so out of place in the daylight.

I examined the child for a moment. His cheeks were flushed red, but he remained asleep.

I went back down the hallway and followed the sounds of that familiar *pok-be-cock* passing through another hallway into a large, spacious kitchen in which the aroma of coffee hung in the air. There was a huge island, a black granite countertop, and a sprawling cherry oak table in front of numerous curtained windows and tall French doors that led outside. The curtains were a silky navy blue that flowed to the ground. Somehow the light managed to filter through and illuminate the hardwood floors, dark cabinetry, and the tall leaning figure who pored over a newspaper while holding a corded phone to his ear with his shoulder. He was angry.

"Right. Actually, I *do* understand what the word *protocol* means. I'm just saying that we've got a small child up here who is very sick, and I don't know how to take care of him," Roden spoke firmly into the phone. "He has something called 'night terrors.' And a fever. And did I mention? *No parents.*" A pause. "What he *needs* is a *doctor.*"

I heard an exasperated sigh from him as I began opening cabinet doors in search of a coffee mug. After seeing about four empty shelves, I finally opened a door with three presumably clean mugs turned upside down.

"A care package," I heard Roden mutter into the receiver as I poured from the tall, steaming percolator. He looked up at me briefly before shifting his weight and looking back down at the newspaper again. "I don't want to have a housewarming party. I just want us to get out alive." I sat down and listened, curious.

"I'm sorry—exactly how long do you expect to leave us here? *Weeks.* Okay... That's—yeah, that's not going to work. What am I supposed to do for the boy?" Silence.

I stared up over my mug as I waited.

"To begin with, they need new clothes. A small boy, maybe five or six years old and a..." He looked up at me, uncomfortably. "Twenty-something female. And we need food. And ammo. Look, I'll call you back with the details."

He hung up the phone and began to pour himself a cup of coffee, letting out a frustrated sigh as he poured.

"Who was that?" I asked.

"An agent from the CDC." He sat down across from me at the dining table.

"Weeks?" I said, raising my eyebrows at him.

His expression was grim. "At the very least, yes."

"But, why?"

"Protocol." He spat the word out with disgust. "Because it's an unknown disease, and they don't know how long the incubation period is yet. They're learning about it as we speak, but it could take a while to gather enough data to be convinced that we wouldn't be putting the rest of society at risk by leaving the refuge."

"Ahh," I said as though I understood. But really I just felt myself sinking. I wanted out. *Now.*

"Meanwhile, they're sending us a care package."

"How are they going to deliver it?" I asked.

"On the balcony, by helicopter. We're fortunate to be in this house at a time like this, to have a safe way to receive supplies." I listened to the slurp of his coffee before he continued. "I can't imagine what other survivors are going through. And aside from the shelter, this is probably the safest place in the refuge right now."

"It must be incredible," I muttered, letting my eyes roam around the room. "Living in a house like this." I admired the ornate designs on the ceiling. Was there an end to the opulence?

"I suppose so. I never spent a lot of time indoors before."

"That's so hard to believe. There's just so much potential..."

"Maybe, but after a while, it seems to just blur into one room after another. It usually feels more like a museum than a place to live. It's damn hard to keep up."

"Huh," I inadvertently huffed. I was thinking about how spoiled a person must be to not appreciate a house like this.

"Right," he said, looking away. "Well, if you could write down everything you and the boy need, I'll let the agent know, and we should have the package in a few hours. Is that okay?"

"Sure," I answered.

He stood up abruptly and walked away, leaving a trail of dirt from his muddy boots and the echoing sounds of his footsteps in his wake.

I WAS SITTING on the edge of the couch, where August was propped up against a large pillow. I held the cool, damp washcloth to his burning forehead and watched as his dim eyes slowly opened and closed as they had been doing for some time. I'd walked him to the bathroom once, and it seemed to take all of his renewed strength in that one task. Also, he had begun to sweat through his borrowed, clean clothes. Things were not looking as good as I'd hoped.

"August, are you feeling any better?" I asked. After a moment's hesitation, I watched as he slowly shook his head.

"No? Well, could I get you to drink some water, please?" He nodded then, and so I held the tall glass up to his clammy hands and helped him to the water. I'd eaten a little food from what I could find in Roden's kitchen, which wasn't much. And I'd especially brought a banana and some peanut butter for August, but he refused it.

"We're going to get you some medicine soon, okay? And some new clothes..." I tried to sound cheerful. "And some chicken noodle soup. Do you like chicken noodle soup when you're sick?" He slowly nodded again, licking his dry lips.

"Well, it will be here in no time. I just need you to drink lots of water and tell me what you need. Can you do that?" He nodded again.

Then he closed his eyes and soon emitted that gentle, rhythmic hum that told me he was asleep.

I GLANCED AT my reflection, relieved to be in new, clean clothes. I rolled up the long, warm sleeves of my shirt and threw on a hooded sweatshirt before making my way to the mansion's foyer. I'd barely persuaded August to eat a bowl of chicken noodle soup and take some medicine before he was fast asleep again. Meanwhile, I hadn't seen Roden since he hauled down the backpacks and packages from the helicopter and I helped unload the bags of food in the kitchen. Imagining that August would be asleep for quite a while, I decided to take my time drifting in and out of every room and haunt my way down every corridor at my leisure.

I began at that grand staircase, feeling the willow-shaped newels with my fingertips and taking in the delicate curves and that leaning pose in which they had been formed, as though they were falling over in slow motion. I walked up the many steps, carefully shifting my weight from my throbbing ankle as I went, and silently thanking God for painkillers. I reached one hand out to feel the dark oxblood wallpaper with its lacy gold damask designs as I climbed the steps.

Once at the top of the second floor, I leaned over the railing and looked down at the foyer, at the doors and sea of marble. There were two large windows on either side of the French doors, covered in heavy drapes that matched the walls. From this height, I imagined looking down at guests who were just arriving, taking off their mink and suit jackets and handing over their bowler hats and sharp, black umbrellas.

I reluctantly turned around and leaned back against the railing, attempting to decide which hallway to explore first. There were two corridors, one toward the right wing, the other to the left. A Robert Frost poem flitted through my mind. Unfortunately, there was no way to tell which path was more or less worn than the other. So I took the left.

I soon came to the first empty bedroom. It was fairly large and complete with an antique dresser and queen-sized bed, a vanity table, and a large closet. The bed had four posts with rich plum curtains streaming between them. A window held white eyelet curtains and a view to the second-floor balcony. On one wall there hung a painted portrait of a woman with porcelain white skin and a piercing stare that seemed to be trying to communicate something. I gazed back at her for some time, waiting for a change of features or gleam in those dark eyes, which I half expected to see at any moment. I found it strangely difficult to look away.

I moved on to the next room, another bedroom. This was similar but in soft peach tones and gold. It had a large old-fashioned desk and light blue, round, velvet pillows on the bed. And then I saw a large bathroom with two sinks and another claw-foot tub with a modern shower setup. I paused to look at another old portrait, a woman with porcelain skin and large, round eyes. This one reminded me of Anna Karenina, and I found myself a little frightened of her.

Down another corridor, I found some kind of a study or library with towering shelves of books. I perused the bookcases briefly, finding several familiar bindings: Maugham, Fitzgerald, O'Connor, James, and Wharton. I touched my finger to their spines as I recognized them, as though doing so might bring them back to life. And then I passed through to more bedrooms. All of them were sublime, perfect, exquisite. And yet, they all held the same sense of vacancy. Of waiting and...incompleteness.

I moved down to what appeared to be the end of the hallway, but it unexpectedly curved. I followed the walls and parade of black sconces in my dimly lit path, and for a moment I began to question whether I was dreaming again. The flooring had changed to marble and took on that swirling fog appearance I'd seen in the foyer. Once again I wondered if I might fall through or vanish into its murky depths. I stepped uncertainly across that phantasmal, whelming flood until I arrived at two French doors standing wide open into a large room.

It appeared to be some kind of ballroom. All the walls were covered in mirrors, giving the appearance of an overwhelming expanse of space. Here, more than anywhere else I'd been in the mansion, the sense of vacancy overpowered every bit of grandeur.

As I stepped onto the floor, I immediately had the impression that it was especially designed for dancing. My shoe somehow felt lighter on the smooth, cream-colored flooring, which reminded me of a giant pearl. In the center of the room was hung another large chandelier in shimmering crystal and sable.

Taking off my shoes, I padded across the dance floor. The room had somehow grown sacred in my mind in those few seconds since I'd first glimpsed inside. Standing beneath the chandelier, I glanced around the room at the multitude of Charlottes, all standing clad in vivid inadequacy with an unrefined expression, painfully out of place amid all the splendor. I closed my eyes and slowly, deliberately replaced each of the images with one dressed in a fine black lace dress and a sleek Grace Kelly bun at the nape of my neck that shined in the light from the chandelier.

I watched them smile softly, with elegant neck and shoulders bare and upright and dazzling. There were no bruises, no sense of added weight to my features from fallen tears and heartache, no hint of damaged goods. And for a moment I was fine, and my skin was smooth and glowing, and my face healthy and pure, brightened with the incandescence of innocence and hope.

But then the images changed. The crowd around me transformed into a room full of people wearing brilliant and bizarre Halloween costumes. Jackie Wilson music blared from the speakers while the crowd around me chatted and laughed, played games, and danced. But in my mind, I was looking for him. I was looking for Gavin.

"Did you find what you were looking for?" I heard a deep voice say from the entrance of the room. My eyes flew open in surprise, but for a moment, all I saw were the disappointing Charlottes that surrounded me. All of them looked as though they had been caught in something childish. And maybe they had been.

Then I caught Roden's upright figure sprinkled throughout the crowd of Charlottes and turned to look at him in the doorway. He had changed into a navy blue shirt and denim and looked as out of place in the ballroom as I felt. I closed the distance between us, looking down at the shoes in my hand, uncertain how to answer his question. When I looked back at him, he was obviously uncomfortable.

"Did you...find the balcony entrance yet?" he asked.

"I haven't even seen the staircase for the third floor," I admitted, feeling foolish as I put my shoes back on.

"Yes, well all this opulence can be overwhelming. I'll show you the lesser-known ways around if you want. That is, if you're interested in all that secret passageway, hidden door-type stuff."

"Have you ever met anyone who wasn't?" I asked.

"I don't know." He surprised me by laughing lightly. "It isn't the kind of thing I go around asking."

We walked past the French doors of the ballroom back toward the way I'd come. I followed him into that room with the small library and watched as he moved to stand in front of that same bookshelf of classics. He ran one finger across the spines of several books, just as I had done when I was alone, but came to a stop at a thin, midnight blue binding of *The Great Gatsby*. He tilted the top of the spine back, and I heard a low knocking sound emit from the wall behind the bookshelf. It was the sound of wooden cogs and the mechanics of an older generation. The soft green wallpapered structure was pushed back and slid to the left behind the bookcase.

Roden stood beside the opening, indicating that I should go first. I entered a dark landing on a narrow black staircase, which spiraled both below and up above, between cherry oak walls lit with golden sconces, I leaned over to look down at the spiraling handrail, which reminded me of an old Hitchcock movie I'd seen. Then I went up, slowly urging my weak ankle and sore bones to keep moving as I held tightly onto the handrail. Roden followed silently behind.

We came to a final landing where there stood a small black door. I hesitated on the landing, suddenly uncertain if I was really allowed to enter. Roden reached around me and turned a brass doorknob, nudging the door open for me. Before us was a small room with ivory textured walls. Scattered throughout the walls had been painted small black bird silhouettes. The birds were in flight, in varying postures and sizes throughout the walls, and as I looked up, I saw that they were even on the ceiling.

"Weird, huh?" Roden asked.

"Fantastic," I answered, admiring the walls and ceiling. There was another door, this one white with small windows at the top, revealing a glimpse of the blue-gray sky. I opened the door, which reluctantly gave way with a soft crackling of old paint, and stepped forward out into the windy air of the balcony.

The view was breathtaking. As I stepped across the wet stone with its scattering of orange and yellow leaves and black twigs, I took in the vast treetops, the hills and valleys, and slanting cabin roofs in the distance. I could just glimpse between the fiery trees the bridge I'd once stood on, having looked back up here with that rowing crew to my back and Danny at my side. There was no one on the water now.

I saw smoke rising in the distance and could just make out that thick, intriguing scent of danger.

"I wouldn't look down if I were you," Roden said quietly as he bent down to pick up a pair of binoculars. I kept my gaze on the treetops, the horizon, and the clouds, resisting the temptation to peek down at the gristly scene that was surely displayed on the ground. For the moment, the air was even devoid of the sounds of wolves. And I knew that it would not last.

"This is so incredible," I said into the October wind, pausing to pull my sweatshirt tighter at my neck. Meanwhile Roden peered through the heavy lenses at something I didn't wish to see before setting the binoculars back down, apparently satisfied with what he saw. "But I'm sure you hear that every time you have people over."

Roden stood beside me, leaning over the railing with me. A cold wind blew through the top of his dark hair and caused him to blink at the sting of it. That's when I noticed tiny, barely visible lines curving from the outer corners of his eyelids. It was difficult to imagine that they might have come from a time when he laughed often. But lately it seemed that anything was possible.

"I paid someone to clean once a month," he said. "And she was pretty excited about the tour on her first day."

I laughed at his peculiar statement, saying, "Yes, but what about friends and family? My grandparents have a house less than half this size and have always thrown the greatest parties." I remembered one from my childhood, when the weather had been just like this. "It was complete chaos... kids running around everywhere, spilling food on the sofa, people laughing until the walls shook upstairs..." But then I remembered the Halloween parties and suddenly lost interest in the topic.

Roden had been facing me as I spoke but turned his head away ambiguously in the silence. I heard the scrape of his shoe against the balcony's debris, and he leaned over with his elbows on the railing. The wind breathed out its calm whisper as it blew my hair around and gave off that mysteriously intoxicating scent of autumn...and smoke. I closed my eyes and breathed deeper.

"Since I moved in, I haven't been in much contact with them, my family," he said. "My grandfather rebuilt the Willow Mansion just before he passed away, unexpectedly. And I didn't move in until a couple years ago. But I think it was intended for that sort of thing."

"You mean, for people?" I asked, finally opening my eyes to glance at him.

"Yes, for people," he answered, looking back at me with the faintest hint of a smile.

"Well, that is a pity, isn't it?" I asked the treetops. Their fiery orange leaves shook free in another sudden gust of wind. The horizon was dotted with red maples, some with their hues lightened at one side or bearing patches of green and yellow, while others had quickly turned to russet in anticipation of the winter.

"You know I saw you up here once. From the bridge?" I asked. I recalled once more my first day in Willow's Bend and wished with all my heart to be there again.

He looked down at his feet for a moment before looking at me and answering, "No, no you couldn't have."

"No, I'm sure I did," I insisted. "At least, I saw *someone*."

"Well, I don't remember seeing you." I watched as he pulled the edges of his collar up to his chin.

"That's strange," I muttered.

"Maybe..." he started hesitantly. "Well, there have been some sightings..."

"Sightings?" I prompted.

He cleared his throat. "The original owner was known to be pretty eccentric. The story that's most generally accepted is that the house burned down in the night by a conspiracy of the bitter townsfolk. He owned everything nearby, you know..." he said. He pointed his finger toward the west as he spoke. "There was a general store there, a silo, and a small factory... And then toward that way was a cotton field and a pecan grove."

I followed his gaze for a moment, trying to imagine the Willow's Bend of so long ago. Then I turned and leaned back against the rail with my arms folded, taking in the scene of the third-floor doors and windows, the enormous chimney, and black rail posts and arches.

"Anyway, he also had some kind of special currency—Mexican, I think—that was hidden in one of the stairwells. So the main story is that some people got angry, or maybe jealous of those coins, and burned the mansion down in the middle of the night. But the *other* story...is that his wife was unfaithful."

"Ahh," I said. "There is always that. The unfaithful wife version."

"Yes, well you know how women are." He laughed jokingly. I looked disapprovingly at him. "Anyway, so he uh... supposedly set the bedroom on fire in a heinous crime of passionate jealousy."

"And then the house burned down and everyone died?" I remembered Danny's history lesson.

"Something like that," he said. "Except for the gardener of course."

"Interesting. But how do we know the gardener is innocent?"

His face immediately became more serious, and there was an uncomfortable silence between us before he spoke again.

"Because he was my great-grandfather."

"Oh. I'm sorry," I muttered. "And um...what does this have to do with you not being on the balcony, again?"

"Well, there have been some sightings of the owner's illegitimate son. On the balcony...on the front lawn beneath the willows, through the windows, that sort of thing." He stepped away from the railing for a moment, rubbing his hands together and blowing into them to stay warm. "So, maybe that's who you saw. And if you see a small, pale child from the turn of the century again, you'll know it's just Ambrose."

"Oh, well it was definitely not a child. Whoever it was, he was distinctly tall, dark, and...unhappy."

He shot me a surprised look at that last word but turned his head away evasively. "Sounds like you got a good look for being so far away."

"I guess it stayed with me."

I turned back to the picturesque view and unwittingly let my eyes quickly scan the slopes below. Just one brief glance was all. The earth-green and rust-brown tones on the ground were speckled with bright shades of red, not unlike the firewheels in the dandelions. But the flecks of red were too big, and we were too far away to see the dandelions. I stared down at the face of the mansion, seeing the green vines that had climbed up and taken hold in places. Something about the view reminded me of a memory I thought I'd forgotten. I couldn't quite put my finger on it, but it filled me with a profound sadness.

My thoughts were interrupted as the sound of the baying wolves rose up in the distance like a hellish choir; the lower, more sinister bellows supporting the higher yips and gravelly, deep-throated howls. And for that moment, I forgot where we were and who had been standing next to me. The sunlight was gone. The trees, the beauty, the conversation all evaporated from my mind and made room only for that song and its impenetrable darkness. A moment later, piercing through the abysmal black, I saw the flashing red lights of an ambulance.

Suddenly, my forearms were being clutched tightly. I inhaled as though I'd been trapped underwater for a long time. The fog began to dissipate as my ears rang and hissed with white noise.

"Charlotte? Can you hear me?" Roden's voice reached my ears as if from some distance.

"Y-yes, sorry," I muttered out of my confusion, blinking to see that Roden's face was only inches away from mine.

"Well, let's um..." he began, still gripping my arms and moving me backward, "stay a little farther from the rail, okay?" I nodded as he let me go and turned his back toward me, swearing under his breath so that I could only make out the consonants.

When he turned back to face me again, I thought he was going to yell at me, from the look on his face. Instead, he spoke quietly. "You almost gave me a heart attack, you know that?"

I stared back, confused. Inside the mansion, I often heard the sinister, distant sounds of howling, but out here, the sound was much louder and somehow managed to get under my skin.

"Did I...almost go over?" I asked, once I had finally regained my breath and my ears had stopped ringing.

To my surprise, he chuckled, an empty sound before replying, "Yes, yes you did."

I stepped back up to the rail, causing Roden to raise his eyebrows at me. "I'm fine, really," I insisted. "I'll be more careful, okay?" His eyes lingered on me doubtfully.

I took in a deep breath and exhaled, as if to prove that I was okay, and looked out again over the treetops and the white wisps of clouds decorating the boundless azure of sky. I heard the tremor of trees in the wind, but the wolves were silent once again, leaving me to wonder if I had really heard them in the first place.

"I spent the summers here, growing up," Roden began, as he too surveyed the distance. "When my grandpa lived in a small cabin nearby—before he rebuilt this place—he'd send me out on 'expeditions' into the woods alone. When I came back, we'd spend the evenings on the back porch, where he'd drill me about everything I saw." He paused, leaning sideways against the railing now, lost in his own vision of the past. "I scouted out paw prints and tracked bird nests and collected rocks. I learned to know these woods like the back of my hand." He laughed softly. "It was a boy's dream, I guess. Of course, then I grew up, went away to school, and got a career..."

I turned to look at his hesitating features, the cut on his cheekbone that was still healing, the dark stubble on his chin, and the furrowing of his thick eyebrows. I had to admit to myself that while he wasn't remarkably good looking, there was something about him that kind of made me want to look again.

"It's funny, when I heard what Grandpa was doing, he told me he would eventually leave it to me someday. And I was really...thankful. Before he passed away, I'd envisioned something specific in mind." His lips parted and closed again. I waited. "Well, as you've probably guessed, things didn't go quite as planned."

"No, I guess they didn't," I muttered. I breathed into my cupped hands and rubbed them together several times. A bright red cardinal landed on the railing post a few yards away from me. I watched as he cocked his head and looked questioningly at the rooftop, then a tree. He shuffled his feet and surveyed it all again before abruptly flying away.

"So, answer this for me," he said. I watched him step on a piece of rock and grate it against the stonework with his shoe, as though he were trying to spell something out with it. "Why does someone like you come out to the middle of nowhere and rent a cabin in the woods alone? I mean, weren't you a little uncomfortable? And what were you trying to accomplish in that, anyway?"

I puffed out a sigh, deciding which questions to answer and how much of an answer to give. When I finally did speak, the phrases came out slowly, with long pauses filled with uncertainty and nervous glances back toward that bridge.

"I guess you could say I was encouraged to...take a break. Think through some things. And get my health back under control. And, yeah, I wasn't sure if I could do it at first— stay alone in the woods, I mean. But I've spent my life being afraid and dependent, and I guess I finally grew tired of that. Besides, it doesn't take a house to be haunted, you know."

"Is that so?"

"Yes. Besides, I had Cleo. And Charles and Hamlet."

"So...you were sick?" He placed his hands firmly on the railing and looked down at our shoes.

"I was making myself sick," I confessed. "Pushing myself too hard, I guess. In school. And work. Et cetera."

"And why would you do that?"

"Because I..." I felt the words stall, unwilling to rise up. I set my hands down and grabbed onto the railing as I'd seen him do, perhaps for some sense of strength or balance or... something. And then I threw caution into what Danny called "that great Oklahoma wind of ours."

"I lost someone," I said. "How do you...how do you communicate something like that?" The questions rose up with a startling sense of desperation and urgency. I heard them resonate. I heard them plea. "How do you put it into words that he was killed by a drunk driver? And that it completely destroyed me?"

I stopped to wonder what I was saying, and who I was saying it to. And then I pressed on, because I realized that the only alternative was to scream at the top of my lungs over the trees and the hills and the universe. And maybe I would get to that too. "You know...it's so strange, hearing it come out of my mouth like that. Like a simple equation. It feels so irreverent and unfaithful. It's just so...not enough. It couldn't possibly communicate what that did to me, to my entire life, to my soul. I didn't know a human could survive that kind of pain."

I took in a deep breath before more words gushed out at their own will, flinging up and out like paper-thin leaves into the vastness of the sky, which somehow invoked an irresistible intimacy. "And they say hindsight is twenty-twenty, but when I look back, nothing adds up. It's all chaos and misery."

I covered my mouth with one hand as I inhaled sharply. Whether it was to regain my composure, or to stop myself from talking, or to breathe warmth into my cold bones, I wasn't sure. But after a long silence, I looked beside me to see whether he was even still there. He was. I was surprised to see that he was very much still there.

"Charlotte, I'm very, very sorry," he said. But his gaze was steadfastly fixed on the railing.

"Thank you," I muttered, blinking in confusion at what I'd said and slowly awakening to the fact that I'd made him uncomfortable again.

After another silence, I heard, "I guess we'd better go check on August." And I watched the whites of his knuckles fade back to their original tan as he slowly released his grip on the railing.

"Yeah, we'd better do that," I agreed quietly, but the words felt painfully gauche. We walked quietly away from that rail and that view with all of its magnificence and grandeur and purity. And away from the blood stains in the grass.

I heard that wind to my back shaking the trees vigorously and felt its invisible hand caress my hair up from around my neck and out of my stinging eyes. I watched Roden turn the handle on the door and listened to the paint crack and flake as he very quietly, gently, forced it open.

CHAPTER NINE

Dear Heart,

*Nothing is sane. Nothing makes sense anymore. The world
has gone mad—absolutely mad. The impossible has
happened, and yet, it does not bring you back. I cannot
remain the way I've been. Something must give.*

*I don't know what this means. I don't know what to do
with this newfound sadness. But I feel that something must
change. Perhaps change is happening with or without my
permission—with or without your consent.*

*So what does this mean? What would you say if you were
here? But you are not here. Your memory remains, but your
presence is gone. Is there forgiveness for me—even for me?
Or am I merely failing again, in some new, twisted way—
in the worst way imaginable? Will you condemn me for
choosing to live?*

—R.A.

"ARE YOU FEELING better at all?" I asked in hushed tones. I was sitting on the edge of the couch, where the child's limp figure was bundled against blankets and his head was turned away from me toward the empty hallway. He'd refused to eat anything for dinner, forcing me to eat the cold sandwich and warm soup that I'd brought to him. The care package had arrived right on time, which was fortunate since Roden had nearly run out of groceries before we even arrived.

He slowly shook his head in response. His blue eyes were glassy, and his cheeks were still tinged red with fever. He had a hint of a tan on his somewhat chubby arms, around the thin, cotton soccer T-shirt that had come in the care package. I wondered what he used to be like before everything changed for him. I wondered what he was like a week ago, when he was still a child with a family staying in a refuge.

"No? Not at all?" I asked. He was barely even conscious at the moment, and I couldn't tell if the dampness on his pillow was from sweating or from shedding silent tears. As I gazed down at his features, which had an abnormally aged look to them, I was reminded of an old black and white photograph I'd seen of a little boy during World War I. The weariness around his eyes, the heaviness upon his brow... There was something like that about August's face now. I tried to remember if he'd looked that way the first time I'd seen him. I couldn't recall, but I feared that he had changed a great deal since Roden first found him hiding beneath the kitchen sink.

The edges of his mouth were pulled into a subtle frown that reminded me of an expression my grandpa might wear at a funeral. It wasn't the kind of look you'd expect to see on a five-year-old. At least, I guessed that he was about five, but I knew it was the wrong time to ask.

"Well, what are we going to do about that, August?" I asked, interrupting the heavy silence.

His glassy blue eyes blinked but didn't meet mine.

That's when it occurred to me. Perhaps he didn't *want* to get better. After all, he must be at least vaguely aware of what he'd lost in the last few days. *He'd lost everything.*

The illness, the tragedy, the fear... It could all easily devour him at a time like this. And if it did, he may never recover at all. I had to do something.

"What about..." I began, trying think of something to cheer him up. I remembered that when I was a child, my mom used to sing to me when I was sick. "Do you like music?"

His eyes briefly met mine before he nodded. A miracle.

"What if I sang to you some of my favorite songs? Would that be good?" I asked, still carefully cultivating a tone of enthusiasm. His eyes met mine again, lingering this time. Then he nodded.

I began singing a slow song, fighting the discomfort of hearing my untrained voice, which sounded too loud and coarse in the presence of another human being. I'd been used to singing in church congregations and alone in my car, but that was all. I had no illusions of being a gifted singer. But as I continued the lyrics and melody of the old song, I gained encouragement by August's fixed gaze. He seemed to like it.

"Would you like to hear another?" I asked, after finishing the song. His nod was accompanied by a crooked smile on his cracked lips. I felt my own lips soften into something very close to smiling.

I sang another one of my favorites, remembering the way my mother's voice soothed me through every storm and ushered in peace where there had been chaos. And as I sang, I felt the pristine memories of my own childhood come back to me from someplace where I thought they'd died. I remembered running down our old hallway in my yellow Sunday dress and laughing at everything and nothing. I remembered tucking marigolds into my mother's hair beneath the maple tree and making hair wreaths of henbit and dandelion in the grass.

August and I continued to watch one another as I began yet another song. I remembered kissing my baby brother's feet and making him laugh through the bars of his light blue crib, a memory that hadn't surfaced in many years. It was a silly, bubbly laugh that only a baby could make, and I could hear it now. I was crazy about that laugh of his. I remembered the sunlight through the stained glass windows and hymns I'd long since forgotten. And when they came back to me, they seemed to resonate richer, deeper, and breathe life back into my darkness.

As I finished the last song, I realized that August's gaze had long since subsided and that he had fallen asleep again. But his features appeared softer and seemed to regain some of their lost innocence. And perhaps mine had too.

Following an impulse, I reached out a finger and ran it across his forehead, as though to smooth out the slightest hint of a furrowed brow. There was a part of me that was a little afraid of this newfound love. This giddy, ebullient joy that was filling my chest as I watched over him. Because I knew even then that there was no turning back from it. Because I knew that I couldn't undo the binds that were strengthening by the moment; these roots that were deepening and intertwining would not be easily untangled.

I picked up my dishes and started toward the kitchen, deep in thought about what these new sensations meant and where they were taking me. I tried to imagine a scenario in which these longings would not be disappointed and unfulfilled in the end. This boy I barely knew but somehow felt profoundly bound to—what would become of him? This boy who was orphaned and sick and vulnerable. Who was I to take care of him? I could only foresee a future of foster homes and school counselors and absolutely nothing to fill the void of his lost parents.

Then again, perhaps he had relatives who would take custody. Or perhaps he did, but they would not want him or would not love him. As I walked across the room with my heavy thoughts, I was surprised to see Roden's tall form leaning against the doorway in front of me. My cheeks felt warm as I walked past him into the hallway, realizing that he must have heard me singing. I continued down the hallway straight to the kitchen sink with August's dishes and turned the crystal knob on the faucet.

"I just wanted to tell you," Roden said from behind me, surprising me a second time, "they sent vaccinations."

"What?" I turned to face him where he was leaning against the island's granite countertop, partially bathed in the dim light between us. Behind me the water continued to rush and gently gurgled down the drain.

"They're for regular strains of rabies, so there's not a lot of hope that they'll help at all. But I understand that they won't hurt anything either. So...we should probably take them just in case they could save our lives later on."

"Why didn't you say something earlier? We could have given it to August this afternoon."

Roden answered with a sigh. "Actually, for August it could be dangerous. That's why I didn't bring it up earlier. Preferably, we should wait until he's over this illness before giving him a vaccination. The shot could spike his fever."

"I see. Well, I couldn't possibly take the shot before he got his."

"I know," he said. "I figured you'd say that. Still, I think we should take them as soon as possible. And if his fever has gone down a bit..." I read the look of hesitation in his eyes as he paused. "I think we should go ahead and vaccinate him tonight."

"Tonight?" I asked incredulously.

"The fever has gone down, hasn't it?"

"Well, yes, I think so. But it's coming and going right now. I'd feel better about it in a few more days—"

"Charlotte, I think there's something you need to understand. If someone manages to break in here, we may not have a few more days to wait. While I'd like to believe we're perfectly safe right now...it's really not that simple. Someone *could* get in. We don't have the luxury of a tall fence to keep danger out like at the shelter. I'm being as vigilant as I can, and there hasn't been much activity on our hill. But they are out there. And if they find us, we'll need to be as ready as we possibly can. I don't like the idea of endangering August any more than you do. But we have to weigh the risks here, and I really believe that this is the best thing."

Certainly I had taken it for granted that we were safe in the mansion. Maybe it was the façade of luxury, or perhaps it was Roden's formidable presence, but it hadn't yet crossed my mind that anyone could break in. Still...I would never want to do anything that put August in more danger than he was already in.

"But it probably won't even work, right? I mean, you just said that yourself. Besides I..." I made the final decision to voice out loud a thought that had been bothering me off and on for the past two days. "I think Danny might have been infected. And he told me he'd been vaccinated specifically for rabies."

Roden looked silently at me for a moment before speaking. "That can't be right. We've both seen what the infected victims are like. If he was infected, he would have killed you."

"He was really on edge, not at all like himself," I answered. "When the men showed up, his behavior changed a lot. He was fearless...but something more than that. It was as though he was becoming more like them, more violent. It was as though he was looking for a fight as much as they were." I replayed the facts in my head, surprised at how easily they came back to me. I told Roden everything I remembered that seemed relevant while trying hard not to relive the scene in my mind: the dog bite, the strange behavior, the tan-colored eyes that replaced the familiar irises I'd come to know and trust...

I looked down to see Roden scribble furiously across a notepad as I finished speaking.

"The authorities will want to know all of this. Any clue could be helpful in getting us out of here sooner." I watched his handwriting make its way across the paper, the script forming a peculiar slant. The tails on his y's, g's, and f's formed long, oblique lines on the page, as though the ink were actually black rainfall coming down hard and fast. I continued to rest my eyes on his notes, though I could feel his scrutiny rest on my blackened eye. "So, was Danny responsible for that handiwork?"

"Actually, no. Danny only protected me. But just before the attacks started, we had a visitor. Some guy Danny knew, or I don't think he would have let anyone in. He took all our food and...I said something I probably shouldn't have."

"Did he have a name?"

For a moment, I couldn't remember. I thought back to that day, the sinister look that the man wore, his patronizing manner, and the sickening glow he had about him just before he hit me. "James," I answered at last. "His name was James."

A knowing look passed over Roden's face. "And Danny trusted him?" he asked. But something in his voice told me he wasn't waiting for my answer. He shook his head before changing the subject. "Well, even if Danny had become more violent toward the other infected men, the infection definitely explains his behavior."

"Does it?"

"Like I told you, Danny and I have known each other for a long time. I've never known him to have much of a temper. I mean, don't get me wrong, he definitely isn't perfect. Well, *wasn't.*"

I folded my arms then, trying to stifle the wave of sadness as the reality hit me once more that Danny was dead. But like standing in the ocean while looking the other way, the strength of the wave hit me unexpectedly, knocking the air out in one ruthless push. Inwardly I tried to maintain some form of balance, but the sand was shifting beneath my feet.

"But," Roden continued, his voice just enough to bring me back, to anchor me where I stood, "I know that in his right mind, he'd never go looking for a fight. I just know it."

"How did you become such good friends, anyway?" I asked.

A corner of his mouth subtly twitched before he answered. "Long story." And it was as though a wave had just unexpectedly come and passed for him as well.

"Well, why did you stop talking to him?" I pressed, curiously watching him recover from the impact.

"An even longer story. The important thing is that we make the best decision for August based on what we know."

"Well, we know the vaccination didn't save Danny," I replied. "And I just couldn't live with myself knowing that I'd made August's fever worse if...if it killed him."

"I know," Roden answered, exhaling deeply in a way that convinced me that he did indeed know. "But you won't have to take that risk. Because I'm going to do it."

I WAS THINKING of bravery while I carried a backpack down a corridor, searching for what would become August's bedroom. Roden's willingness to do what was best in spite of the risks made an impression on me that evening. I flipped on any lights I could find along the way as I made the distance to the bedroom according to Roden's directions, readjusting August's backpack where it was slung across my shoulder.

I couldn't find a hallway light switch, so it was dark along the way. I passed a sitting room and could see floor-to-ceiling windows across the length of the room. It was covered in a soft baby blue wallpaper, and the furniture was cream and suede.

My thoughts soon turned to Ambrose and that ridiculous story of the boy ghost. I heard a distinct creak behind me. I turned around to see a shadow following me. It was just a shadow, doing what shadows do, and nothing more. It was not the shadow of a hundred-year-old child. In fact, it was the shadow of a foolish young woman called Char. I continued down the corridor, determined to put Roden's ghost story out of my mind.

I stepped into the bedroom that would be August's on the opposite side of the hallway. This room was decorated in a similar fashion to the other, with baby blue walls, light-grain wood, and cream fabric. The difference was that there were no windows in this room. Roden and I had agreed that we would be safer in the inner rooms, away from windows, so this would be August's room for now.

I took in the small bed, with the posts chiseled and shaped into twisted tree limbs. I imagined that it looked elegant in the daytime, but here at night, even with the light on, it felt oddly sinister. I immediately registered a loud, sonorous *tick-tock* and saw a grandfather clock mounted on the wall with a bronze pendulum swaying left and right in perfect rhythm. Its sound punctuated the silence of every moment, and each time felt unexpected and startling to my ears. I noted that there was something childlike about the room's decor. A large brown bear sat in the corner of the room next to the bed. And a soft, yellow cotton blanket laid across the foot of the bed. I was reminded of the children's book *Where the Wild Things Are.*

I moved to a small wooden dresser and began unloading the backpack of August's things. But as I did so, I had doubts that I was doing the right thing. An hour ago I would have hastened to unpack everything, ready to settle in. But after Roden's reminder of our vulnerability, I thought that perhaps we should keep his bag packed for an emergency. I shut the dresser drawer with a creak and a thud and opened the backpack on the floor. I took out the thermometer, children's Tylenol, toiletries, and a set of pajamas with monster trucks on them. The rest could stay in the bag.

I turned to glance at the doorway, suddenly uncertain if that last *tock* didn't come from somewhere behind me. There beside the doorway hung one of the few pictures in the room. I hadn't noticed it until now. This picture was a large photographed portrait of a small boy with a piercing stare and straight dark hair parted down the middle. The black and white photograph portrayed the boy in turn-of-the-century attire.

Next to the framed portrait, I saw a figure emerge from the darkness.

"I see you've met Ambrose," Roden commented as he carried in a sleeping August and laid him gently down on the cream-colored bedding.

"You mean, that's him?"

"In that photo? Yes," he replied. His voice lowered slightly, "I think this was remodeled after his bedroom. Of course, I don't think there's a room in this house he doesn't hang out in from time to time."

"Great," I muttered.

"You're not scared, are you?" He crossed his arms, grinning slightly.

"A little creeped out, maybe," I admitted.

"Well if it makes you feel any better, I don't think he's the violent type."

"Ah, that makes me feel much better," I muttered, standing up to approach August's bed. My sarcasm made Roden laugh. But he immediately stopped when August began to stir. I stood uneasily over the child, softly shushing him to go back to sleep.

Roden left the room, saying he needed to move his things to a room nearby. I took August's temperature, just managing to get him to sit up at an angle against the pillows.

I sat down in an old-fashioned rocking chair I'd pulled up from a corner of the room. My elbows were balanced on my knees, and my chin slumped against my hand as I waited out the *tick-tocks* of the clock for three full minutes. It's strange, observing time measured out that way. What was it T.S. Elliot said? Something about measuring out life in coffee spoons.

Here it was measured in stoic rhythm. Hard, cold thuds of small, blunt pieces of metal. *Is it too slow? Is it too quick?* It always seemed to be one or the other. But just now it seemed to be something different altogether. It seemed crass and irreverent. It was as though you could scientifically measure out life and come to a decisive conclusion about its worth, its value. *What does all this mean?* I thought, yawning. *Probably nothing.*

The *tick-tocks* chanted louder and louder in the room, like the words, "Stop, stop," being commanded again and again. *Stop* the chaos. *Stop* the oceanic tide of horror and despair. *Stop* the world with its violence and rage. *Stop* the ominous black rain from slanting across the page.

"Are you sure you're okay?" Roden said from the doorway.

Obviously I'm losing my mind, I thought. But instead of answering, I leaned across the bed and eased August's thermometer out of his mouth. I scrutinized the glass and mercury in the light, reading out loud, "One hundred point one." The medicine must have brought the fever back down a little but not enough to make me comfortable.

Roden softly swore from the other side of the room. I had never before met a person before who could swear softly. But that's exactly what he did, so much that I began to doubt the very crassness of the words. "What are we doing wrong?" he asked.

"I don't know," I answered. "Something. Maybe everything. *Probably* everything."

"Well, we'll just have to keep doing what we can."

"Yeah," I muttered, standing up from my chair and sighing again. "So, I guess you still think we should do this?" I looked nervously across the bed at Roden. But what I really wanted to say was, "Please, let's not do this."

He held up a small zipped bag. "I think it's for the best."

"August," I said softly, bending over the sleeping boy. "I need you to wake up just for a minute, okay? We're all going to get our shots, and then you can go back to sleep."

He blinked at me.

Roden got the syringe and vial ready, having been given specific instructions from our contact with the CDC earlier in the day. We gathered the gauze, alcohol, and a small Band-Aid, laying them out on the bedspread. I persuaded August to sit up and pulled up his sleeve. He didn't make a fuss. In my mind, I heard the words *stop, stop* grow louder once more. But as Roden stuck him with the shot, August merely looked across the room with a glazed look on his face and didn't move a muscle.

"You did wonderful, buddy," Roden said, pressing the gauze against the child's little arm. "You're very brave, you know that?"

I stuck the small, neon blue Band-Aid on his arm, saying, "That's right, you did perfect." Then I saw the tears run down his cheeks. He leaned back against the covers and cried. I couldn't stand the sight of him in that condition. I couldn't bear the sight of the tears, nor the intuitive feeling that he wasn't crying about the shot at all.

In a moment, Roden had my shot ready. It had always been a kind of superstition of mine to never look at the needle when I received my shots. I suppose I'd always believed that if I didn't look at it, then it wouldn't hurt. But this time I stared hard at the syringe and the metal as it pierced my skin, taking it in with my eyes like a religious laceration to my soul, as though willing myself to feel physical pain. But it wasn't nearly enough. Not enough to make up for August's loss. Not enough for Danny's death.

"You're very brave," Roden said, once again interrupting my dark reverie with the unexpected levity in his voice.

I laughed in spite of myself. I continued to watch as he pressed a small neon Band-Aid on my arm. "Pink, huh? I don't even get to choose?"

"Sorry," he answered. "Protocol."

I SPENT THE next few hours pacing across the bedroom floor, taking the child's temperature, and suppressing the very natural urge to panic.

Then his fever rose.

"Charlotte," Roden said, beckoning me out into the hallway. I joined him just outside the door, where I slowly, methodically wiped a stray tear from my eye. I knew that I needed to hold it together. I was going to be genuinely brave for once in my life. That single tear was all I could afford, all I would permit. "It's normal for the fever to get worse before it gets better. Everything is going to be okay. Do you understand?"

"Of course," I answered vacantly. "He's going to be fine. I know it." And I did know it. At least, part of me knew it. The only problem was that the other part knew just the opposite. And maybe more strongly.

"Well, I'm glad to hear you say that," Roden said, turning away from me and running one hand through his dark, unkempt hair. We were both incredibly tired. It must have been past one o'clock in the morning, and I couldn't imagine sleeping anytime soon. "Because I have to admit, I was getting a little scared, myself..."

That's when I lost it.

The thing about "losing it" is that you really have no idea how small the thread you've been hanging on to is to begin with until that very moment when you let it go. The absolute fragility of your own peace of mind is underestimated and elusive to your rational faculties until then. My illusions of bravery now obliterated, I cradled my face in my hands and let the tears burst forth. I walked quickly down the hallway, afraid that August might hear my outburst, and continued to cry. To my surprise, Roden had followed me into the living room.

"Hey, did I say something wrong?" he asked.

I just managed to shake my head, trying to get ahold of myself. I was never the type of person to cry in front of other people without embarrassment. "No, I just...I'm just so tired of losing people I care about." In truth, there were a hundred different things I could have said. I could have mentioned how physically exhausted I was, or how much I missed my family, or how shocked and horrified I remained at the things I had seen and heard in the woods that week, or how afraid I was that we'd made a mistake in vaccinating August. Any of those explanations would do, and certainly many more contributed. But in the end, the answer I gave was as sufficient as anything and everything else.

Then, I'm not sure why I did it, but I hugged Roden. It was all a little uncomfortable, to be honest. I mean, I never think about how tall people are until I hug them. And he wasn't the type of person to get a lot of hugs, from what I could tell, so perhaps he wasn't comfortable either. To my satisfaction though, he did hug me back. And I kept choking out a steady and profuse stream of tears. It was sticky and unpleasant, and I almost felt guilty for crying on his warm, dry shirt, though I was comforted by that warm, dry shirt as well. After all, it was flannel.

Then I silently conceded to myself that it was a new, wonderful sensation to have a shoulder to cry on. In the last few years, I'd cried a lot but almost always alone. The more alone I'd felt, the more I felt I could contain and control the pain, like pressing down on a wound to stem the blood flow. This was much better.

And maybe it was nice that the person I was crying on had saved my life—more than once. But I didn't overthink it, not this time. I just stood there hugging this fellow human being, crying, and every now and then getting a whiff of cinnamon and pipe tobacco. There was something reassuring in the scent that sort of overpowered the initial awkwardness of hugging him. I took a deep breath and released it.

"Me too," he muttered against my ear, but I'd already forgotten what I'd said to him. I was starting to pull myself together but didn't pull away just yet when he continued, "And

I do care about him. A lot. But there's something I can't seem to figure out."

I stepped away at last, wiping my face and moving to sit down on the couch in front of the dying fire. He sat down next to me as I swallowed the last of the tears. "What is it?" I asked.

"Well, I know that for myself, I feel indebted to August. I mean, I know I did what I had to do. But still...being responsible, even in part, for making him an orphan....I know that I need to do everything I can for him. But you? What can you possibly owe him?"

I thought about his words but couldn't quite wrap my mind around owing him, or loving him because I owed him something. No, it was more than that. I remembered the day in the river. And then I remembered the dream and knew that it was that more than anything that forged the bond between us.

"I met him before," I said. I recalled the intermingled scent of sulfur and sunscreen. "He was drowning in the river, and I pulled him out of the water."

"You mean, you'd already saved his life before all of this started?"

I looked up at him, confused. "Well, it never felt that way. I guess, I've seen some pretty horrible things happen, and I've never had a chance to stop them from happening, you know? But August gave me that chance. I was able to do something truly good for the first time in my life. I've always been a victim, but loving August makes me feel like a hero. He makes me feel strong. Honestly, it feels like August saved me. And although I didn't see him again until that day in the woods, I already felt so...bound to him. It's like he gave me something I'd never had before. It's like he gave me——"

"Purpose?" he asked.

"Yes. That's it."

"I know exactly what you mean. I've been alone for so long I'd forgotten what it felt like to think about someone else and live for someone else. But it's a really good feeling."

"Yeah, it is. And I love him. I don't know how else to explain it, but I really do."

"I know. I knew when I heard you singing to him."

"Well, his mom is gone, and my mom always sang to me when I was sick." I shrugged, my voice gradually returning from the effects of crying. "It's the sort of thing moms do, I guess."

"Yeah, well, not all of them," he answered. "You're really good to him, Char. Taking care of him...I know it's all a lot more than you bargained for when you rented that cabin alone in the woods."

"Yeah, and we're both a lot more than you bargained for too," I said. Through my blurry gaze, I could see that he smiled gently in reply. "I never really thanked you for saving us. And taking us here. I know you didn't want to be around people."

He raised his eyebrows. "Did Danny say that?"

"He said you didn't think he was worth talking to anymore and that maybe nobody was. He said you'd only talk to me if I was paying you for your time. Something like that."

At my words, he stood up and walked over to the fireplace. He prodded the fire, sending sparks into the dark and quiet room. I waited and listened. The very room waited and listened with me, breathing in and out with dancing shadows from the fire. There was a long pause before he spoke again. Meanwhile, the fire was stoked and reawakened with a gentle roar like a small dragon.

"He was like the little brother I never had, Danny. I knew his family from spending the summer here as a kid. I taught him and his sister how to rock climb, actually." He laughed weakly at some memory that must have come back to him. "She was terrible at it."

"I didn't even know he had a sister," I admitted. It occurred to me just then how little I must have known about my landlord and friend.

Roden sat back down next to me again. "Danny, his sister Sophia, and I—the three of us were really close. And," he looked down at his hands before continuing, "I was engaged to her."

"Oh," I muttered involuntarily. I tried to think back to conversations with Danny, but I didn't recall a sister. "It seems odd that he didn't mention her. I thought we'd gotten to know each other pretty well."

"Yeah, well," he said, staring determinedly into the fire once more. His next words came out so quietly, I would later wonder if I'd imagined them. "That's probably because she died three years ago."

CHAPTER TEN

I t was four a.m.
My eyes were fixed on the grandfather clock ahead of
me while August slept. Roden had fallen asleep in another
chair on the other side of the bed. I glanced at his dormant
features slumped against his shoulder, his dark, prickly chin
crumpling the collar on his button-down shirt. But I was kept
awake by the need to see August's fever go down. And maybe,
if I was being honest with myself, also by the unexpected news
of Roden's dead fiancée.

I had a lot of questions, naturally. I sat alone in the measured
silence, in the company of two others but also feeling the
solitude of being the only one awake. I let my mind wander. I
wondered how Sophia died, what had ended Roden's lifelong
friendship with Danny, and why he'd come back to live a
solitary lifestyle in a haunted mansion in the woods. As one
question led to the next, I also wondered why Roden initially
left Willow's Bend, since he'd spent his childhood so happily
here. After all, my curiosity about Roden had only grown
during our few conversations since that first dramatic meeting
in the woods. And here, now, I allowed myself to wonder what
kind of a man had a reputation for disliking people in general
yet sought the first opportunity to risk his life to save a child
he didn't know. Could these two facts truly be reconciled in

the same person? And if so, then precisely how did the pieces fit together?

Confident that he was asleep, I indulged in a long, contemplative look at Roden from across the room. In the dim light of the bedroom lamp, I wondered how old he was. After all, he had one of those complexions that made it impossible to tell. Just now his thin-rimmed glasses and sun-weathered skin lent him a particularly domestic and fatherly appearance. However, I knew that being outdoors had given me the exact opposite impression, and I tried to fit the two together.

Whatever his age, it was cloaked by his person through layers of juxtaposing traits. I recalled the youthful alertness in his eyes against the unmistakable assurance in his gait. There was the bright fierceness shown in his tightened jaw that contrasted with the tiny lines at the corners of his eyes and the slightly weathered look of his tanned skin. The mature intelligence in his carefully chosen words, which were only tempered with the surprising levity in his humor. The way his knowing and skillful presence precluded and silenced the otherwise overwhelming effluvium of fear and replaced it instead with something almost tangibly calm and light.

I pulled the thermometer from between August's arm and his chest, where I'd gently tucked it in a minute ago. The feverish child had begun to sweat through his shirt and took it off, so it was easy to slip the thermometer in while he was still asleep. He lay there with eyes closed and mouth slightly open. His hair was matted against his forehead and the pillow; his cheeks were tinged rosy with fever.

I peered hard at the mercury line in the lamplight on my side of the bed. It read ninety-nine point four. I couldn't believe my eyes. It was actually going down. I exhaled a deep breath and felt the relief wash over me. I glanced at Roden one more time, fighting the urge to wake him up and tell him the good news. I had to stifle a laugh when I looked at him in the lamplight because his mouth twitched while he slept.

Looking back down at the thermometer again, I exhaled deeply, happily. Then I sat back in the rocking chair, closed my eyes, and fell asleep.

I'D WOKEN UP with a start from one of those dreams about Gavin. Lately it seemed like the dreams were occurring more often, and here he was again. But this one was different. This time, he'd gotten up from where he was lying down in a large, cold room. He walked over to talk to me, but this time I didn't care what he was going to say. I didn't wait for his words to chill me like they usually did. In fact, I wasn't even surprised.

"Charlotte, I—"

"No," I interrupted him.

"But Charlotte—"

"You're dead, Gavin."

And the dream ended.

For a moment, I couldn't stop looking around, feeling absolutely certain that someone had been right behind me just a moment ago. *Was it Ambrose?* Whoever it was, was gone now.

I stretched my arms and yawned. It was late morning, and I seemed to be the last person up. Curious, and still trembling slightly, I made my way down the hallway and into the empty sitting room, past the darkened fireplace of ashes. I turned down another hallway, following the unexpected sound of laughter. The sounds of movement and conversation echoed from the kitchen to where I was. I walked in to see Roden and August sitting at the dining table eating breakfast.

"Good morning," I said, as they turned their heads toward me. I was immediately struck by the fact that they were both smiling.

"Good morning, finally," Roden said over a bowl of cereal. There was something unusually playful in his tone. "We were just enjoying our fruity puffs, weren't we, August?" August distinctly giggled, but didn't say anything. "We're not sure exactly what fruity puffs are, but we decided we like 'em."

As I poured myself a cup of coffee, I heard slurping and more giggles behind my back. I turned around in time to see both man and child comically pretending to gulp down spoonfuls of fruity puffs, only to let the cereal splash back into the milky bowls again. I couldn't help but laugh. It was refreshing to see August acting silly, being a child again.

When they both looked at me, they stopped what they were doing. "August, try to be a gentleman." Roden pretended to scold him, though it only led to more giggling as they finished their breakfast. I watched them clink their spoons against their bowls for a while, though my mind went back to thinking about my dream and that strange sensation before I woke up.

I'D STUMBLED on an old hardback collection of Henry James short stories. What was interesting to me was that there were a few I still hadn't read. I was always strangely fascinated with his verbose descriptions and haunted characters, so when I found this edition in Roden's library, I really had intended to read it. I turned a thick, musty page of the lengthy "Altar of the Dead," though the action was merely a formality. The attempt to get my mind off what was happening outside the mansion walls was proving to be futile. Although Roden spent a lot of his time patrolling on the balcony, he didn't report back with much information. And while a part of me was grateful, the other was painfully curious as to what was actually going on out there. I watched as water sprinkled the page and felt it hit the back of my hair.

"Hey, buddy, try to keep the bath in the tub, will you?" I asked. But I was relieved to have an excuse to close the book and set it down. As I turned around to face him, August smiled behind a large beard of bubbles. "Oh, I beg your pardon, sir. I thought there was a small child in there, not a distinguished old man." I'd already decided to take cues from Roden and try to keep August in a good mood. Keeping things lighthearted seemed like the best plan for August's sake, but I also had to admit that I was enjoying every moment with him.

He smiled again before throwing a handful of bubbles into the air. "It's okay," he said in a mock deep voice. We laughed.

His head fell to one side, and he yawned. That's when I noted the redness in his cheeks and glassiness of his eyes. I'd almost forgotten that he was still recovering from a serious illness. "Are you feeling okay?" I asked, still surveying his features.

He shrugged, but there was a trace of a frown on his face. "You look kind of sleepy," I observed. He shrugged again before confirming my statement by rubbing one eye with his hand. "Well, just let me know when you're ready to get out." I picked up my abandoned book and flipped forward to the familiar "Sir Edmund Orme" instead.

I was thinking of the Jamesian ghosts of the nineteenth century and my own experiences with the undead. While I had never been a fan of pop culture horror, there was something oddly alluring about the apparitions of James's fiction. Perhaps it was their gentlemanly tendencies, or their mysteriously hushed presences in the lives of the living, like hovering silhouettes amid Victorian era teatime.

And yet, I'd always felt that more than anything, it was James's portrayal of the destructive nature of fear itself that stood out to me. Whether we are haunted by something real or only in our minds, it is the fear that gets the best of us in the end. Fear was always the real enemy.

"Are they gone?" August asked quietly after some time, interrupting my reverie.

I lowered my book, realizing yet again that I wasn't retaining anything I was reading. "Are who gone, sweetie?"

"My mom and dad."

I sunk back against the bathroom wall, immediately feeling the weight of his question. As I surveyed the child's upright form, his bare chest jutting out in an effort to brace himself, to be strong, I literally ached for his loss. My chest felt too full, painfully full, and too exasperated for the routine ins-and-outs of oxygen that it was wired to perform. *What could I possibly say?*

"Yes, I'm afraid they're gone," I said at last.

His bottom lip trembled for a moment but then stopped. He glared down at some unseen shape in the bubbles as his mouth formed a bitter frown. His clammy pink skin faded pale then flushed red once more. I groped for some words to throw out there, like a safety net for someone who was clearly falling.

"But Roden and I are going to take care of you, and you have nothing to worry about." I tried not to think about the holes in my words—the unmentionable, unknown future.

Doesn't he have something to worry about? And what happens when we all leave? Where will he go? How will his life be different?

"I'm ready to get out now," he choked out at last. And I jumped up to retrieve his bath towel, mostly because I couldn't bear to look into his watery eyes a moment longer.

MY HEART WAS heavy as I climbed the stairs to the second floor. It was heavy when I thought about the orphan asleep downstairs. It was heavy with thoughts about the future, about the inevitable aftermath of the destruction of Willow's Bend. My heart ached with lingering sorrow over Danny. And it throbbed with having just performed the pointless task of leaving a message on my parents' home phone.

I still couldn't bring myself to unload all of this on my brothers. All I knew was that no one was home and that the phone at my cabin was probably ringing off its hook right now. And I missed my family. I missed spending time with my younger brothers, hearing my father's gruff voice, and talking to my mother about nothing.

"Char?"

I stopped. I had been walking past door after door, not exactly conscious of where I was going or what I was looking for when I heard Roden's voice call out to me. As I peered into the large room he was in, I took an involuntary step backward.

The room was full of guns.

A gun on the desk, on the shelf, in an open case... I counted three different guns in plain sight. Deer heads peered vacantly from their mounts on every wall, their dark eyes remaining forever innocent and curious. Even in their rigid elegance, I perceived ominous warnings to stay clear of such powerful weapons, as though each of these creatures had naively wandered into this same room only to meet their deaths.

"Hey, what's wrong?" Roden asked. He continued cleaning some type of gun where he was sitting at the desk. Whatever it was, it had fortunately been taken apart into several pieces. I exhaled a little. "What's with you and this fear of guns, anyway?" he asked, pausing what he was doing to look up at me.

"I uh..." I leaned back against the nearest wall, which was decorated innocently with plaques and a shelf of trophies. "I witnessed a murder when I was really young."

The answer, though simple and true, sounded strangely fictional spoken aloud. "Wow." He raised his eyebrows in genuine concern. "Really? How young?"

"I was nine."

He swore under his breath and was silent for a moment. "Well, that has to change, you know."

"Excuse me?" I asked.

"Cinnamon?" He abruptly thrust out a bag of raw cinnamon sticks as he leaned in his office chair toward me. In the process, I caught sight of those scars sprawling down the length of his forearm. In this lighting they looked less like vines, more like barbed wire.

"No, thank you," I answered, frowning. The spicy warmth of the cinnamon just managed to reach me from across the room, strangely juxtaposing against the foreboding presence of metal and lead.

"I think you need to learn how to shoot a gun, Charlotte."

"No, thank you," I started, taking another step back toward the hallway. "If there is one thing I should not do on God's green earth—"

"We're not just on God's green earth anymore—we're in Willow's Bend. And I just happen to be a professional shooting instructor." He stood up from his chair, picking up a rag and began wiping off his hands. "And knowing how to use a gun could save your own life, my life, and August's life. Plus, it would do you some good to conquer your fears." The readiness of his argument made me suspect that he had given the situation a lot of thought.

"Roden, I appreciate your concern, but that is not even up for debate right now. Besides..." I shook my head slowly, looking for the right words to explain my conviction. "I could never do what you do."

"You mean, hit your mark?" I saw the faintest hint of a half-smile on his face.

"I mean *kill people*." My words came out more harshly than I'd intended. But I meant them. I couldn't look at a gun without the conviction that it only existed to steal lives. To destroy fathers and mothers and children.

I watched as his eyes fell to the floor, and he gave off the tiniest nod before leaning back against the desk and folding his arms. But he didn't answer.

I started to turn away then, but I was held back by his words. "Hey, Char? Can I ask you another question?" He still wasn't looking at me.

I nodded anyway.

"Was his name Gavin?"

At his question, I dropped the Henry James hardback I'd forgotten was still in my hand. I knelt down to pick it up before asking, "How did you know?"

"You were talking in your sleep," he answered. And after a pause, he added, "You told him he was dead."

I swallowed hard. But there didn't seem to be anything left to say. Then he stood up straight and took two measured steps toward me. I wondered if this was the way he approached deer too, or if one had ever seen him coming. "What happened to the drunk driver, Charlotte? The guy who killed Gavin?"

"What?" I gripped the hardback tighter.

"Did he go to prison for what he did?" He took another step closer, with a distant yet intense look in his eyes. "Did you hate him? Do you still hate him?"

"What are you talking about? It was an *accident*, Roden."

"No, it wasn't." His voice grew louder as he spoke. "It was a choice to get behind the wheel when he shouldn't have. And that choice killed Gavin."

"Why are you doing this?" I shot back, mystified. I couldn't understand why he would possibly want to know how I felt about the drunk driver. In fact, I hadn't thought much about him in the last couple of years. After all, hating him wouldn't bring Gavin back, I knew.

But in the beginning... *No, it was a long time ago.*

"Because I need to know, that's why." At his words, I took a cautious step back, away from the verbal assault. A step back away from the memory and the raw emotion that threatened to resurface.

But he took a step forward. *"Did you hate him?"*

"Yes!" I spat the word at him, as though it would hurt him more than it hurt me. And I felt ashamed to admit the bitterness that I'd harbored those first few weeks. Maybe months. It was an anger I'd scarcely ever admitted to myself and certainly never voiced to anyone else. But in a moment of feeling tired and pushed and provoked, I was overcome with the need to justify myself. "Of course I hated him!" I yelled across the room, and by now I knew that I wasn't yelling at Roden at all, but instead at a man whose name I did not even know. "He took *everything* from me!"

I felt the shame of it, the moral weakness of my hatred that had been buried for so long that I'd forgotten it was there. With no monument, no marker in the dirt to remind me of those emotions, I'd scarcely stopped to mourn them, to acknowledge them.

"Are you happy?" I asked through stinging tears. This was acutely directed at Roden. Because he had unearthed it, bursting the dirt-stained box wide open to reveal the lowness, the cheapness of my innermost feelings.

"I'm—I'm sorry," he said abruptly, surprising me and maybe both of us with his sudden retreat, blinking and turning away from me in that shrinking and claustrophobic gun room. Whatever dark curiosity had gripped him a moment ago, it had vanished just as quickly. "I don't know why I... No, I'm not happy." He walked toward a tall window on the other side of the room. I continued to watch, uncertain if he knew that I was still in the doorway, uncertain why I was still in the doorway. The light from the window cast strange shadows on the side of his face, distorting the contours and deepening the crevices until he was a different person altogether.

I was still breathless and tense, fixated on the new, darker person before me, when I heard it—the sound of his voice faltering, the impression of something crumbling. "I'm sorry." And the tenor of his voice frightened me, for the very singular way it echoed my own feelings, a startling replica of myself, my voice, my remorse.

I left him staring pensively out the window with that gun still strewn out all over the desk in pathetic pieces, impotent and forgotten. And I couldn't shake the impression of a child with a broken toy.

I walked away keenly aware of having just had a fight with a person to whom I owed everything. I felt at once betrayed and guilty of betrayal. Or perhaps like I'd just been yelling at my own reflection. And yet even then I wasn't certain it had been a fight at all. It was too fresh, still too emotionally charged, like an ancient battlefield on which the cannon smoke has not even cleared. *Did we win? Did we lose? Who is left alive, and what are the casualties?*

I came across the study on my way back to the staircase and decided to put that book away at last. As I stepped through the doorway, I was first struck by the way the sunlight illuminated the room peculiarly, casting a dark red light through the curtains onto the floor and oxblood leather furniture. Subdued and atmospheric, the blue spines of the books became deep purples, the greens earthy browns, the yellows dark orange. It was a subtle yet striking transformation. A part of me just wanted to sit down against the wall and fall asleep there like a daydreaming child.

Reluctantly I slid the book back onto the shelf between two other dusty tomes and then stood back to survey the shelves again in all their multicolored glory. None of the titles seemed interesting, relevant, or comforting in the way I wanted. Nothing resonated or called out to me the way a person wants a book to do in a bookstore or a public library. And perhaps this was because I was inconsolable, distracted, and too tired to engage in anyone else's world.

I stepped away with a sigh and glanced around the room. That's when I saw the large, ornate hardback of *Walden* by Henry David Thoreau.

It appeared to have fallen between the desk and the wall, haphazardly balancing on the rounded foot of the desk at an odd angle. I never would have found it if it hadn't been for the way the sunlight illuminated everything so peculiarly through the curtains, touching even that precarious spine with its metamorphic powers. But there it was, and I couldn't pass it up.

As I picked the book up off the floor, I was surprised at how light it was. Curious, I flipped open the cover without a moment's hesitation. But as I stared down at the book in my hands, I was shocked at what I found. It wasn't the real book at all but a hollow box. It was one of those boxes made to look like books to hide a life's savings inconspicuously on a bookshelf, assuming that the thief is too shallow and illiterate to see the value in classic literature.

But there was no money inside this box.

Instead, I found a stack of several pieces of paper, each folded in the same way, one stacked compactly on top of the other. I glanced at the empty doorway and then sat down at the desk to pull out the first page. As I sat down, my fingers held the first trifold with the innocent steadiness of one who is merely curious. But as I unfolded the paper, something at the back of my mind told me that I was trespassing. Somehow I knew that the contents of the page were neither irrelevant nor impersonal. They weren't the obscure artifacts leftover from a forgotten generation. And as I glanced at the unfolded page, perfectly creased in two places, my fingers began to tremble. For I knew that I was crossing over from innocent curiosity to guilty intrusion.

And I knew that the letter was written by Roden.

I recognized the small, bold print with the f's and g's slanting sharply down the page. It was black rain.

As soon as I began reading the cryptic phrases, I knew that it was a personal letter. It was clearly a very personal letter written to...it didn't say exactly. It was dated with yesterday's date and signed with Roden's initials. I set aside the first letter to read the second. Then the third.

That's when my conscience finally overpowered my curiosity. I folded up the three letters with shaking fingers and closed the book. I carefully placed it exactly where I'd found it, between the wall and the desk leg, balanced on that mahogany wood. And I walked away from that desk and that room that had been so beautiful and alluring just moments ago. And I walked away from the light that changed everything. It was only the intimate, forbidden phrases that I took with me as I made my way through the corridors and down the stairs. And maybe a softening toward that mysterious, tortured soul who hid himself away in a room full of guns.

CHAPTER ELEVEN

Whether I was haunted by memories of Gavin or involuntarily clinging to them, I couldn't say, but this memory was crystallized in my mind and left utterly perfect. While I had sincerely hoped to leave it behind when I made my journey to the refuge, I knew now that deep down, I didn't want to forget what happened because I didn't want to forget Gavin. After all, that one memory of what happened was all I had left of him. The memory was tragic and nightmarish but perfect in that it was untouched and unchanged in the two years since it actually happened. And it all started on Halloween—what promised to be a fun celebration just like any other year. I had no idea that this one would be different, that it would change everything.

At Nana's house, Halloween was enchanting. My grandparents' luminous three-story house, flanked on either side by maple trees adorned with glittering lights and Chinese lanterns, stood with its austere white façade and striking black shutters and seemed to swell and sway with the movement of the people inside. I was greeted with robust laughter, Jackie Wilson music, and friendly chatter from the open windows as I walked up the brick path and inside the gate toward the front porch.

I tugged hard on the heavy, black front door and was instantly accosted by twenty different aromas: dark crystal molasses cookies, pumpkin loaves, recently dusted costumes, and a myriad of candles that created a subdued ember glow from the fireplace mantle and atop the mahogany furniture. Black metal cauldrons were filled to the brim and spilled over with their enticing, brightly lit hoard. The capacious kitchen, I knew, was full of deliciously festive foods, such as ladyfingers, midnight bourbon balls, and elaborate chocolate cupcakes that glittered an incandescent orange. My grandparents were exceptional party throwers.

As I lingered near the doorway, I found myself swept up in the loud, chattering crowd, brushing up against the unrecognizable mob of voices and costumes that I knew to be relatives, neighbors, and friends. Standing idly in hallways and upstairs and here in the foyer, were fairy princesses, shady-looking old men, giraffe women, toddler tigers, and any number of brilliantly masked characters. There were ball gowns and circus clowns, renaissance masks, and movie stars. The sounds of their voices, incessant laughter, and sudden boos and shrieks of delight reverberated off the walls, staircases, and bat-covered ceilings where white webs were strung.

I saw him from across the room wearing a pizza delivery boy costume, complete with the red shirt and cap and standard khakis. He was helping a small girl untangle some spiderwebs from her ladybug wings just outside the kitchen. I made my way past them to the apple cider and gazed out the window to the glittering veranda just beyond the back door.

I stepped aside as I was passed by Scarlett O'Hara and General Lee, who were talking animatedly. When I turned back around, I was surprised to see the guy in the pizza costume reaching across for a glass and the ladle.

Fortunately, I had just taken off the fake mustache that came with my mechanic's suit when our eyes met.

"Hi," he said, nodding politely. "Do you always come to these parties?"

"Oh, hi. Yes, I do." I watched curiously as he filled his cup with cider and peered around the room innocently.

"My name's Gavin," he said as he reached his hand across to mine.

"I'm Charlotte," I replied. "My grandparents are throwing this party. You know, Dinah and Pete?" I prompted, trying to figure out who had invited him.

"Oh," he said hesitantly. "Yes, Dinah and good ol' Pete." He nodded before taking a swig of cider. "It's a heck of a party, that's for sure."

I felt my brow furrow as I regarded him with disbelief.

He looked directly at me for a moment, before letting out a dramatic sigh. "Okay," he said at last. "I wasn't technically invited to this party." He took off the cap and ran his hand through his light blond hair before putting it back on again.

"Technically?" I asked.

He leaned in conspiratorially. "This uh, isn't a costume. I just delivered six of our Hawaiian specials and five orders of breadsticks." He hitched a thumb toward the dining room.

I laughed out loud. "So you're basically crashing this party?"

"Well, I was sort of invited. At least, the pizzas were. But yeah, maybe I am." He paused. "You aren't going to tell on me, are you?"

"No, I'd better not," I said.

"Oh yeah? Why not?"

"I'm not in costume either. I just changed a carburetor."

For a moment, he looked stunned. Then we both started laughing. People started to stare at us from across the room. We stood there catching our breath as I noticed that his irises were a murky shade of blue and that he had kind, thin lines curving away from his eyes. His features grew serious before he began speaking again.

"I'm sorry—you were joking, right?" he asked.

We both started laughing again.

I nodded in reply, taking a sip of cider to try to get ahold of my nerves. He smiled as he looked me up and down, apparently taking in the oil stains and smudges on my suit, face, and arms.

"Listen, I actually have to get back to work. But you're not, um...I mean, I get off in a couple of hours..."

"So you'll come back?" I prompted.

"That depends. Am I invited?"

I took a deep breath and made a show of considering my answer. "Okay."

"Okay?" he asked, beginning to laugh again.

"Yes, please come back. But only if you're wearing a costume, of course. If you show up without a costume, I'm afraid they won't let you in the door."

"Wouldn't dream of it, Charlotte. Will you save me a cupcake?" He readjusted his cap as he retrieved a red pizza warmer from the table.

"I'm afraid I can't make you any promises. They're a hot commodity around here."

His eyes turned serious again as he looked back at me, wordlessly. And while he looked at me, I realized that I wasn't breathing. But a smile broke out at last as he said, "You know, I think I'm enchanted? And that's something I never thought I'd say to a mechanic." He should have been walking away, but he remained. I bit my lip before sipping more cider and sort of smiling down at my feet in disbelief. Oxygen came back to me powerfully, mysteriously, flushing my cheeks and tingling when I exhaled.

When he spoke again, the regret was thick in his voice, and his eyes shone sincerely. "I'll be back soon. And remember, if you see another pizza guy around here, he's an impostor." We laughed again. He winked before he turned and walked out of the room.

I spent the next couple of hours in a kind of nervous stupor. I wandered from room to room, carrying around a small round plate with a brilliant orange cupcake as music blared, and I ignored everyone I passed. I blew off every invitation to join the rest of the crowd.

I wandered outside to the veranda, where I inhaled the scent of honeysuckles and watched the wind chimes dangling down from the eaves. I swung slowly back and forth alone on the porch swing. There was a game of charades going on in the game room, and I could hear the voices through the windows. But for the most part, the night air was pretty serene. It was just me and the locusts.

As I sat there, I tried to think about other things, but I just couldn't stop thinking about Gavin. I was thinking how bizarre the evening had been—how drastically life had just changed. And I was thinking how impossible it was to fall in love with someone I'd just met.

And yet I was more in love than I'd ever dreamed possible. In the night sky, I couldn't see any stars or hear the rushing of the wind through the trees. I saw Gavin's face and heard his laughter, the sound of his voice. I saw our first date, our first kiss, our first road trip to Austin. I saw myself introducing him to my roommate and her elated facial expressions. I saw his introduction to Grandpa Pete and that first all-important handshake with my father. I was wondering if he preferred Robert Burns or Robert Frost, Elizabeth Barrett Browning or Elizabeth Bishop, the summer or the winter. In short, I was entirely out of my mind.

I was awakened from my reverie when I heard a haunting, eerie howl from far away. I heard several different howls rising and weaving in and out of one another for several minutes until they finally died away. It wasn't uncommon to hear coyotes on the edge of town, but their sound had an unsettling effect on me. That's when I started to get really nervous.

"He's coming back," I told myself. I looked down at my watch. It had been over two hours. *Where is he? Did he change his mind? Was it all a ruse? Was he just trying to get an extra tip?* And I knew that I was doing it again. I was letting fear control me. I had to get a grip. I finally went back inside the house.

I stopped in the living room, where some white eyelet curtains behind the couch were blowing from a cool breeze outside. From the living room windows, I could see the lights cascading down the brick path and the tall black poles lighting the street and the crowd of vehicles parked there. I was gazing expectantly out the window, hoping against hope that he would show up at any second. I was hoping, begging, praying that it wasn't all a dream. I craned my neck in a painful desire that he would appear before my eyes.

And for a brief moment, he did.

I heard the roar of an engine, then a sickening thud and crash. I gasped, feeling the air leaving my lungs in one swift blow, knowing then and there that I'd never be the same.

It would be days before I could even process clearly what had happened. Looking back, I recall that people immediately ran out into the street as I stood there in disbelief, trying to breathe, trying to understand. I'd just had time to recognize Gavin's blond hair as he pulled a yellow construction worker's helmet on. He emerged from behind a parked car before a truck came speeding down the hill, ran straight into him, and then plowed into two other parked vehicles. Yes, the others took off running to help him. But if they had seen what I had seen, they would have known that there was no rush. There was no reason to run out into that dangerous street where anything could happen. No reason at all, because he was already too far gone.

My vision swam as the driver climbed down from his enormous truck and staggered to the ground. I was later informed that the man who accidentally killed Gavin was on his way home from another party and was extremely drunk. He never even saw him in his way, they say. Of course, he was very sorry. He wished he hadn't done it. He was a Methodist. He would undo it if he could.

But he couldn't.

I didn't think people dreamt after passing out, but somehow I did. The next thing I knew, I saw Gavin's face looming over me in a surreal image. "Charlotte, are you going to invite me? I'll be back, okay?"

I screamed something at him, though I'm not sure what it was. I imagine it had something to do with the truck.

He replied, laughing as he spoke, "I'm just going to catch this ladybug. I'll be right back. Just wait for me, okay?" His face was a little blurred, but his voice rang out clear and so realistic, that when I finally came to, I woke up with tears already streaming down my cheeks and knowing deep down that I'd wait for him for the rest of my life.

What happened that day, everything about it, was so surreal. From the bizarre costumes, painted faces, cobwebs, candles, and the taste of cider on my tongue to the howling dogs and the roaring engine—it was all made into a sickening caricature in my dreams.

No matter how many times I told myself it was impossible to fall in love with someone I barely knew—or perhaps, really didn't know at all—I knew it didn't matter. It's amazing how useless statistics are when a very unlikely thing is actually happening. It doesn't matter if the odds were fifty/fifty or one in a million. Either it happened or it didn't. It didn't matter that it was impossible. *It happened to me.*

That's when the dreams began. As much as I wanted to leave that day behind, part of me must've desperately wanted to stay there. What was so startling in those first few months was that his voice—the cadences and tone and slight imperfections—made the dreams feel so real that I began to wonder if they were. I mean, I knew they were just dreams. And yet something about them gave me the impression that I'd known Gavin for years—that I had to have known him for years to dream it, to get it all so right. It was like listening to a part of myself I never knew was there before. But it had always been there, and it would always be there afterward.

The hours that followed his death slowly spun out into days, weeks, and months. Somehow, although stretched to impossible lengths, time dragged by. It seemed peculiar to me that the world kept moving on as though nothing had happened, as though it hadn't just ended. Because it had.

Nothing seemed to drown out the memories. Because it all came back to pain. It all came back to Gavin, to a Halloween party, and an order of six Hawaiian specials and five orders of breadsticks. It all came back to a drunken man who used an F-150 to destroy the only thing I ever wanted.

I TURNED OVER against the soft cotton sheets, attempting to yield myself to their gentle comfort. This was the first night since coming to the mansion that I was sleeping in a bed. Of course, I use the term *sleeping* loosely, as I lay awake beneath closed eyelids with a mind that would not stop roving over my conversation with Roden and the vivid memory it had conjured. I lay there face to face with that day once again, trying to come to terms with the past and aching from it all over again. Yet it occurred to me for the first time that perhaps I wasn't meant to face it alone.

Although August was still recovering from his illness, he was sleeping alone this time. I'd taken up a room near his, the closest with no windows, and I knew Roden was somewhere down the hall.

Even from this room, in the interior of the building, I could just make out the sounds of wolves howling in the distance. I had mostly learned to block the sound out, but not tonight. Tonight it pierced the night air with a special eeriness, filling up the room with a potent mixture of fear and loneliness. It resonated louder than it actually was, perhaps more an object of my memory than the perception of my eardrums. But somehow, it found me.

I raised my head up to flip my pillow over. Again. But I knew I couldn't sleep. Roden and I had scarcely spoken all day, and after a quiet dinner with August, I'd come to suspect that Roden was avoiding me as much as I was avoiding him. *What is he hiding?* At last I got up from the bed. I slipped down the hallway as quietly as I could, glancing warily around once or twice for any sign of Ambrose. I made my way to the nearest bathroom and shut the door.

As I stepped into the tub, the hot water sprayed across my face in a hard, fast rush. It was getting to be that time of night when things feel surreal. I closed my eyes, letting the water soak my hair and flood my face with warmth. I inhaled the steam, remembering an old song about walking in a garden, and imagined that I *was* that garden.

The grass was sticking up between my toes and the scent of fresh soil was on my hands. My hair was made of roots, with clean dirt hanging in tiny clots. And my arms and back and legs were covered in green vines like tattoos. Or maybe like scars.

I was surprised to find that small patch of neon pink on my arm and found myself gazing at it for a long while before peeling off the thick, rubbery bandage. I took my time washing, taking each sensation in slowly, drifting back and forth between reality and my imagination before I finally turned the faucet off and started to dry.

The mirror was fogged, but I reached across the sink and wiped it off with my hand while I was still wrapped up in a towel. I dried my hair slowly with a smaller towel, trying to catch the fat drops of water at the tips and at my chin and elbows. Then I just sort of stood there, looking at my reflection and inhaling the humid air.

I'd done this a thousand times before, but here I was doing it again. My eyes peered back at me beneath a quizzical brow as I looked hard for some sign of a soul within those ambiguous amber rings. I saw the lights and darks of my russet skin, with various nondescript planes and contours, high cheekbones, and a defiant upper lip. My black eye had all but healed, leaving just the slightest hint of a bluish-purple ring as a vivid reminder of the danger outside. I saw a high hairline and a prominent chin and black eyelashes fanning off the wide, almond-shaped eyelids. I saw the hint of bronze reflecting in the bathroom light, but mostly a heavy veil of thick, black hair that weighed down just past my shoulders.

What is there? I implored those amber irises that I was certain were not mine. I begged them to give up their secrets, to reveal the woman I had been searching for all these years. I saw my mother's skin and hair. I saw resemblances of aunts, my mother's mother, Grandpa Pete, and Nana. I saw hints of my father and my brothers and past generations I'd only seen in photographs. But I didn't see what I was looking for. I searched for self but couldn't find it no matter how hard I looked.

I leaned in closer, begging the same questions again. I wondered what was in the way. Was it the glass? Or the thick, humid air that separated me from my reflection? Or the questions themselves? *Where is Atsila?* But she wasn't there.

I dried off and changed, shooting the same silent questions at my reflection the whole time. I made my way back to the bedroom, tripping through the darkness without any answers. I clutched at dripping strands of hair through a towel and shivered at the cool night air as I entered my bedroom and sat down.

And I shuddered at the sense of loneliness that enveloped me.

Sitting with my heels digging into the bed frame, I silently begged, pleaded Roden to come in and talk to me, breathe with me, sit with me. I asked him to tell me everything or answer nothing, to just come and be. I lay back down against the comforter in those pajamas that were not mine but were given to me as a victim or patient or prisoner—I couldn't remember which. And I stared into the bleak darkness, waiting. He couldn't hear me though. At least, he didn't come. But I lay awake anyway, for a very long time.

Then I heard the scream.

I sat up in the bed as the sound erupted from across the hall. I moved from the bedroom to the door in a panic. It was late and dark, and though I hadn't fallen asleep, it hadn't yet occurred to me when I yanked my door open that there was nothing I could do for him. And in the end, I doubt that it would have mattered anyway. I would have wanted to be there, to wait out the struggle until he woke up.

I didn't make it to August's bedroom before the unintelligible screams changed to distinct pleadings for his mom.

"Mommy, please, don't!" Even amid the noise, I heard a door bang loudly from somewhere down the hall as I neared August's bedside. "Daddy, come back, Daddy! Please come back, *please!*"

I sat down on his bed and made an involuntary *shhh-ing* sound, though I knew he wouldn't hear me.

Unexpectedly, he woke up from the nightmare and lunged at me in the darkness. With his little arms clutching hard around my neck, he sobbed a gut-wrenching cry against my shoulder. I held my arms around the child, trying to keep him steady, keep him close. His body shuddered with the intensity of his weeping, and his drool began to dampen my thin gray t-shirt.

"They left me." He sobbed. "Why did they leave me? Why?" His voice didn't sound like his own. And perhaps it wasn't his own. And I wasn't my own, and we were different people altogether.

He continued in this way for some time, and I began to slowly rock him, *shhh-ing* all the while because I didn't know what else to say. And maybe because I was crying too. I'd closed my eyes, ducking my chin down against his soft, blond hair, and sort of just tried to hold him all together. I held on for dear life, as though we both might fall apart without my arms around him.

"Hey, champ." I was startled to hear Roden's voice so near my ear. But he spoke softly, gently interrupting my chorus of *shhh-ing*. His voice sounded a little hoarse, causing me to wonder if he always sounded that way when he'd just woken up. I opened my eyes to see Roden sitting on August's other side, reaching a hand out to touch him on the back. "Everything's going to be okay. I promise."

Roden must have turned a light on in the hallway, because half the room was illuminated so that I could see his arm, bare beneath a plain white undershirt. And from beneath the thin, white shirt sleeve, I saw the scars snake out, sprawling down the length of his arm.

I'd never seen so much of them since the draftiness of the mansion warranted long sleeves. But here they were, illuminated in the light, irreverently and unromantically. And so I realized I'd been wrong about them. They were not vines or barbed wire or anything else. They were just scars in random patterns, veering off in random directions. And even as I clutched the weeping child to my shoulder, I ached for those scars too.

My eyes flitted up in time to see that I'd been caught looking at them. And he dropped his gaze to look back down at them as well. August pulled back from me a little and turned toward Roden, sniffing and wiping snot and tears all over his own arm as he had done to my shirt. For a moment he didn't say anything. He just looked at Roden, and Roden looked back at him.

Then August spoke. "What happened?" he asked. He wiped away more tears as Roden just sort of stared back at him, probably still thinking of those scars. "To your face," August prompted, simply.

Roden reached a hand up to his forehead. I hadn't noticed it before, but it was bright red in the light from the hallway. "I, um, ran into my door," he admitted with that hoarse and groggy voice of his.

I remembered the sound of the door banging. Squinting, I could just make out the contours of a knot forming on his forehead above his right eye. August began laughing, a comically distorted, post-crying laugh. I couldn't help but catch the infectious mood and was soon laughing even harder than August. Then I detected Roden's hoarse voice, probably laughing more at us than anything else. And the laughing grew louder and funnier sounding.

Between the three of us, there was snorting and giggling and gasping for air. Three human souls, all of us damaged and scarred by the past and struggling after a myriad of ghosts, laughed through our tears and our snotty noses, causing the bed to shake and the howling of the wolves to be drowned out by our own hysterical voices.

I AWOKE to the sound of hammering.

I threw back the covers and made my way down the hallway, annoyed. I was still rubbing the gunk out of my blurry eyes when I stopped to peer into August's room without even making the decision to go there. But he was miraculously still asleep.

I smiled at his dormant form as he lay facedown on the sheets with one pale arm dangling off the side of the bed. I gently pulled his door closed and continued following the jarring sounds that had awoken me.

I eventually came to stop behind Roden, who was on his knees in front of a large window in the mansion's foyer. He had a long board held up across the bottom of the window and was hammering a nail through the board into the frame. He was wearing a faded blue T-shirt and jeans that were stained and fraying at the bottom. A delayed yawn escaped my lips just as he paused to pick up more nails from off the ground, letting them clink and roll across the marble. He turned to look at me, surprised by the sound.

"Morning," I muttered. "Doing some remodeling, I see."

He stopped to wipe his hands on his T-shirt, smudging the blue with dusty grays and browns. "Something like that. Helicopter dropped them off early this morning. I just brought them down from the balcony. I don't suppose the helicopter woke you up?"

"Nope," I answered. "Just the hammering."

He looked up at me with a smirk on his face. "Are you always so snarky first thing in the morning?"

But before I could fathom an answer, he continued, already turning away from me, "Coffee's brewing in the kitchen, actually. If you don't mind, I could really use a cuppa joe, myself."

I muttered some kind of assent and turned to walk away as he resumed hammering.

"Oh—Charlotte?" Roden said suddenly, though the words were muffled through clenched teeth. I turned back to see him retrieve two nails from between his teeth before he spoke again. "I take my coffee black."

"Right," I mumbled as he turned away with the vaguest hint of a smile on his lips. "Somehow I figured as much." But my voice was drowned out by the hammering.

When I reached the kitchen, I was welcomed by the sight of the percolator puffing out its last bursts of steam and the aroma of coffee wafting toward me. I poured two mugs before retracing my steps back to the foyer. By the time I arrived, he'd covered the first two windows on the first floor, though the glass proceeded upward to face the balcony.

"Thank you," he said, dusting himself off with one hand before taking the mug in the other. We sat down on the lower steps of the staircase. I could smell the wood and something like sawdust as he took his place next to me against the ornate railing. His expression grew more serious before he spoke again.

"Charlotte, I'm really sorry for what happened yesterday. For what I said."

"I know," I answered. Our eyes met for a brief moment as I tried to decide whether I should probe for more answers, confess about the letters, or just try to forget it altogether.

I hadn't made up my mind when the ring of the kitchen phone reached our ears, echoing off the walls and marble in that nerve-racking old-fashioned tone. I watched Roden stand up and walk away, gripping his coffee cup with one steady hand, the tip of one finger just touching the rim. As he turned the corner, I noticed the redness on his forehead again. I had to turn my head away to keep from laughing.

After he left I found myself thinking about the night before and the experience in August's room. The surreal memory... the intense sorrow and the profound comfort...the new intimacy I felt with both of them, whether I wanted it or not... I wasn't sure what to make of it—if I was the only one changed and maybe a little startled by what happened.

I stood up, deciding to stick close by to August's room until he woke up. I couldn't imagine he had the first floor quite figured out yet, and I didn't want him to get lost or feel alone. But just as I was passing through the living room, Roden emerged from a hallway.

"Char," he said. I stopped to look at him, surprised by the urgency in his voice. But he just sort of stood there, looking me up and down before continuing. "It's for you." It took me a moment to register what he was talking about.

I suppressed the urge to run toward the phone. When I finally picked up the receiver from where it had been lying flat against the countertop, I realized I was holding my breath. "Hello?"

"Char, is that you?" my mom's voice answered on the other end of the line.

I exhaled at last. "Mom! Yes, it's me. Thank God you got my message!" I couldn't make out her reply because her words were choked up by tears. "Mom, what's the matter? Why are you crying? What is it?" I could tell that she had covered the phone with one hand as my heart thudded dramatically.

"I'm sorry. It's nothing, it's just...I didn't think I'd hear from you again."

I exhaled in relief. "You scared me."

"Me?" she said, indignantly. "We've been trying your phone for days now! All we've gotten is that busy signal—we just didn't know what to think until we finally got through to someone at the CDC—"

"Did you say *busy signal?*" I asked. For a moment, I found myself trying to recall whether I'd left the phone off the hook.

But then I remembered the mayhem—someone must have knocked the phone off the counter.

"Yes! We didn't know if you were on the phone with someone or if the phone had been knocked off its hook and you were unconscious somewhere, or... Oh, Char, we've been so worried. We heard about the quarantine on the news, but they aren't giving out much information. Please tell me what in the world is going on."

"I will, I will. It's just...it's so good to hear your voice, Mom," I admitted.

I spoke to her and my dad for over an hour.

Surprisingly I found myself mostly talking about August—how brave he'd been, what a miracle it was that we found him, and how connected I felt to him. I talked to them about the night terrors, the way he lost his parents, and about how we had to vaccinate him.

"What's that sound in the background, sweetie?" My dad asked at one point. I heard the sound of hammering again.

"Roden's boarding up the windows in case someone tries to break in."

I could hear the anxiety in my dad's voice as he spoke. "We could leave tonight, you know. We could be there by midmorning tomorrow."

"Dad, there's nothing you can do from out there, and there's no way you're getting in here," I said. "Roden will protect us if anything breaks in. And the authorities are dropping off all the supplies we need to survive. We just have to wait things out and hope for the best. We'll be fine." Though my words sounded sure, my heart ached to ask my father to come save me. I wanted so badly to crumple beneath the strain, to give in to the fears of the danger lurking outside the mansion walls, to curl up and weep like a child.

There was a long pause on the other end. "You're absolutely right," my dad said at last. "You're going to be just fine."

AUGUST AND I spent the day together taking care of all the meals, laundry, and even sweeping the floors that had been tracked with mud and dirt. Of course August mostly contributed by keeping me company, but he seemed happy to be helping me around the house. Meanwhile, Roden spent most of the day boarding up windows, slowly transforming a historical luxury home into something that felt more like a war bunker.

After dinner I let August and Roden wash the dishes while I finished cleaning the kitchen. Roden slipped away while I got August ready for bed and tucked him in. He asked me to sing to him until he fell asleep, informing me that he thought this would keep the nightmares away. I happily complied.

After kissing the top of August's head, I went back to the kitchen and made hot chocolate on the stove. My mom and I had come up with a special recipe years ago that had completely ruined me for the store-bought variety. I even added a tiny splash of rum from a bottle I found in the back of Roden's cabinet.

I made my way to the staircase, following an instinct that I'd find Roden on the balcony. I zipped up my jacket as I climbed the steps, trying to figure out why he seemed so distant and closed off all day. *Was it the phone call? Did my parents say something that upset him?* I couldn't figure it out, but I wasn't going to spend yet another sleepless night without at least a few answers from him.

I clutched the two steaming mugs against my chest with one arm as I turned the crystal knob with the other. The night wind blew the door toward me so that I had to push hard against it as I stepped out onto the balcony.

For a moment, I thought I was alone.

A thin cloud of smoke to my left caught my eye, and I saw Roden's figure standing at the rail with a pipe in one hand. There was a light near my head attracting fat moths and other bugs making their loops and buzzing circles in the air. I pulled the door closed behind me, hearing the stubborn creak of wood and old paint.

In the lighting I caught the side of Roden's tan face and thick, dark hair and tried to decide whether he realized he was no longer alone. His mouth made a slight movement, a downward twitch or...something. It gave me the distinct impression that I was trespassing again. It was too late to go back though, I knew. The mugs burned through my sleeve, reminding me of why I'd come. Roden slowly turned his gaze toward me but didn't speak.

I stepped across the balcony, now holding a mug in each hand, which burned my palms though my fingers remained stiff with cold. "I brought you some hot chocolate," I said, handing him the mug. Then I stopped to inhale the night air, thick with the scent of pine and cedar and...wood smoke. There was a hazy ember glow in the distance, perhaps a cabin that had caught fire.

But I was distracted by the scent of Roden's pipe tobacco, much stronger than anything else. And I felt inexplicably emboldened by the scent, enveloped in its complex flavors and that subtle hint of danger.

"I'd really love to know what you're thinking up here all alone."

Roden took a sip of the hot chocolate and stepped away when he started to choke on it.

"You don't like it," I said, laughing.

He coughed a little before taking another sip and swallowing. "No, no I do." He took another sip to prove it and then chuckled lightly. "I just didn't expect to like it *quite* that much. I take it you found the rum."

I nodded, waiting patiently for him to begin speaking again, but time passed slowly as the last of the cicadas chanted out their songs in the woods around us and the wind blew her biting chill through the treetops. The sip of hot chocolate burned my tongue as it went down but remained rich and sweet at the edges of my lips. Instinctively I licked them, trying hard not to shiver as I waited, feeling our jacketed elbows touch as we stood at the railing. I clung hard to the hot mug with my bony fingers and let the warmth of the alcohol fill up my chest and my cheeks and my limbs like a flicker of light in the darkness.

The full moon reflected light just beyond one of the rooftops of the third floor, with that bear standing ominously over the baby. I liked to think that he was protecting him from some unseen dangers, maybe wolves or snakes or men with guns. Of course, for all I knew, I could have it completely wrong. The bear could be the most dangerous of all.

A hazy ring encircled the moon like a halo as I contemplated the scenario. My thoughts were interrupted by the sound of howling, which rose and fell with the wind. Like a foreboding tide, it seemed to grow resolutely nearer.

"Danny and I met when we were really young," Roden began. "I remember we'd been friends for about a week when we came up with this game out in the middle of the woods. We'd pretend one of us was a hunter and the other was a wolf, and we were both just sort of hiding and hunting one another with slingshots and rocks. We called it Wolves and Men."

"That doesn't sound like a very good game for little boys," I commented.

He chuckled, as though admitting I was right. "One day, I slung a rock at him pretty hard and thought I'd knocked his eye out. I remember we both started panicking, and I practically carried him all the way back to his house.

"When we got there, his mom made such a fuss over him. And she wouldn't even *look* at me. She just kept muttering to herself, 'Oh, Danny, my poor baby boy,' and ignored me altogether. I went home and cried my eyes out. I felt so bad. He was a few years younger and smaller, and I knew I should have taken care of him. Instead, I'd hurt him."

He stuck the pipe back into the side of his mouth, letting the puff of smoke fill the air between us like a thin and fleeting veil. I caught myself inhaling it as I watched those tiny lines at the corners of his eyes and wondered again at how they got there. "I was just thinking about Danny's mom. Someone's going to have to tell her that her baby boy is dead." Perhaps they were not laugh lines at all. Perhaps it was merely genetic.

"I miss him, too, you know," I confided, sipping the hot chocolate with both hands wrapped tightly around the mug for heat. Roden turned toward me slightly when he answered.

"No, it's so much more than that. Char, it wasn't supposed to end like that. I never meant to let things get so out of hand..." I waited to hear him complete his thought, to unravel some elusive mystery about himself, but he stopped instead.

"I guess I took it for granted that there'd be time to say what I needed to say."

I looked past Roden at the incandescent moon. "What is it you needed to say?"

"That I'm sorry. Just that I'm so sorry." He leaned against the railing with the hand that held the pipe, setting the mug there as well. I watched him peer hard into the darkness, though I knew he didn't see anything aside from what was playing in his mind. "Now I have to tell his mom instead."

My chest physically ached, and perhaps it was merely a chemical reaction of the cocoa and rum. But I like to believe it was seeing Roden leaning against the rail in the cold and the bleak canvas of shadows and the moonlit rooftops and tree limbs and chipping white paint. I turned my head away from him and gazed off into the same dark abyss. I peered hard and tried to let myself get lost in its vastness and obscurity. But it wasn't dark enough for that.

There was a moment when I thought I saw Danny's athletic figure standing on the bridge in the distance. I knew it was a phantom of my imagination, but even so, the image was burned into my mind. The bridge, with its white and gray stone appearing sleek and soft through the treetops, was bathed romantically in moonlight. It was glowing and seemed to be just waiting for someone to recite poetry. Struck by the unexpected sight of my phantom, I fought hard not to crumple against the railing and weep for Danny.

Somehow I stood my ground. I took a deep breath and drew a strand of hair from my eyes, the muscles in my jaw feeling tense and strong.

"Do you have family worried about you, Roden?" As I spoke, I turned away from the phantoms and the sorrow.

He laughed bitterly. "I doubt it. My father drinks like a fish, always has. And my mother..." He wore a sort of bitter smile on his lips. "She ran off when I was in high school, actually. Last I heard she was looking for herself in Paris. But that was several years ago."

"C'est tragic," I muttered. "Je suis très désolé." As I grew colder, I tried harder to refrain from shivering out loud like a child.

"You speak French?"

"Very little," I replied honestly. "I lived with a French roommate for two years. I suppose it was inevitable I'd pick up a few phrases."

"Two years is a long time in roommate years," he commented, suddenly turning his full attention toward me. I wondered if he was trying to distract himself too. "You must've been very close."

"Umm, not really."

My reply made him laugh, causing the pipe to tremble on his lips.

"I guess we probably should've been close, but in the last couple years, I sort of kept to myself. To be honest, I think I started pushing people away."

"Let me guess. Because of Gavin?" It was strange, hearing Roden say his name. And yet a tiny wave of relief swept over me when he did.

"Yes, because of him," I answered. I took a long drink of hot chocolate before continuing. "I guess I believed that nobody understood my loss—it was just too unbelievable, and I couldn't really blame them."

I'd always heard that you couldn't miss something you never had, but suddenly all those friendships I didn't make in college seemed to leave a vacancy. And I realized that whatever I thought I'd been achieving by keeping everyone at arm's length for the last two years...I'd had it all wrong.

"I don't think it's so hard to understand," he said. "Losing someone you've known for a long time is just really hard for anyone."

"Yeah, I guess so." My answer came out quietly, cowardly. I wasn't sure I could bring myself to explain to him why my case was different. I clenched my teeth to keep them from chattering in the cold, but it only reinforced the feeling of being a coward. "Actually, this...this was different." I exhaled a heavy puff of air, feeling like I'd already accomplished something. But I knew I wasn't finished.

"Oh?"

"I only knew him for two hours," I answered. I glanced at Roden's face but couldn't find the skepticism I expected to find there. "And...I'd fallen in love with him." I said these last words looking away into the darkness, too uncomfortable to watch his reaction. I heard him move somewhere next to me, but he didn't respond right away.

"Wow." He said the word quietly, reverently.

"I know," I said. "It's completely unbelievable." I wasn't sure what I'd expected, but the effect of having told him everything was somehow less than satisfying. I was beginning to regret coming up here and ever confiding in him in the first place. But somehow we seemed almost incapable of having casual conversation when we were alone together. When we spoke, it was always big and heavy and honest.

"No, it's not that," he said abruptly. I realized that he was turned to face me now. "It's just that I feel like I understand completely. Sophia and I had known each other for a long time, but sometimes I think what hurt the most was that I'd had this whole future planned out in my mind where we would always be together. Not only is this person who you loved gone but so are all the time and memories you were supposed to share together." It must have been the cold air around us, because it looked like his eyes were watering. "And I can see why it would be difficult to share that with people."

"Yeah, I guess, as hard as it's been, and as terrible of a job as I've been doing trying to cope with it, I just always imagined it was safer to keep it to myself."

"And...do you feel safe?" Roden asked, looking thoughtfully back at me.

"You mean, right now?"

He gave a terse nod. I took another sip of hot chocolate, surveying his features.

"Of course I do," I answered quietly before finishing off the thick, dark chocolate residue at the bottom of my cup. It was chalky and grainy but satisfying. And I swallowed down the last hint of rum as well. I glanced at the moon's image over the rooftop once more, suddenly convinced that the bear was protecting the baby. And I looked beside the small cloud of pipe smoke, at the pair of hazel green eyes that watched and waited for my answer. "I'm with *you*."

CHAPTER TWELVE

August and I had been preparing dinner together before we decided he needed an afternoon nap. I took him back to his bedroom, where we went through what was quickly becoming routine. Once snuggled beneath the sheets and blankets, he was out before I got halfway through the first song.

Or so I thought.

I stood up and began to cross the room to the door when his sleepy voice stopped me. "Char?"

I turned, surprised, and made my way back to his bedside. "Yes, sweetie?"

"Are you going to leave me?" he asked.

I sat down next to him on the bed, brushing his hair out of his gorgeous blue eyes. "Oh, no, sweetie. I will not ever leave you." There was so much more that I wanted to promise him, but even the words I'd just spoken felt like a half truth. I would never leave him as long as we were in Willow's Bend, but once we got out, everything would change. Wouldn't it?

"I will always be here for you, August," I reassured him. That somehow felt more true. In whatever way I could be, and whatever way he needed me to be, I would be there for him.

"How about one more song?" I asked. He nodded, his chubby chin brushing up against the top of the covers.

After singing the song, I slipped out the door and made my way back to the kitchen to finish cooking dinner.

I could hear Roden unloading an armful of logs into the fireplace down the hallway, and I wondered what he would think of August's question. I went to move the large bowl of green beans from the island to the other counter, when something caught my eye.

Next to the pantry, there was a calendar hanging on a nail in the wall. It was strange that I hadn't noticed it before, but then it was in a corner of the room and nearly blended in with the wall color. Shifting the bowl into the crook of one arm, I approached to get a better look. The month still read January of this year, so I reached out my free arm and began flipping through the months.

For a moment, I had no idea what the date was. I thought back to the last date I could remember. It was the day Danny came by to pick me up for pizza, the day we found out about the quarantine. After that, I remembered, was the day I ran away.

I counted the days we'd spent in the mansion. Then I recounted. Staring at the month of October, I touched each box with my finger, doubting my calculation. But each time, I landed on the same date.

The bowl slipped from my arm, shattering loudly against the floor and my foot. I winced where I stood, barefoot in a sea of shattered glass and green beans, swearing under my breath at having been so clumsy. As I bent over and began to grope after the shards of glass, my hand must have knocked off the calendar because it fell at my feet as well. The sounds from the fireplace had stopped, and I knew that Roden was coming. My face flushed red as I searched for a safe place to step. But the top of my foot was bleeding as I crouched down and began picking up green beans from the hardwood kitchen floor.

"What's wrong?" Roden asked, still wearing those tan work gloves. He rounded the island and stared down at my mess. "Hell, Char, what happened?"

"Nothing happened," I said angrily, already flustered and defensive. "I just dropped a bowl, that's all."

"You're bleeding," he observed.

I stopped picking up green beans. "I can see that. Thank you. You can go back to work now. I'm fine."

"I'll grab the broom," Roden said, not bothering to take off his gloves.

"Roden, please, I'm fine—" I started, but as I moved, I stepped on glass again, feeling the cut through my skin on the bottom of my foot. Groaning, I froze where I stood, crouched on my heels and feeling rather stupid for cooking barefoot in the first place.

"Right, I'll get the broom," I heard Roden mumble before turning to go.

I'd always gone barefoot when I could, since childhood, so it wasn't unusual for me to be seen cooking without shoes on, even in the colder months. Suddenly though, I was embarrassed to be caught like that.

Once Roden was gone, I took the opportunity to drop the green beans back onto the pile of broken glass and ducked my head into my hands. *What just happened?* I thought. I took a moment to breathe deeply and tried to pull myself together just as Roden came back into the kitchen with the broom, dustpan, and a box of Band-Aids. He swept a clear path for me before stopping and reaching out his hand. I took it, balancing my weight on my unscathed foot and hopping away from the mess. I picked up the bandages and set to work cleaning up my foot.

"Are you sure there's no glass in your foot?" he asked, sweeping up the shards on the floor. I looked up from where I sat in a dining room chair.

"Quite sure, yes," I said. And then, "Really, I can clean it up, Roden. You don't have to help me."

"I know you can clean it up, Char." But he kept sweeping anyway. He was using his condescending voice, and it drove me crazy.

I started testing out my foot, to make sure I could put weight on it now that all the glass had been wiped away and the wound was covered. I looked up at the sound of Roden's voice.

"Hey, that's something," he said, putting the calendar back onto the wall with the nail. I carefully lowered my gaze back down to my bandage as he spoke, dreading what he was about to say. "I didn't even realize today was Halloween."

IT WAS WITH a certain distracted bitterness that I finished preparing dinner and we all sat down to eat. I don't recall much of the conversation or the flavor of the food. I did eat and made a comment or two to encourage August to eat more of his vegetables. I remember the sound of ice clinking in our glasses of tea and the gentle *thump-thumping* of August swinging his legs in his chair so that he kicked the table with his socked feet. I heard Roden and August say something about playing games and having a sort of a party upstairs. It was supposed to be some kind of Halloween party they were planning for tomorrow night. But even that conversation didn't hold my attention.

I was once abruptly brought back out of my thoughts when Roden momentarily choked on his food and pushed away from the table to cough.

"Are you okay?" I asked without thinking.

He cleared his throat a few times before responding with, "Are you?" I looked up to see his features portraying sincere concern.

His question took me by surprise, but I answered with a stoic, "Of course," before letting myself fall back into my thoughts.

Perhaps *thoughts* is an inadequate word. My overwhelming impulse was the very letting go of ideas, memories, and emotions. If I was forming thoughts, they probably amounted to nothing more than, "Let go, let go, let go..." an incessant chanting, pleading, and prayer that formed and dissipated and reformed again. Precisely whom I was trying to let go of, or which memories, was unclear.

It was Halloween. Nothing more than a particular square on a calendar. A number, a date, an advertisement for candy and face paint and cheap costumes. It was not death. It was not love. It was not fear. And yet there was this desperate pleading at my core to recoil and let go and release something...but what? What had I not let go of already? Whom had I not mourned and buried and confidently informed, "You are dead"? What was left to let go of?

After dinner, I cleaned the kitchen while Roden helped August get ready for bed. But when they returned, August asked if he could stay up with us for a little while longer. It wasn't terribly late yet, so Roden volunteered to make us Halloween s'mores at the fireplace, and August asked to look at a book that had been sent to him in the care package. After our dessert, I settled onto the couch with a book of T.S. Eliot poems and continued to try to "let go" against the back drop of "Waste Land" and August and Roden's conversation. Roden stoked the fire as they talked about August's book, and I tried to focus my thoughts on Eliot's verses.

We spent some time in this way, which once again struck me as a peculiar family, though still that same huddle of shipwreck survivors clinging to the same piece of driftwood.

I looked across the room at the child and wondered once again at his age. And then at my age, and then at Roden's. Weren't we all adults by now? August, who had lost some measure of innocence, seemed to rise above so many stories in books dubbed as "coming of age" so that they now only amounted to a pile of sex-saturated best sellers. August, who had really come of age, not by temptation or some great heaping of responsibility being thrust upon him, but by the bare and fusty bones of tragedy itself. August, my old man. August, the survivor.

And what was my age now but a composition of erroneous numbers being added and divided and subtracted and then multiplied all over again to some arbitrary sum that was meant to speak volumes of who I was and where I'd been? But it could not and did not encapsulate the sound of gunshots on a playground, nor the sudden, feverish ripening of young love and the gut-ripping tragedy of a senseless car accident. It did not embody or give shape to Danny and Cleo and strange men transmogrified into grotesque and ferocious predators.

No, that too was left to the bare bones of tragedy, and that was my age now.

And Roden, I knew, had some number assigned to him like any other human being, but like August and myself, that number was necessarily wrong and misleading and shapeless. We are not ages, then, but stories. And our stories are, like us, old and matured and steeped in timelessness and the rich, sepia-hued shades of reality.

And I had just gotten this, just digested what I thought was a perfectly accurate picture of us, when I heard a movement and saw August stand up and drowsily approach me.

"I guess you're ready for bed, huh?" I asked, letting the sounds of the crackling fire hiss and pop around my words.

He stood in front of me as I closed the book I was holding and started to sit up. But much to my surprise, he began to climb onto the couch, yawning.

"Hey, don't you think you'll be more comfortable in your bed?" I asked, though I found myself making room for him at the same time.

He shook his head as he continued to get comfortable until he was snuggled up against me. I heard his sleepy voice mutter something about wanting to stay with me.

That's when I realized that I'd been wrong. Or perhaps if not entirely wrong, then I'd at least oversimplified my conclusions about August. It's true that he was much more than his age, but as much as he was older than any number, he must have been younger as well. And maybe he was only as young as we all are. But his youth and needs for comfort and human contact were as valid and pure and relatable as anything, and I had to remember that. He may have been an old child, but he was a child who warranted all the nurturing of a young, tender orchid—with all the care and attention and resources I could possibly offer.

I put my arm around him, kissing him on the forehead, as though giving him permission to be just a child for the rest of the night. And I let myself fall asleep, feeling the sweetness of indulgence and the simple pleasure of giving him something he wanted, if not needed. And at least for the moment, the bitter and jarring ticker tape of thought had stopped.

It is a strange and mysterious chamber to which our minds retire when we sleep. Sometimes the dreams are so vivid or realistic that we have trouble coming to terms with reality upon waking. Other times, however, we wake up entirely uncertain as to what had taken place in that realm of imagination; yet we awaken changed by it. It was this last sensation that I experienced when I awoke on the couch.

I couldn't have been asleep for long, for Roden was still stoking the fire in the same position as when I closed my eyes. Nothing in the room had changed—none of those subtle details within a room that always change with the passing of time. And yet I awoke possessed with a certain conviction, already having made a firm decision without having any clue as to the thought process that led me there. I was going to learn how to use a gun. I had to learn how to use a gun. And I had to do it tonight.

I whispered Roden's name, causing him to turn around to face me, and suggested that he carry August to bed now. At my words, he searched my face as though I had already said something surprising and out of character. As though I had already told him that I wanted him to teach me to use a gun.

He complied, however, leaning over the both of us with the vaguest scent of cinnamon and tobacco still lingering on his person and intermingled with the vague and indefinable scent of his skin and hair and firewood. He gently scooped up the child into his arms. And in those brief seconds, it was as though some scene from my already forgotten dream drifted back to me. It was vague but potent—the impression that Roden was there, whether in my dreams or merely in some subdued recesses of my thoughts. Had I dreamed of him? I watched him disappear from the room as I tried to remember. But all I was left with was the impression that I'd been found out. That something had been revealed and laid bare and vulnerable between us without my noticing and without my permission.

When Roden returned, I had already folded up blankets and cleared the coffee table of our s'mores and milk glasses. He walked in the room and paused, as though instinctively waiting for me to announce something strange and startling.

And feeling the weight of this, the sheer and impossible predictability of the moment as though we were both acting according to someone else's script, I told him what I wanted to do.

"You what?"

"You heard me," I said, still feeling predictable but submissive. "I'd like for you to teach me tonight." Somewhere a clock ticked loudly, its sound forming a third presence in the room with us, tapping out its contribution to our awkward conversation, as though trying to make it less painful, more normal.

Roden looked down at a large leather watch on his arm before exhaling his answer, "It's getting pretty late, Charlotte." Or perhaps that wasn't Roden at all, but the clock itself. "Are you sure you want to..." But his voice trailed off at the end as his expression suddenly changed. "I'll meet you upstairs in a minute." With that, he turned and headed in the opposite direction.

"ALL RIGHT, we're going to start with the basics," Roden said. "I'll primarily be focusing on getting you comfortable with the Walther P22, because the kickback is comparatively minimal. Obviously we won't be able to fire any shots, so we just have to do the best we can for now." He pulled out a black handgun from a small case, though he made a point to aim it at the wall away from us.

"Okay," I said, determined. I thought that sounded confident, but my palms were sweating, and it was hard to tell.

"Always assume the gun is loaded. Never aim it at anyone or anything unless you intend to destroy that person or thing. And just for clarification, that means *do not aim it at me*, even during this lesson. No matter how certain you are it is unloaded, treat it as though it were. And do not shoot without aiming." His voice was commanding and confident, as though he had gone through this spiel a hundred times before, and maybe he had. I nodded, gazing at the Walther P22 with a mixture of terror and deep concentration.

I began to find it difficult to concentrate on Roden's words, however, which was unfortunate. After all, I knew that all of them were essential. It wasn't for lack of trying; I just couldn't seem to tear my eyes off the gun. And I couldn't stop sweating.

"This is not a Hollywood movie," I heard him say, when I finally glanced up. "When you do use the gun, the shot will be extremely loud, and you will need to be prepared for the kickback. Your adrenaline will be running very high, which is normal. Just remember to breathe and go through the steps I've taught you. You will not be doing any rolls, cartwheels, or shooting with two guns at once."

If I hadn't been focusing so hard on taking normal, steady breaths, I might have actually laughed at that. There was no oxygen to be spared for laughter.

"You will check for yourself that the gun is unloaded," he said. I extended my hand to grasp the metallic pistol while peering into the empty chamber and suppressing a cowardly shiver that ran down my spine. I fought back the haunting presence of playground memories as I followed Roden's instructions for gripping the pistol in both hands. I listened intently to the carefully measured cadences of his voice, which remained confident and calm most of the time.

However, I heard the slightest hint of alarm in his voice every time he said, *"Finger off the trigger, please."* This came up frequently and was the only time he sounded the least bit uncomfortable during our lesson. When he finally took the gun back, I'm certain we were both relieved.

He led me through various demonstrations, carefully explaining his every move step by step. I wondered if he was always so thorough as a shooting instructor or if he was taking extra pains for my sake. As I watched, I had to admit that he looked amazingly comfortable with the weapon, reminding me of his skillful shooting that saved my life just days ago. And I couldn't help but admire that.

Of course there were a lot of things I'd come to admire about him in the last few weeks. But maybe these feelings came naturally toward someone who saved my life and were not at all authentic or personal. There had to be some kind of psychological explanation for what I was feeling. Some explanation that would make these feelings void and null. After all, we were trapped in Willow's Bend together, forced to depend on one another, forced to trust one another. We had no choice but to make the most of the situation. Surely this is all that our relationship amounted to. Whatever it was and wherever it came from, it left me with a terrifying sense of intimacy. And I had to snap out of it.

"And if you are aiming, you are shooting to kill. Understood?" I nodded, refocusing my attention on his instruction. "You don't shoot to warn or to wound, because doing so may only make your target angry and eliminate the advantage of surprise. You have to understand that the moment you point a gun at someone, you are making the decision to end their life forever. Period."

I swallowed hard at the gravity in his voice.

Roden taught me how to do a drill next, to prepare me in case I had to get to the gun and shoot under attack. I did the drill several times while Roden watched and coached me through it. After a while it started to feel natural enough that my mind was wandering again.

"You know, I think you're really getting the hang of it," Roden said. I found his statement to be awfully ironic, as I had just been wondering what in the world I was doing and why everything suddenly felt so complicated. Until that day I was convinced that there was nothing in the world that I was more afraid of than a gun. And perhaps that had been true before the quarantine.

But everything had changed.

I had just handed the gun back to Roden and was looking forward to leaving that room and Roden's presence for the evening. Maybe then I'd be able to think clearly, to make some sense of everything. I heard Roden make a sound when he put the gun away in its case. The corners of his mouth twitched as though he were trying to hide a smile.

"What is it?" I asked.

He stood up straight then, glancing at me and looking away again, still fighting a smile. "It's nothing," he said, looking at me again. "It's just that you've got some..." He leaned forward and rubbed a calloused thumb across my chin. "Marshmallow."

CHAPTER THIRTEEN

The record began to spin on the turntable. It was a large, vintage piece of work we'd found in the corner of the ballroom. I caught the hiss and gentle tap of the tone arm touching vinyl, feeling a wave of excitement as I released my delicate grip. Static intermingled with brass instruments before Perry Como's crooning voice sang out, drenching us in all of its retro glory.

I smiled down at August, who was gazing in awe at the booming contraption. After more of his night terrors last night and my sudden, agonizing insomnia, tonight's party would be a welcome distraction for both of us. Regardless of what the future held, the three of us would have the time of our lives tonight.

"Come on," I said, speaking over the lively music. I took his hand in mine. "Let's go help Roden."

We made our way to the room where Roden was fighting with an old door, jerking on a stubborn brass handle. "Jammed," he muttered darkly. "But I know," he said between efforts of turning the handle and pulling in different directions, "this closet was once a goldmine..." He paused before turning the handle all the way to the left and giving it a fierce yank at an odd angle.

The door finally gave way, causing him to fall backward onto the floor at our feet. A stack of boxed board games fell down from a top shelf onto the floor in front of us. An array of dice, game pieces, and cards scattered across the hardwood floor. "Of games," Roden finished.

August was the first to laugh that time.

We decided to set up our party headquarters in the ballroom, as it seemed to be the most appropriate place for a party. With all the reflections moving around us, the room almost felt crowded with just the three of us. I threw down blankets and pillows to make a pallet on the hard floor while August jumped around in his pajamas and made faces in the mirror. I glanced up in time to see him pull at the insides of his mouth, sticking his tongue out and trying to cross his eyes.

I laughed out loud, just as Roden walked in carrying a pile of board games. "Whoa, buddy," he said, catching August's face. "Save it for a camera." He set the games down on the floor before turning toward me. "I'll go grab the popcorn and root beer floats while you guys pick out the first game and get us set up."

August and I agreed that Candy Land was a good game to start with since we were both a little disappointed about celebrating Halloween without any real candy. When Roden returned, we started our evening of fun playing three highly competitive rounds of that game before moving on to the next. I had the misfortune of getting transported back to the beginning of the board every time I got close to the finish line, which was incredibly frustrating for me and hilarious for Roden and August. Meanwhile, Roden's immediate strategy was to make obvious and ridiculous efforts to cheat his way to the finish line while August fell over backward on his pillow every time we caught Roden in the act.

We played August's specialty, slapjack, next. I quickly discovered for myself the arm the kid had on him when I narrowly got to a jack before him. After four rounds of the game, I could actually see a hint of red on my hand. "Good grief, August!" I exclaimed, shaking my hand in the air to recover.

"You can't say I didn't warn you, Daffodil," Roden said through laughter. "If you can't take the heat..."

"Yeah, yeah," I said. "It's your turn to shuffle. And we'll see who the daffodil is when I dominate every round of spoons."

"Is that so?" he said, eyeing me skeptically.

"Oh, you just wait and see."

"What's spoons?" August piped in.

"You haven't learned spoons yet?" I asked, looking wide-eyed at August. "You poor, deprived child. Well, lucky for you, you just happen to be in the presence of *the* reigning spoons champion of my Sigma Tau Delta chapter in college. Gentlemen, prepare to be amazed."

"Ooh," August said appreciatively between handfuls of popcorn.

During our fourth round of the game, I had already established a solid winning streak when I saw that there was only one spoon in the middle of the floor. That's when I spotted the spoon in August's hand and the grin on his face.

"What the—" I muttered, but Roden heard me and quickly acted. We both dove for the piece of silver, somehow causing it to sail across the floor to the other side of the room.

"No!" I yelled, getting up to run for it. Roden must have been dead set on ending my winning streak, because he tore off after it as well. Our numerous reflections flew across the room as we made our sprint for the utensil, which clattered against the wall. What followed was a bit of a blur, to be honest. I know that at one point I slid across the hard surface and collided with Roden. He had just reached the spoon, when I slammed into him, knocking it away from his hand.

By the time it was all over, there had been an animated debate concerning who was disqualified and who smashed whose finger. I came out victorious in the end, as Roden eventually conceded defeat.

It was only afterward that we discovered that August's hand only held three nines and a six.

"Fair is fair," Roden said nobly as he stood up between August and myself. I was beginning to make sense of the laugh lines on his face, as the three of us had been smiling and laughing almost nonstop all evening. "And while I fully hold you responsible for what may or may not be a permanently broken pinkie, I also have to give credit where credit is due. And so, I propose a toast." He lifted his half-empty glass of root beer and ice cream in front of him with an exaggerated air of reverence. "To the Queen of Spoons."

Then he looked down at August, where he and I were still sitting on our blankets and pillows. "August, would you like to say anything?"

August burped before replying, "Can we have some more popcorn?"

"Here, here," Roden answered before taking a swig of his drink.

"Amen to that," I added, before tipping my glass back as well.

IN THE DIM light of the kitchen, I began rummaging through the cabinets. I thought I heard a thump from upstairs, where I knew Roden and August were picking out the next record to put on the turntable. I stopped at the sound and felt the hair on the back of my neck prick up. There was quiet again, and I had to laugh at myself for getting so easily spooked.

I began unwrapping the microwave popcorn that August had asked for when I caught my own reflection in the microwave door. I saw to my utter surprise that I was still beaming. I'd hardly noticed my reflection in the ballroom all evening, being too distracted with all the games and silliness of our party. But here, in the light of the kitchen and the microwave window, I saw that my cheeks were flushed red and my eyes brightened in a way I couldn't ever remember seeing before.

I laughed to myself at the ludicrous idea that I was having the time of my life. Here, with two people I'd never have met if it wasn't for the spread of an unprecedented strain of rabies in the woods of Willow's Bend. Here, with a shooting instructor who avoided people as a way of life and an orphan with night terrors and the most striking blue eyes I'd ever seen. It was preposterous and impossible. And yet it was happening.

Interrupting my reverie, something caught my eye in the directions on the popcorn's box, which specifically stated to microwave for two minutes and thirty-eight seconds, though "time may vary according to microwave." I smiled to myself, thinking how bizarre it was and wondering if it was a typo. Or perhaps there was a very real, special magic about that specifically allotted amount of time. I frowned down at the bag before deciding to give it a shot.

I threw the bag in and clicked the microwave door shut. I pressed the magic numbers, two, three, then eight. The buttons *beep, beep, beeped,* as I pressed them. Just then, I thought I heard another thump. I could have sworn this time that the sound had come from outside.

I waited.

No, it was nothing. My eyes kept flitting to the boarded-up glass windows and locked French doors to my right, which were still covered in luxurious, navy blue silk curtains.

Suddenly, I could just barely make out the sound of laughter from upstairs. August's little boy's laugh and Roden's new laugh—the kind of laugh he must have had years ago but seemed to be rediscovering all over again tonight. I loved that sound. It was the sound that told me everything was fine.

I heard the record player begin to play upstairs. It was the Fleetwoods' nostalgic melody that somehow found me through the labyrinthine passageways, corridors, hidden staircases, and bedrooms. "Come softly to me," I heard the teenage voices sing. I chuckled once more to myself, releasing those stubborn muscles in my neck and shoulders and returning my gaze back down to the microwave. I reached out and pressed the start button.

But I didn't hear the beep of the start button.

I heard the slamming of metal against metal and the shattering of glass as I turned my head instinctively toward the boarded French doors to my right.

The first thing I registered after the sound was the sight of the two French doors flinging wide open into the kitchen, sweeping in a gust of cold air and the scent of wood smoke. A woman covered in filth and scrapes and bruises emerged from the darkness outside, looking around the room before locking her eyes on mine. Something about her straight blonde hair and tall stature looked familiar. Maybe from an old nightmare.

Five other women followed her through the open doors as I reeled backward. That first woman carried a metal golf club in her hand, what I think they call a driver, though I immediately spotted with terror the small pistol tucked into the band of her ragged pants as well.

"Is he here?" the woman with the club and gun shouted. She quickly closed the space between us, her boots crackling across the sea of shattered glass that had flooded the kitchen floor. As my mind scrambled to understand what was happening, her eyes flitted toward the living room. "I'll ask you one more time," she said, pulling the gun out and aiming it at my chest. "Is he here?"

"Who—who are you talking about?" I stammered, though my eyes were locked on the gun. Her finger was resting precariously on the trigger. I was as good as dead.

"No one's here, Jess," a younger woman said, her voice rising as she spoke. She put a hand on Jess's shoulder, saying, "I told you he's dead! Hell, I'm the one who shot him!"

Jess lowered the gun at her words and shoved it back down into her pants again. "Okay," she said. At her word, three women lunged at me.

I just had time to start down the hallway when I felt a firm jerk on my hair and I was pulled backward. I hit the corner of the countertop with my head as I fell backward onto the floor. Two hands pinned me to the ground at my shoulders just before someone pounced onto my legs. "We'll hold her. You guys get the food," the woman at my shoulders said. I looked up to see a middle-aged brunette with a scar on her forehead and a nasty bruise on her neck. "Hurry up!" she shouted.

I heard cabinet doors slamming as I glanced at the girl sitting on my legs. She was the one who had yelled that someone was dead. She dug long, dirty fingernails into my arms, pinning me harder into place on the floor. It was startling to realize that she couldn't be much older than fifteen. She was filthy, with dirt and leaves in her hair, sunken cheeks, and dark circles beneath her eyes, and she smelled strongly of ashes. Then she put two dirty hands on my throat to strangle me.

And I was certain that her distorted, malicious features would be the last image I'd ever see.

I couldn't scream. I couldn't breathe. My body went into panic mode as I tried with all my might to writhe and struggle against her hold. But I couldn't move. I could only stare back into her dim, yellow eyes and cracked, bleeding lips as she pressed hard onto my throat.

Suddenly, I was released from her death grip and immediately struggled to inhale air again. The girl was standing now. Before I could catch my breath, I was kicked in the head—a clean, direct hit that jerked my neck around until I heard a frightening crack and hit the ground with my face, landing on my stomach.

I was trying to decide whether my neck was broken or I was paralyzed when an order was called out.

"All right, let's go!" The voice belonged to Jess. Or maybe the brunette. I lay there on my face and the dirt from their shoes, coughing like mad but thinking with some relief that they were leaving.

The next thing I knew, I was grabbed by my hair again and shoved back onto my back so that I was facing the sallow girl with the nails again. She sat down hard on my chest before I could respond, pulling her arm back and hitting me brutally in the face. My cheekbone first. Then my teeth and my chin felt the impact of a ruthless punch. She was wearing a ring. I remember thinking that her eyes shone with pure terror, masked with cold, lifeless hatred for me.

And then she hit my eye. And again. Those were her best hits yet.

"Emily!" someone shouted. Emily hit me two more times before spitting on my face. Then she was pulled off me by two other women, shouting profanities. The saliva ran down my cheek, intermingling with my blood, warm and sharp. I saw her eyes one last time through my right eye and wondered vaguely if her friends were aware that she was infected. I watched Emily from where I was left on the floor. Emily was dragged backward toward the broken window, still filling the air with grotesque obscenities and insults. Emily had begun to cry.

I closed my eye. There was shouting and footsteps. Then I heard the gunshot. My ears rang. Someone screamed. Strangely, that's when I recognized Jess as the woman from the shelter. The *nice* woman from the shelter. Jess screamed from somewhere across the room. More shouting. Another shot. Running footsteps.

The music continued to play as I sank in and out of consciousness. Blessed unconsciousness. *Just a little further*, I thought.

It was the beep of the microwave that drew me back for a moment. The popcorn was done. One last sensation met me where I lay on the floor before I lost consciousness completely: the smell of burnt popcorn.

I plunged back down into the dark abyss at last.

I DON'T REMEMBER Roden picking me up off the kitchen floor and carrying me out of the room. I don't remember August crying next to my bed while Roden went downstairs to board up the kitchen door again, though I'm certain these things happened. I do remember Roden's hand brushing my hair back out of my eyes, though where and when it was I can't be certain. After all, it might have been a dream.

I remember a damp washcloth, the stinging cuts on my face burning, and the scent of rubbing alcohol. I remember coughing a lot and touching my sore neck where I could still feel those nails digging in. And I remember the first time I had the nightmare of the sallow girl strangling me in my sleep.

At least, I thought it was the first time.

I was woken up by the sound of my own scream, sitting bolt upright in the bed. Just as I was beginning to come to, I saw that Roden was firmly holding onto my shoulder and my arm. "She—she—" the words stuttered out of my mouth between desperate gasps of air as I registered that no one was strangling me. "She's gone—where is she—"

"It's just a dream, Charlotte. I promise," he'd say. I couldn't figure out why it sounded like he'd said those words so many times before.

"No, she was here—I swear she was just here—" I felt the tender skin on my neck with my hands again. And I felt the sting of tears threatening to fall. Not from sorrow but from terror.

"She's gone now, and I'm here. Nobody is going to hurt you—I'm right here, okay?" I looked back at him through my one good eye, surprised at the calmness in his voice and the solemnity etched in his features.

"Where is August?" I asked, feeling hot, irrational tears slipping down my face. I tasted the wet salt on my lips, always such a surprising sensation in the midst of fear or pain. My right eye scanned the room for him while my left remained swollen tightly shut.

"He's safe," Roden assured me. "He's in the next room, sleeping. He's safe."

"C-can you check, please?" He looked doubtfully back at me. "Please, just check for me, please? *Please, Roden.*" I knew that I sounded like a child and that I was hysterical. But I watched him slowly stand up from the chair he'd pulled up to the side of my bed and walk out the door. As I wrapped my arms around my body to stop the trembling, I again had the sensation that we'd gone through this more than once before, but I couldn't recall for certain. I panted breathlessly as I tried to place which room I was in. It wasn't the room I'd been staying in. At one end there was a window that remained uncovered, so I knew I must be upstairs.

Roden walked back into the room, leaving the door open as if to prove to me that he was keeping an eye on August. "Sleeping," he said with a gentle but forced smile. He sat back down in the chair next to me, leaning forward on his elbows. I saw his face in the moonlight that poured in through the blinds and could see the dark circles and glassy eyes of a man who was exhausted. "He's been worried about you, of course." He spoke softly through his fingers, as his chin was propped up by his hand. And his words came out calm and calculated, perhaps the way a doctor speaks to a delicate patient. "But I told him you're going to be just fine—just need some rest and someone to look after you for a while."

"W-what if they come back?"

"They aren't coming back," he answered patiently.

"How do you know?"

He sighed before speaking, picking up my hand that had been gripping hard onto the comforter and holding it in both of his. "I know. They thought I'd been shot and killed in the woods a long time ago, or they never would have risked breaking in. They've probably been scouting out empty houses for food, and they thought this was one of them." I forced my hand to relax as he spoke, feeling the calloused texture of his fingertips on my palms. "But they aren't coming back."

"Are you going to leave me?" I blurted out impulsively. Yet again I had a feeling of déjà vu. There was a long pause before he answered.

"No, I won't leave you, Char. I'll be right here." Then I remembered with a sense of irony that August and I had the same conversation recently. And I wondered if Roden's answer felt as conflicted as mine had been.

I started to lick my cracked lips, realizing I felt dehydrated. But my bottom lip was swollen and tasted of blood. "You're thirsty," Roden said. He jumped up to retrieve a glass of water from off the dresser. "Here you go." And he helped me hold the glass as I just managed to sit up enough to drink. But it hurt to swallow.

That's when I noticed the way Roden was looking at me.

I lowered the glass, handing it back to him slowly. I couldn't quite figure it out, what that look was supposed to mean, but it gave me a very bad feeling. And I knew that, even more than my cuts and bruises and swelling, something was very wrong. I wondered vaguely what that something might be, even as I lay back down and fell asleep again.

And I slept peacefully.

I remember waking up to hear the sound of crying. It wasn't the sound that woke me up, for it was much too quiet. But when I heard it, I was surprised to find that it wasn't me. I turned my head groggily. Roden's head was buried in his hands, and the sight of him broke my heart. It was the saddest thing I'd ever seen, and it was a little frightening too. I struggled to say something, anything, to make him stop.

"You okay?" I managed to say, though my voice sounded hoarse and unrecognizable in the darkness. I had this desperate need to comfort him, to fix him, but for the life of me, I couldn't understand why he was crying. *Is someone hurt?* I thought. Then I remembered.

His head jerked up, causing me to see the circles beneath his eyes and the tears that glistened in the moonlight in two vivid streams. Something about the streaking tears reminded me of smeared ink, like the oblique tails of f's and g's in some old love letter, but he quickly erased them with his hand. "I'm so sorry I let this happen," he said. His features crumpled and contorted as I watched him attempt to stifle the tears. "I'm so sorry, Char."

I tried to smile at him through the darkness, but something seemed to be wrong with my facial muscles. "Oh, I see," I muttered in that aged and raspy voice of mine. And I remembered the game he played with Danny, and the guilt he felt after hurting him. "Wolves and Men, huh? But you didn't even do it, remember? Not this time. You're off the hook."

"It's not a joke, Charlotte. I thought I could protect you, and you were nearly killed down there in my own house."

I looked away from him, sort of marveling at the effect of the moonlight in the darkened room. The lateral lights and darks through the blinds, the yellow streams against the blue-grays and midnights that reminded me of family vacations when we spent nights in a roadside hotel. It reminded me of those late nights filled with anticipation and the constant rush of highway traffic outside the windows. It came back to me then, the sound of a fan, my brothers' snoring, and my father flipping through TV channels and casting those vivid flashes of light all over the room.

But it was quiet here now. And dark. There was no traffic, no television. There was only the sound of Roden trying to pull himself together.

"It is a shame, you know," I croaked out. I turned to look at his face as I spoke and realized for the first time how much I liked it. His features struck me quite suddenly and unexpectedly, more vividly than they had out in the woods that first time. I liked his face with all its peculiar contours and angles and ambiguous shades, in crying as well as laughing. And those eyes. I decided to look at them more often. "I really loved that song that was playing." I turned my head back to stare up at the ceiling, listening to the song in my head as I slowly fell back to sleep.

But it didn't quite sound the same anymore.

CHAPTER FOURTEEN

"R o-den," I half whispered in the direction of his chair. But my voice was hoarse, and half of his name was silent while the other was much louder than I'd intended, cutting across the room so that I cringed at the sound. The early morning light was pouring in through the blinds behind his slouching figure where he slept—the same way he had the night August had his fever. I sat up in the bed, ignoring the spasms of pain and dull aches and leaned across the space between us. Just as I put a hand on his shoulder, his head jerked up. At the same time, in the same motion, his hand twitched to his side, where I caught a metallic gleam in the morning light.

There was a flash of something in his eyes too. It was that thing I'd noticed earlier but couldn't quite put my finger on. I knew what it was now. And the impression was only heightened when I realized that he was wearing a pistol.

"It's okay," I assured him. "I just need to go to the bathroom."

"Oh, I'm sorry," he said, standing up to help me walk. My leg was sore, and it was difficult to walk even a short distance without his support.

"I'll be okay. I just—" I began, pausing to hiss at a stabbing pain in my ribcage, "—couldn't remember where the bathroom was."

He helped me two doors down the hall to a bathroom, where I closed the door behind me but for some reason didn't lock it. I immediately leaned across the sink, taking in my distorted features, but honed in on one particular detail: my eye color. I scanned my iris for the slightest hint of yellow, a symptom. Because the look in Roden's eyes, that indefinable something, was a look of fear. And it was the very real fear that I might be infected.

After all, Emily—that raging, crying, violent figure of my nightmares—was infected. And after giving me so many cuts, she stopped to spit on my face.

Diverting my attention away from the closed-up bulk of flesh that covered up one eye, I gazed in relief at the other. At least for the moment, I was convinced of still being myself. But I didn't know how long it would take for the transformation to occur if I was infected. After all, symptoms for regular rabies strains could take several weeks to show up. So the questions haunted me: Am I infected? Am I dangerous?

I wondered too about my sudden thirst for water. Was it a symptom of infection in the form of dehydration? Or was it mere thirst? I remembered Danny's cracked lips, his refusal to drink water. It was as though he was frightened of it. I reassured myself that when I drank water the effect was satisfying. Surely the only pain was due to my sore neck and having been strangled by Emily. Not to mention all the screaming I'd been doing...right? Or was I just kidding myself?

I tried not to think about what would have to happen if I started showing more definite symptoms, what Roden would have to do for August's protection, for his own protection. By this time tomorrow, my mind may be lost. My body may be transformed. And what would Roden do? Would he lock me in that bedroom and flee with August? No. They needed the mansion to survive, to be rescued. He would have to get rid of me then... And yet I couldn't imagine him actually following through with that. So what *would* he do?

I shook my head, knowing that I was in no condition to sort through worst-case scenarios, even if they were probable scenarios. But I couldn't quite get them out of my head.

While Roden helped me back to the bedroom, it occurred to me that he had spent a lot of time on the phone with the CDC over the last few weeks. He probably knew more about the infection than I did.

"How long?" I asked on the way to the bedroom, with one arm still around his shoulders so that he carried some of my weight.

He helped me to the bed before handing me a glass of water and two more pills.

"How long what?" he asked at length. But he wasn't looking at me.

"You know what," I answered. Of course he knew. "How long until we know for certain if I'm infected?"

He slowly shook his head. "Listen, you need to focus on getting better, okay? Don't add to everything else by worrying about that."

"She tore into my skin and spat on my wounds, Roden. I think it's reasonable to be concerned, don't you?"

I watched his reaction closely, as it occurred to me that he may not have noticed or been aware of the saliva at all. But if he was shocked by the news, he wasn't letting on. He sighed as though until now part of him knew and the other part refused to consider that I was probably infected. "We don't have much to go on besides what you told me about Danny and what we know of the other strains of the infection. But judging from what you said about Danny, I'd say anywhere from twelve to forty-eight hours just to have some idea, just to rest a little easier."

"What are you going to do?"

"I'm going to make some breakfast and see if August is awake yet," he answered as he crossed the room to leave.

"That's not what I mean," I said, the tenor in my voice already verging on desperation. I wanted a straight answer. Suddenly I had to know. "What are you going to do when you see symptoms? How are you going to protect August and yourself? How are you going to—"

"Char, stop!" he nearly shouted. The sound of his voice made me immediately and unexpectedly aware of his height and his age and his past—all of which towered over me impressively despite the space between us. He shook his head at me silently, as though this gesture in itself was intended to answer all my questions. As though he could just say "no" to everything I'd asked. No to the infection. No to reality.

At length, he spoke again. "I'll bring up breakfast in half an hour. Try to get some more rest."

And he was gone again.

THERE WAS a soft knock on the bedroom door.

I closed the book I had been holding for the better part of the last hour. I'd been trying to get my mind off my physical pain, but reading with this headache was nearly impossible. I set the book down on the bedside table just as the door slowly opened. It was the middle of the afternoon on my second day of recovery, and my plate from lunch was still sitting on the table.

"Are you doing okay?" Roden asked. He carried in his hands a wooden box with a small book on top.

"Well, I've definitely been better," I said as I painfully sat up straighter against the pillows and reached for a sweatshirt. Pulling the thicker second layer on carefully over the T-shirt, I slung my denim-clad legs over the side of the bed to face Roden.

"I thought you might be up for a game of chess," he said, pulling up a small table and a chair.

"I'm better at Candy Land," I admitted. "But I'll give it a shot if you'll go easy on me. I'm a bit of a sore loser."

"I know," he answered with a slight grin.

"Well, now I'm a sore loser with a headache, so you'd better watch out."

"You like Swinburne?" he asked, nodding to the book of poems I'd pored over late into the night.

"I think so," I answered. "I guess he's somewhat extravagant for my taste, but his verses are beautiful." I watched Roden set up the board as I reminded myself of each of the pieces and their names and roles and abilities. I thought of the queen moving around the board to protect the king, who always seemed so vulnerable.

"You know..." I began at last, after we had been playing in silence for a while. "I don't want you to feel bad about what happened to me. I mean, I know that there was nothing you could do."

He moved a pawn before speaking. "I'm afraid that there are several different things I could have done," he answered solemnly. "I could have been alert. I could have kept the music turned down so that I could hear the damn door get busted. I could have kept the gun nearby so it wouldn't have taken me so long to get to where you were." I opened my mouth to reply, thinking he was finished, but he continued, "I could have boarded up the doors in the first place, but I didn't anticipate being attacked by the non-infected, which is the only way anyone could have gotten in so quickly. I didn't, but I *should* have. I could have—"

"Okay, okay," I stopped him, realizing that I wasn't going to win that argument. I shook my head as I moved a bishop across the board. "You know, if it wasn't for all the pain I'm in, I'd think it was all just a nightmare. I can't explain it, but it genuinely felt like they broke into the mansion just to torture me." My face flushed at the degrading memory, the sense of fear and powerlessness I felt on the kitchen floor. And maybe I was humiliated to be found in such a state of utter weakness. *Always the victim,* I thought.

"They didn't come for you. They came for food," Roden said, using that stoic tone of his. Strangely, this had never entered my mind. "Not to justify anything, of course, but I think you were just in the way."

As we exchanged moves across the board, I listened to the wind blowing through the trees outside the window. A thin, gray branch grated up and down the glass as though begging to be let inside. It was growing colder outside. An early winter, perhaps.

"I can't believe Jess was with Emily," I muttered, waiting for his next move. "I mean, she had to know that she was infected. And we both know how determined she was to keep her distance from anyone who might even possibly become infected."

"Maybe she hadn't noticed," Roden replied with a shrug.

"That just doesn't make sense to me," I said, resting my chin in my hand as I spoke. I recalled my only other encounter with that fierce woman and her utter refusal to allow August shelter. Of course, that was before any of us knew that females could be infected. "Of all people, I would expect Jess to notice the symptoms right away."

He captured my last rook. "Yeah, well, I guess we all have our breaking point. After all, Emily was Jess's sister."

I sat back against the pile of pillows. Suddenly everything made sense. Jess must have known about Emily's deadly condition and refused to accept it as truth, or just refused to act on it. Perhaps Jess lied to herself, put herself and others at risk because she couldn't bear to consider any alternative.

"What are you going to do, Roden?" I asked, looking up from the chess board after moving my knight.

"About what?" he asked, elusively. And maybe he had already begun to forget. After all, so far I'd shown no symptoms.

"If I'm infected. How are you going to protect him? You know you have to protect him."

"It's been almost forty-eight hours, Char." We each moved our pieces across the board as I considered my reply. I wanted to feel safer. I wanted to hope. But I also didn't want to lie to myself about the reality of my condition. While I knew that the mansion was safer from intruders than ever, I was much more concerned about the danger already inside these walls; despite the time that had passed, I still *could* be infected.

"Forty-eight hours doesn't mean anything, and you know it. I may just not be showing symptoms yet. Tonight, tomorrow, the next day... What happens if I start showing symptoms then? What will you do?"

"I'm not going to do anything but take care of you and August, because you're not infected."

"But what if I am? We both know that's why you refuse to be unarmed for even a moment," I said, nodding toward the pistol at his side. "Because you need the mansion, and if I become dangerous—

"This is for our protection—yours, mine, and August's. You're not infected. I told you I'm not leaving you, and I meant it."

"We had a deal, remember?" I said, recalling one of our first conversations out in the woods. "If one of us shows signs of infection—"

"That doesn't work both ways," he cut in firmly, almost angrily. "We never made a deal that involved me leaving you to die."

"Roden, if I ever hurt him, I couldn't live with myself," I said, hearing the emotion in my voice that I was trying so hard to keep at bay.

"I know. But I won't let that happen." He moved his bishop before sighing and leaned back in his chair resigned and unhappy. "Checkmate."

I STARED DOWN at the object in my hand. It was a small brown seed that had been cut solidly in half.

"What is this?" I asked, looking up from my desk chair at Roden. He set my bowl of soup down on top of the mahogany desk where I had been poring over an anthology. I'd ventured to the library down the hall from the bedroom, having grown exhausted of my confinement to the same small space and healed enough to walk on my own.

The lamplight that had illuminated the stack of poetry books and short stories I'd accumulated that evening now also illuminated my outthrust palm beneath its bulb so that I might get a better look.

"It's a persimmon seed," Roden answered over my shoulder. "Look there, in the middle."

I peered into the waxy gray substance. In the middle there was an intricate white shape. "It's a spoon," I muttered in disbelief.

"Exactly," he said. "Some people use it to predict the weather, you know. My grandfather always said that a spoon means heavy, wet snow for the winter."

"That's amazing."

"Yeah, and if you see a fork, it's a mild winter. And a knife indicates a lot of ice. Crazy, huh?"

"Yeah, but does it work?" I asked, picking up my bowl. Although a helicopter had been dropping off supplies pretty regularly, Roden somehow convinced them to make an extra drop of food supplies the day after the attack, without telling them the attack had ever happened. However, the ample amount of groceries did nothing to improve Roden's cooking skills, and all indications told me this was another meal from a can. I was grateful nonetheless.

"I don't know. I guess we'll see," he said, glancing out at the window in front of us. "No snow so far."

I stared down at that tiny shape again, finding it incredulous that nature could mimic dining utensils while predicting weather. There was something so mystical about it, so awe inspiring, and yet...domestic.

"He misses you, Char," Roden said, sitting down on the floor against the opposite wall. "Maybe you could come downstairs in the morning."

"No," I answered flatly, automatically.

"Well if you don't feel well enough, I could bring him up here..."

"It's not that, and you know it." I took down a spoonful of mushy vegetables.

"It's been long enough, Char."

"No, it hasn't," I shot back. I ate another bite before continuing, trying to get it over with. "I'm not putting him at risk any more than I have to, Roden. I can't do that. I just can't."

He stood up, casting long shadows into the hallway behind him. "I won't let anything happen. I swear it. But he needs you. He keeps asking for you and worrying about you... And I think you need him. We need each other to get through this, and deep down, you know that. You know it as well as I do."

"I also need to not put him in danger," I said. There was a framed picture on the wall just beside Roden. In it, the lamplight reflected my face. It didn't show the remaining bruises and cuts on my skin and surrounding my eye. Instead, it reflected some vague illusion that I was normal, unbruised, and whole. I was staring back at that illusion when I heard his voice again.

"Listen, Char. Whatever we do, let's not let this thing keep us from each other, you understand? That's the worst it can do, and we can't let that happen. *We can't.*"

I turned away from that framed illusion to look uncomfortably back down at the persimmon spoon. It predicted snow. But it couldn't tell me anything about our future— none of the important things that I needed so desperately to know.

"We need each other, Char. You know we do."

"I'll think about it," I answered, but I was still looking down at the seed when he finally left.

I MOVED SLOWLY down the staircase, less certain with each step that I was doing the right thing but also feeling a small sense of accomplishment that I was doing *something*. I ran my fingers against the falling willow newel post at the landing as I turned toward another hallway on the ground floor. Once there, I listened for voices, for laughter, for some sign of life to tell me that everything was okay. But there was a lingering fear that the entire ground floor was unsafe now that it had been compromised and that I would run into something much more sinister than Roden and August.

As I passed cautiously through the hallway, glancing back in each room on my way, I finally heard a voice.

"Okay, right," the voice said. And I knew it was Roden. I exhaled my lingering fears as I emerged through the kitchen doorway. Roden was looking down as he scribbled something on a notepad while holding the telephone receiver to his ear. I glanced to my right to see August sitting at the table, also facing away from me, swinging his legs like he always did while he picked at the scrambled eggs and sliced banana on his plate. "So what time was that, again?"

Suddenly it felt almost too good to be true to be back in the kitchen again, to see August's small form looking healthy and animated as any little boy should. I could tell as I surveyed his boyish, flaxen hair, red pajamas, and what he called "snuggy socks" on his feet and realized that Roden had been taking good care of him. Of course he had. That was perhaps the one thing that I never had to worry about during my recovery upstairs.

It was better than I'd remembered, more than I'd expected. And I couldn't help but smile. The effect on me was profound, and I immediately felt healthy and whole again, as though the ugly past had never separated us to begin with. My world was back on its axis, and I couldn't remember why I'd waited so long to do this.

I fought the urge to scoop him up in my arms in a bear hug and forced myself to walk around the side of the table to face him. "Mind if I join you?" I asked. He perked up in his seat, throwing his shoulders back and raising his eyebrows.

"Chaaarr! You're back!" He threw his arms around my neck, cheering loudly against my ear.

"I know. I'm finally back," I said, laughing at his very childlike behavior. I loved to see him behaving as a five-year-old should. This morning he was as buoyant and lively as I'd ever seen him.

"Two days..." I heard Roden say behind me. "Slow down, slow down. That was at...four o'clock? Okay, we'll be ready. Got it. Okay, thank you, Mr. Ashkenasi, thank you, sir. Okay, goodbye."

He hung up the phone with a glazed look in his eyes, staring off into space. He quickly snapped out of it though and made eye contact with me instead. "Well, it's about time," he said, amiably, allowing a broad smile to sweep across his features. "Can I get you some breakfast?"

"I'd love that. Thank you," I answered. "Was that the CDC?"

"Actually, yes. It was," he answered. "Coffee?"

I nodded as he passed a mug of hot coffee to me. My gaze drifted over to the boarded-up doors of the dining room, the very place where the women had broken in the night of the party. Scanning the floor, I saw that Roden must have found the time to thoroughly clean the surface of all the filth and glass and blood. Thinking back, I was fairly certain he had shot someone. I began to wonder who it was and how he disposed of the body. I pictured him sweeping up the glass, hammering boards over the door in the middle of the night while I slept upstairs. I wondered if he vigilantly looked over his shoulder while he worked, if he wiped a nervous bead of sweat from his brow and wondered if anyone else would return before he could board up the door. Or perhaps he really had been two places at once, upstairs with me and down here alone, accomplishing the impossible only because it was necessary to take care of August and myself.

"Well, I have some good news," Roden said, mercifully breaking my train of thought. But I had trouble imagining good news, so I just accepted the plate of scrambled eggs and toast in silence. "We're leaving Willow's Bend in two days."

CHAPTER FIFTEEN

A ugust was bouncing a tennis ball against a bare wall in the next room. The loud thud of the ball punctuated our conversation as we spoke.

"They're arranging a rescue team to come by helicopter," Roden said while submerging our breakfast dishes in hot, soapy water. "We're supposed to be at the phone at noon sharp to do one last verbal check that we're ready to go and, well, still not infected. Then we proceed upstairs to the main balcony, where they will extract us and take us to a special quarantine hospital waiting for us and any other survivors. We'll be in isolation for some testing for a while, but at least we'll be safe."

"I can't believe it," I muttered. "But wait, do you think we'll be isolated from each other?"

"They didn't say. I'm not sure. But I'm sure the testing won't take too long. Anyway, the important thing is we're getting out of here, right?"

"Oh, right, of course," I replied. That was the important thing, wasn't it? So why did it not feel like the important thing? "But—wait a second, just like that? So soon?"

"Well, yeah. You didn't think they'd leave us here forever, did you? It's been nearly a month, you know." As he spoke, I retrieved one of the dishes and rinsed it in the sink of hot water before starting to dry it off.

"But...Roden. What about me? What about my attack? Wouldn't I be considered at higher risk than you two?"

"For the last time, Char, you're fine," he answered evasively. "I really wish you'd accept that and move on."

"Roden... You didn't tell them, did you?" I stopped drying to stare at him, but I noticed that he went on washing dishes, staring into the depths of the sink.

"Not emphatically, no. I don't think it's necessary to tell them every detail..."

"But, will they even take me once we tell them?"

He finally stopped what he was doing and looked directly at me. "Of course they'll take you, because we aren't going to tell them. It's just not necessary. What *is* necessary is getting out of here. Right? We can work out the details later, on the other side of that gate, surrounded by medical professionals and wearing those ugly no-slip socks and stupid gowns—"

"They need to know that I could be infected. It might be a big deal."

"It's been several days, Char. You're fine. End of story."

"But we have no idea, really. And when they come for us and see me like this, what am I going to tell them? I fell down the stairs?"

"Only if you think they'll believe it. Look, you tell them whatever it takes. You tell them... You tell them I did it, for all I care."

"Excuse me?"

"You tell them I'd been drinking and lost my temper. You tell them I'm crazy—listen, it doesn't matter what you tell them, but you don't say a word about the attack until you're in the damn hospital."

"I would never—"

"You tell them whatever you have to," he cut in sharply, putting his hands firmly on my shoulders. "You understand? You tell them whatever it takes. That's all that matters now, and I don't care how you do it. But telling them you were attacked at this point could mean the difference between getting rescued and getting abandoned. It's the difference between life and death. And it's an unnecessary risk. They're coming to rescue all three of us, and we can't do anything to jeopardize that. We just can't. And I could never leave without you. Do you understand?"

I looked back at the green and hazel shards surrounding his irises like a subtle mosaic or some stained glass pieces stolen from a church's baptismal window and was stung again by the beauty of that glass and wondered at the light that shown through.

"Yes, I understand," I answered breathlessly. "I fell down the stairs."

He let his arms fall down to his sides. "Good," he muttered, a little breathless himself.

"YOU'LL STAY with us, of course," my mom said on the other end of the phone. "Until everything settles down at least. And we're going to throw you a party at Nana and Grandpa's— supposed to be a surprise, but I thought you might have had enough surprises for a lifetime. Listen, do you think you'll be released by Thanksgiving?"

"I don't know, but I hope so. I've missed everyone so much," I replied. "It will be so good to see all of you."

"Oh, Char, I'm so sorry for what you're going through. I had really hoped this retreat was exactly what you needed, that you would be able to really work through some things at last. I guess I thought it would be a new beginning for you."

I listened to her with the phone cradled between my shoulder and my ear as I scribbled mindlessly on a notepad. I found myself doodling firewheels, marking over the same lines and curves over and over again. But Roden and August entered the kitchen noisily, causing me to look up at the sound. August was getting a piggyback ride as Roden made dramatic motor sounds with his mouth, his glasses perched slightly askew on the bridge of his nose as he jogged around the room. He didn't seem to notice.

"Vssshhhhhnnn...mbrrrr... Rrrrt!" He stopped by the island to let August pick up an apple before they zoomed back out of the kitchen, August laughing buoyantly all the while.

"Obviously you should have stayed at home with us where you belong," I heard my mother say. But I was staring off at the place where Roden and August had just been a moment ago. "I can't tell you how much I've regretted encouraging you to go to Willow's Bend in the first place. I've already been in contact with Dr. Morgan this morning, and he assured me he would squeeze you in the moment you're discharged from the hospital. I'm sure the two of you will have a lot to talk about."

I heard Roden and August's laughter in the living room, their cheerful voices reverberating off the corridor walls.

"Char? Char, did you hear me?"

"Y-yes, I heard you. I'm just...I guess I'm just really looking forward to being back home." It was one of those moments when you realize that you just said the opposite of what you felt and you're not even sure why. I'd had no intentions of lying to her. But that statement, so easy to say, so obviously the right thing, left me perplexed and deep in thought for the rest of the day.

"WHAT'S GOING to happen to him?" I asked in hushed tones. I was standing outside August's bedroom door, where I'd just tucked him in for the night. Roden had just been passing through when he stopped to look in on him. He pulled the door closed carefully, noiselessly, before turning to me.

"I don't know exactly," he answered. Shoving his hands into his pockets, he leaned back against the wall. "I think he has an aunt in Wyoming. But he'll probably start in state custody until she comes down or they fly him up there."

"Wyoming?" I asked, incredulous. "I didn't expect... I don't know what I expected, but I hoped to be able to see him every now and then at the least..." I spoke more to myself than to him.

"Well, we really don't know anything for certain yet. The important thing is that he'll be somewhere safe—not in Willow's Bend."

"Yeah, I guess you're right," I muttered. But I wasn't satisfied. Not even close.

"Can I get us some hot tea and try to cheer you up?" he asked. I looked up in surprise to see the smirk on his face. "You just look so sad."

I merely nodded in answer.

A few minutes later I looked up from where I was sitting on the living room floor in front of the fireplace. The furniture wasn't close enough, and I wanted to feel the warmth on my face and my outstretched hands.

"Remind you of anything?" Roden asked as he joined me on the floor with a tray of tea.

"Actually, yes," I said, chuckling to myself. The last time we'd sat this way was my first time to set foot in the mansion. "Good times," I muttered somewhat sarcastically.

"Strangely, very good times," Roden commented pensively. First I threw him a quizzical look. But then I realized that the utter relief of finding safety, warmth, and a place to rest my head that night was one of the best feelings I'd ever felt in my life. I don't think I'd ever been as thankful as I was then.

I took a sip of tea now, listening as the sharp-tongued flames licked at the evening air with tiny, crackling explosions. I let the gratitude wash over me again. *Thank you for hot tea. Thank you for healing. Thank you for clean, dry clothes. Thank you for a bed and pillow and blankets. Thank you for food and water and heat and showers. Thank you for snuggy socks. Thank you for Roden and August...*

But I couldn't separate my gratitude for them from the idea of being separated from them very, very soon. My eyes stung as Roden's voice interrupted my prayer.

"You know, it's strange," he began. "Sometimes I feel like the three of us are so close. And other times I wonder if we're not merely three strangers who just happen to be living out the same nightmare."

"I know what you mean," I answered.

"Do you?" he asked, turning toward me a little. "Do you really? Because I don't want it to be like that. I can't help but feel that everything we've experienced together, as horrible as it's all been, that it happened to the three of us specifically and together. And yet...I don't even know what you were studying in college. I don't know how many siblings you have. Or what your greatest pet peeve is."

"That's easy. Poetry. Two brothers. And..." I paused to take a sip of tea before answering. "When people try to be mysterious rather than being open and honest about their past."

"Okay, I think you misunderstood," he said, chuckling. "Your greatest pet peeve can't be a person. And it can't be me."

I laughed out loud. "Seriously, Roden," I said. "It drives me crazy the way you do that. Me, you can ask me anything, and I'll tell you. I trust you, you know. And you can trust me."

"Of course I trust you. It isn't that," he replied. But there was a long moment of silence. I waited for him to speak, to either tell me more about himself or give me a reason why he couldn't. But I grew impatient.

"What kind of work did you do? Were you always a shooting instructor, or...?"

"No, I was a professor. Just for a short time. I taught environmental science at a small college in Arkansas."

"Unbelievable," I muttered. At first, it was so difficult to picture him in a tie, speaking in a social setting for hours at a time.

"Is it that shocking, really?"

"I don't know. I guess I'm still trying to decide," I answered honestly. Once again I was struck by a startling dichotomy in Roden Adams. Could the same man who rescued August and myself in the woods also have agreed to give lectures from a textbook for a living? I finally decided that if anyone could embody such juxtaposed characteristics, it was the heroic shooting instructor sipping tea next to me. "But that wasn't so hard, was it?"

He chuckled before grabbing the black wrought iron poker and prodding the logs and brittle ash in the hearth. "No, that was easy. I wish it were all that easy." Once again he fell into a long silence. I glanced sideways at him, though he seemed to be mesmerized by the dancing flames.

"Okay," he said at last, setting his teacup down on that tray. "Okay. You want to have this conversation, I understand that. But I have to warn you that you may not like what you hear."

"I can handle it," I said confidently. He stared wordlessly into the fire for a moment as I listened to the whining and hissing and popping of the flames carry on their own conversation with the air around them.

"Listen, have you ever read Thoreau?"

"Just a few pages," I answered evasively, remembering his letters.

"He said that, 'In wilderness is the preservation of the world.' And I came to try to... I don't know, preserve something, I guess. Some part of myself, the part that was still alive—I can't explain it, really. I swore to myself I'd never do something, you see. I never thought I would. I saw myself change in a way I never wanted to, and I had to do something drastic to... I don't know, remain human. It probably sounds crazy, but it's true. I think I really came because I feared for my soul."

"Does this have anything to do with—with Sophia?" I asked, hesitant to say the name out loud.

"No—well, yes," he said, correcting himself as though he were trying to straighten it out in his mind. "It started with Sophia. But it wasn't her fault, really. I could never blame anything on Sophia. But everything changed when she broke up with me. We'd been dating for several years, and we'd just gotten engaged when she broke it off, just like that.

"It was so bizarre...the memory. It was like nothing made sense. But one day she said she never wanted to hear from me again. She'd never speak to me again, and to please respect her privacy and leave her family alone."

"That's harsh," I muttered.

"I couldn't understand it. I never in a million years would have seen that coming. *Never.* Sophia and I being together was the one thing I was sure about. Always had been. And she left me with some lame excuse about needing to find her own way in life. I just couldn't accept that. Over time my frustration became anger, and my anger became hatred. I guess it was the kind of hatred that was really love, a love that has nowhere to go, no way to go on living.

"I think I knew even then that I was missing something, some crucial part of the truth. I think I had a feeling, a premonition if you will. Whatever it was, it was a certain dread that the truth was going to hit eventually and that it was ugly. But I went on hating her, even with that dread eating away at me. And maybe what I really hated was that dread. I don't know. It was all mixed up back then. I couldn't think straight.

"I told myself that she must have fallen in love with someone else, that that was the truth nobody was telling me. I told myself that that was the worst possible thing. But I was very wrong."

He stopped in his monologue to finish off the tea. In the firelight, that teacup looked so small and incongruent in the hands of someone so conflicted and tortured by the past. I stared at it as he spoke, watching him fumble with the cup and turn it around and around with his fingers. But I don't think he realized he was doing it at all, such was the fierce concentration in his eyes on the ghosts of his past.

"Anyway, so at first, I harassed her and her family for answers. I accused her of things, horrible things, just to try to get a reaction out of her. But it was like she had disappeared, because I never saw her. And then I just gave up. I shut down, poured myself into my career, forcing myself to go on these awful dates, each one more excruciating than the last. It was all such a lie, such a pitiful lie, and all just to pass the time before that dread would finally be confirmed by finding out the truth. And it was all just to hurt her—to hurt her just enough to get what I wanted, maybe. Just to get the truth and get it all over with. So I made myself hate her for six horrible months. And then... Then I got the news that she'd passed away."

"What?" I asked, but the sound was muffled as I had been covering my mouth with one hand. "What happened?" I forced myself to pick up the teacup and hold it to my lips.

"Cancer," he muttered. "It was cancer." He looked away before picking up that fire poker again and jabbing at the logs, causing hundreds of tiny sparks to fly into the air like fireflies between the trees. When he spoke again, his voice was changed, breaking up from time to time.

"Just when I thought nothing could shock me, there it was. The ugly truth. And it was nothing like what I'd imagined. I can't explain the emotional...torment. It's an understatement to say it was a roller coaster. The fury melted into self-loathing. The grief alone nearly sent me into depression. But it wasn't just that.

"She left me a single letter, explaining that when she got the diagnosis, she was told she only had a few months left to live. And all she could think of was to spare me some of the grief by pushing me away, trying to force me to forget about her so that I wouldn't have to watch her die. She wanted me to move on with my life as quickly and painlessly as possible, she said.

"But she was wrong—she was so wrong. I would have wanted to be by her side through everything, to the very end. It would have been so much better that way. I can't help but think that things ended in the worst possible way.

"In her letter, she asked for forgiveness. But I was the one who needed the forgiveness, not her. What she did wrong, she at least did for the right reasons. But me? I convinced myself of so many lies... I made myself hate her during the most difficult times of her life.

"And the letter she left me...that letter... It wasn't enough, could never be enough to live on. I'd spent six years loving her, six months hating her and wrongly accusing her, and then she was gone forever. Just like that, I'd never see her again... I never got a chance to set things right... I never got to say all the things I needed to say.

"Danny tried to explain once, but I couldn't listen to him or even look at him—couldn't stand the sight of her family any longer. I could only think they must have been partly responsible for her decision. Maybe they were, maybe they weren't. It's all a blur, looking back. But I was still *reeling* from the pain a month after her funeral when...when I got very, very drunk." He stopped to steady his breathing before he continued. "And I went for a drive. I woke up in the hospital with a headache, a broken leg, and an arm that would never completely heal from the glass of the windshield."

He looked down at his arm where the sleeve was rolled halfway up his forearm. I stared again at the scars, and suddenly it made perfect sense that his arm had gone through a windshield.

"That's when it hit me, what I'd become. I couldn't believe what I'd done, how quickly I'd sunken into the worst possible version of myself—into my father. The one thing I'd dreaded, the one thing I said I'd never do, was become like him. And at the time it seemed like that's exactly what happened. And I'd always have these scars to remind me of my mistakes.

"In the end, nobody understood my decision to leave my career and come to Willow's Bend. I'm not sure even I understand what I was trying to accomplish when I came here. I just knew I needed to make a change, to get away from the life I was living before, from all the mistakes I'd made and the promises I'd broken."

"But didn't it hurt, coming back to Willow's Bend where Sophia used to live?"

"Yeah, it hurt," he answered softly in a way that let me know it was an understatement. "But I guess I felt like I was making up for something too. Forcing myself to be closer to her, to be even more aware of her in the woods she'd known and the places we'd been together, to think I'd hear her in the wind or catch her scent in the honeysuckle vines by the river's edge. It's like pressing on a wound to try to control the pain. At least, I told myself that I was choosing my own fate here, that I could at least be alone and attain some form of peace in my life."

"And did it work?" I asked.

"No. No, it didn't work. For a while, I thought so, but I was wrong." He smiled a conflicted grin at something in his mind. "The residents of Willow's Bend are a curious people.

"Somehow, word got out about what happened, or at least part of it. And so I'm pretty sure you're the only person in the refuge who didn't know. Sad, huh? Coming here for solitude and peace, and I managed to become the biggest piece of gossip since the original mansion burned down."

"Well, it would seem that you can't outrun your problems or hide from them."

"It would seem that way. I probably should have realized that when you showed up with your story about Gavin. Of all the people in the refuge...you and I end up here together. I'm not even sure if I can call it a coincidence. And I've been trying to decide if it's supposed to be some kind of punishment... I guess I've been feeling like you're the last person I would want to know my story. But there it is, in all its ugliness."

"You didn't kill Gavin, you know," I whispered. "You made some mistakes, but you can't take responsibility for every drunk driving accident out there."

He gave me a sideways glance but didn't respond.

"I forgive you for driving that night, and I hope you'll forgive yourself. It sounds like the only thing you killed was a bush on the side of the road."

"It could have been Gavin. It could have been you or August or anyone..."

"But it wasn't. And it wasn't Sophia, either. Roden, it also wasn't a coincidence that you didn't hurt anyone but yourself. It was a second chance. The sad thing is, the guy who did accidentally kill Gavin has probably moved on better than you have. I've never heard of anyone so intent on punishing himself for the rest of his life. It doesn't make sense. Well, that is unless..."

"Unless what?" There was a note of defensiveness in his voice.

"You're afraid. Which is amazing, because I was beginning to think you weren't afraid of anything. But it sounds to me like you're afraid to move on with your life."

To my surprise, he didn't respond. He merely looked off into the flames pensively, leaving me in silence to think of all those letters he wrote to Sophia, trying so hard to respond to her single life-changing letter but knowing they'd never reach her. No matter how close he came, no matter how painful the punishment, he'd never reach her on this side of eternity. And he'd never find her in Willow's Bend.

KNOCK, knock, knock.

I had been sitting on the edge of my bed that morning for some time, processing through our final days on the refuge and what it would be like to return home, when I lifted my head up to the sound. I threw on a sweatshirt over my pajamas and opened the door.

"Char, can you come with me?" Roden asked. I was unnerved to see that he was breathless.

"What is it?" But he had already turned around and walked off before answering. "Roden?" I sped up to catch up with him. "What's going on?"

He didn't pause until we were almost to the top of the steps leading out onto the second-floor balcony. "I—I don't know. I saw something."

"What did you see?"

"I thought I saw..." he began, but stopped and shook his head instead. "I just need you to tell me what you see."

He opened the door and led the way out into the cold morning air. I approached the railing fearfully. If Roden saw something that scared him, I knew I would only be terrified. But I scanned the edge of the woods anyway.

My gaze stopped on a figure sitting on a branch in a sycamore. At first I knew that the hooded figure wearing khaki shorts and dark sunglasses could be anyone. But as I watched, I realized that he was watching us back. He slowly let the hood of his sweatshirt fall from his head and pulled the sunglasses off his face.

I gasped. I couldn't believe my eyes. "Danny?"

"Then you see him too? It's not just me?"

"No, it's not just you," I answered. Danny had come back from the dead. I waved at him, still wondering if Roden and I were both the victim of an illusion. And to my surprise, he waved back. "I was wrong. He wasn't infected. He wasn't killed. That vaccine he'd had must have worked, and he survived the fight at my cabin." Even as I said the words out loud, I knew they sounded absurd. But even from this distance, I couldn't shake the conviction that that was Danny sitting up in that tree.

I waved him toward us and waited for him to jump down from his tree and join us. But he didn't move.

"He must be waiting for you," I said to Roden. He looked back at me with a furrowed brow.

"What makes you say that?"

"Because it's your house," I answered. "And your grudge."

My words must have stung because he turned away from the balcony and headed back to the door. He stopped with his hand still on the doorknob and said something under his breath. Then he exhaled and turned back around. I could see that it was taking every bit of strength he had as he walked back to the balcony beside me.

"Come on!" he shouted the words at the top of his lungs, louder than necessary. I think he was doing it the only way he knew how. It was either that sudden outburst or complete silence.

I watched through the tears in my eyes as Danny jumped down from his tree and walked up the hill at a quick pace. I heard the wolves in the distance, but they were fortunately nowhere near the mansion at the time.

"I can't believe this..." I murmured. I surveyed Roden's features, which seemed strained and dark and broken all at the same time. All the way down the stairs, I couldn't help but wonder if this was only another dream, if something even more strange and unnatural was about to happen to ruin everything.

Roden opened the door with caution, holding a gun in case we were ambushed. Danny walked into the foyer slowly and waited for Roden to close and lock the door before looking up at either one of us. He had put his sunglasses back on. I waited for him to take them off in the dim light of the foyer, but he didn't.

"Danny, I can't tell you how relieved I am," I began. I pulled him into an embrace but was immediately surprised by his rigid posture when I did. I stepped back, realizing that he may still be injured. "Are—are you okay? Can I get you some water or something?"

"Um, yeah," he answered. "Some water would be good, thanks."

I left the two of them standing awkwardly by the door. I took the liberty of putting together a tray of Danny's water, some breakfast, and coffee. When I finally found the two of them, they had moved to the sitting room and were speaking in hushed tones. Something about the nature of their conversation made me pause by the doorway behind them and listen.

"Do you really think I wanted it to happen?" Danny asked. I hadn't noticed before the way his voice had changed since I'd last seen him. It sounded dry and hoarse. "I swear I tried to talk her out of her stupid plan."

Roden stood up and walked over to lean against the fireplace mantle. "I want to believe that, Danny. I do."

"But I couldn't betray her. Not like that, not when I knew she was—" He suddenly stopped himself, as though he couldn't bring himself to say the word.

"Dying," Roden said. "Why can't you say it?" He suddenly turned back to face Danny. "Why can't you just say it, Danny? She was *dying*."

Danny looked away, silent.

"Take off those damn sunglasses and *say it!*" Roden took two steps toward Danny and yanked the sunglasses off his face. Danny dropped his face into his arms.

But Roden must have seen something because he covered his mouth and swore.

Part of me must have anticipated what he saw, though, because I briefly relaxed my grip on the tray I was holding, and it crashed loudly to the hardwood floor. Danny stood up and looked wide eyed in my direction. That's when I saw it, the thing that had horrified Roden. Danny's eyes had transformed into a vivid, creamy yellow. It was the same color I'd seen in the eyes of several infected humans out in the woods.

RODEN HAD QUICKLY helped me clean up the mess from the sitting room floor, though I noticed that he kept Danny in plain sight the entire time. We salvaged some of the food and coffee and sat on a couch opposite Danny.

"I'm not staying long," Danny said. He had put the sunglasses back on, perhaps out of consideration for us. And I was thankful. There was no way I could feel comfortable in the same room with him if I had to face those eyes. "I know I'm infected."

"I don't understand," I said. "If the infection takes so long before inducing violence, then why didn't anyone catch this thing before it got out of hand?"

"It doesn't take this long," Danny replied. "I think it generally takes...hours. For me, it's been several weeks, and I've had better days and worse days. So far I've never completely lost...myself. My control, I mean. I feel violent impulses, but I can control them."

"How can that be?" Roden asked.

"I don't know. There's so much nobody knows about this thing. I think I must've received the vaccine so soon after my infection that maybe it didn't set in as strongly or fully as it has for everyone else. I honestly don't know."

"Then maybe you're fine," I said. "We're getting rescued tomorrow, Danny. We'll call the CDC and make them take you with us."

Danny shook his head. "I already talked to the CDC. They won't take me like this. It would be too risky when the safest thing to do right now is to contain the infection in Willow's Bend."

There was a long silence. I heard a noise on the other side of the room. It was August, who'd just walked in still wearing his pajamas.

"August," I said, standing up. My instincts told me to keep August as far away from Danny as possible. "I'll be right there, sweetie. Can you go to the kitchen and pick out your cereal for me?" He nodded and disappeared.

Danny stood up too. "I'm leaving here soon. I just had to talk to Roden while I still had the chance."

"Danny, it's so good to see you," I said. "Someday we'll meet outside these crazy woods, okay? You're going to make it. I know it."

He cracked a half smile from beneath his shades, reminding me of the easygoing friend I'd known just a couple months ago. But I had to fight the urge to embrace him. "Goodbye, Charlotte."

"No," I said. "Please. Not a goodbye. I'll see you later, okay?"

"Okay," he answered. And so I turned away from Danny's altered form and tried to remember him the way he used to be. I told myself that he would be just fine in a few weeks. Months at the most. But I couldn't avoid the overwhelming wave of sadness that swept over me as I walked out of the room.

"WELL, WE SAID what we needed to say," Roden said. We were on the balcony again, possibly for the last time before we would be picked up by helicopter. Would we ever return to this place? Would we even see each other again? I sent out silent questions over the rooftops and stirring treetops, into the bright, wintery sky with its steel grays and that veiled but incandescent sun. It had begun to snow. Light but fat flakes drifted into our eyelashes and got caught in Roden's dark, unkempt hair. "I believe him now, maybe for the first time. He wasn't responsible for Sophia's death or her final decisions. And I apologized for...well, for everything. For not listening, for not being there for him when he was grieving. And I guess that's all there is to it."

"How does that feel?" I asked.

He inhaled deeply before speaking. "It feels..." he began. He nodded silently into the wind for a moment, as though making up his mind. "It feels good. And what's more, I have hope."

"You do? Really?" I asked. I desperately wanted to have that assurance.

"Yeah. I mean, it's a long shot. But he has a plan. He was planning to head to the other side of the refuge, to the old museum where he thinks there may be a safe place for a supplies drop. But I told him to hang tight for a couple days, and he could stay here instead."

"That sounds like a good plan." My eyes drifted off to the horizon, where I heard the beating blades of a helicopter, but it didn't come any closer. Someone else must have been getting a supplies drop. I wondered if anyone else was being rescued tomorrow, or how they determined who got to leave and who had to stay longer.

"Do you think it's really possible to start over?" Roden asked.

"Well, you can't undo what's been done," I answered. "But you can learn and move on from this place. Everything will change, you know. You can go anywhere, do anything. It will be like a new beginning, a fresh start." I tried to be encouraging, but I knew that he was truly afraid of leaving this place, in spite of what it had become. Since our last conversation, I'd become absolutely certain that Roden was more afraid of moving on than he was of infections or wolves or any other danger lurking in these woods.

"And where will you go?" he asked. "Where does Charlotte Benson go from here?"

"Honestly, I don't even want to think about it." I laughed nervously, and I'm not sure why. I'm not sure why I was nervous or why I laughed at an idea that was so painful for me. But I was, and I did. "I'll finish my last semester of college, I guess. Maybe go back to work at the café or move back in with my parents for a while, or...who knows?"

"So, at this café, I suppose you made espressos and macchiatos, and...I suppose they made you wear one of those aprons and slacks and you went home with the smell of coffee in your hair?"

I furrowed my brow at his peculiar question. "Yes." I laughed unexpectedly, this time freely. "Is that hard to picture?"

"No, I think it makes sense," he answered, looking away over the willows and birches and rolling hillside. He stopped to smile at me before he reached into his jacket pocket and pulled out a book of matches, the cheap kind with the presidents' faces on them. "It's just difficult to think...I don't know, that life will go on when we leave this place." I heard the striking against sandpaper, one, two times. There was a light hissing as he lit the match, cupped it with one hand for a moment, then lit the pipe. He shook the match repeatedly until its tiny flame was extinguished.

"I know what you mean," I said, still watching him through the smoke and falling snow. I tried to picture him as a professor, maybe wearing a tie and dress shirt, but I just couldn't see it. Instead I was getting mesmerized by the dark grays and the pure whites intermingling, colliding in the air. I was reminded of a landscape painting and saw the artist's brush thick and heavy with paint moving across the sky. "It probably sounds strange, but I'll miss Willow's Bend. Everything that's happened here...the good, the bad...it's all been so monumental, so, I don't know...touched by providence, maybe. Sacred, even."

"Everything will change, Char, but everything has already changed too. Willow's bend is not what it was two months ago. We are not who we were two months ago."

"Hmm," I muttered in agreement. I was cold and had to stop to blow heat into my hands and rub them together. I squinted into the brightness of the morning, resting in the quiet sounds of dawning winter and taking in the familiar scents of pipe tobacco, the combination of black tea and vanilla and something indefinable.

"You know, there are still things I can't quite wrap my mind around," I began. "When I was running, when you said you first saw me from that tree...I felt something. I mean, I thought I was about to die, but I could swear something happened. It was as though the wind picked up or...I somehow sped up. I don't even know. I can't explain it. I keep telling myself it was nothing, but I just can't believe that. Do you think I'm crazy?" And after hearing myself voice those thoughts, I was certain that I sounded crazy.

Roden smiled at me, laughing that familiar laugh to himself before removing the pipe from his lips and exhaling smoke in one big puff. Then he replied, "For the record, you're the last person in the world I would ever call crazy. I don't see how a person can live through what we have and not believe in miracles. Actually, I think you'd have to be pretty delusional to convince yourself it was nothing."

I watched his cracked lips move around the pipe, his cold hands rubbing together to stay warm as I'd seen them do so many times before on this very balcony. And I knew I'd miss this. I ached for how much I'd miss it, for how much I already missed these conversations in the cold wind with Roden and his pipe smoke and all his quirks and habits. And it hurt to listen to him, though all I wanted to do was go on listening to him.

"For me, I know there's a reason for all this, though I may never understand it. I'm changed by it, that's for sure. And as for you coming down that hill," he said, turning to look straight into my eyes.

I knew then that I'd never forget his words.

"I saw you. And it was definitely a miracle. *Char, you were practically flying.*"

CHAPTER SIXTEEN

I lay awake the night before our planned rescue, convinced that my mind would never stop racing long enough for me to fall asleep. I was reminded of all those months of insomnia and anxiety I'd suffered before coming to the refuge and of the medication I'd been taking for them. But this was different. I was on the eve of rescue, leaving behind the haunting howls and freshly stained blood of Willow's Bend residents.

I was also leaving behind the two people who had become incredibly dear to me, to the point that I couldn't bear the thought of being separated from them. Looking back, I knew that it was irrational. I could see why any sensible adult would frown upon my thoughts, if only they could have seen them. It was childish to hope that Roden was in love with me—I knew it even then. It was preposterous to even consider adopting August once we were outside the refuge gates. Whatever was required of adoption, I was certain I wasn't qualified. But who can understand the human heart?

I was still tangled up in thoughts of Roden and August when a thought flashed through my mind. It was an image of being in Nana's living room and hearing the ambulance arrive to take Gavin's body away. That's when I heard a foreboding voice in my head say, "You know this thing, this love, is going to destroy you. It's going to hurt, and it's going to hit you hard." I shook my head, trying hard to dismiss the thoughts. And I consoled myself with the thought that it was already too late anyway. I was hooked. And there was no going back.

I suppose that at some point I must have drifted off toward sleep, because I found myself blinking and sitting up in my bed, convinced of having just seen the image of young Ambrose in my doorway. I was never prone to hallucinations. Of course it must have been a dream, because the door was now closed, and it had been so since I'd first turned in for the night. But in that moment, I had seen the boy clothed in some long-since abandoned fashion standing in the open doorway looking quite lost.

Perhaps what was most frightening was not that I believed in this ghost but that I still held in my mind such a vivid impression of his features and demeanor and mood. I saw the lines that rimmed his eyes with sadness and a sense of wandering loneliness. My dreams tended to be of an obscure nature, less definite and concrete in appearance compared to the vision of Ambrose. But more than anything, I recalled that the first impression I had upon waking up from it was one of concern for the long-lost orphan boy. And immediately my thoughts returned to August.

I forced myself to throw back the covers, flinging the stifling cotton sheets away from my body as I stepped down into a pair of shoes. The glass by my bed was empty, and so I thought perhaps a fresh glass of water would suffice to banish all ghostly visitations and fears about the future. I made my way downstairs, as the three of us had kept bedrooms on the second floor since my attack. As I walked, I tried not to imagine the phantom Ambrose. Fortunately he did not reappear on my way to the kitchen, and I felt more brave than before as I walked with my full glass of water back to the stairs.

I paused in the foyer. So far I had been successful in ignoring any bumps in the night, as well as the creaks and the howling of the wind against the eaves. After all, Roden was always somewhere nearby. But it had still been less than a week since my attack. And here I distinctly heard something that made me stop with one hand on the newel post.

Knock, knock, knock. I heard three slow, deliberate knocks on the heavy, wooden front door. Water splashed out of the glass onto my sleeve, dripping down my wrist and forearm. The occurrence of the sound was so unexpected and struck me as so out of place that I wondered if I was still asleep after all.

I waited.

Nothing.

"Ambrose?" I whispered. But there was no response. Certainly a child couldn't knock so loudly anyway.

After a few more long seconds of frightened expectation, I decided that I must be imagining things again. After all, who would be knocking on the mansion's doors from the outside? Were there other survivors? If there were survivors who wanted in, I couldn't imagine them knocking on the door in the middle of the night. I could imagine them banging on the door, shouting, trying to break in. But knocking? It made absolutely no sense. Contemplating various scenarios, each sounding more ludicrous than the last, I went back upstairs with my now three-quarters-full glass of water, fully convinced that the sound I'd heard was as much of a phantom as my vision of Ambrose.

The water must have done the trick, because I soon fell fast asleep.

IT WAS EARLY in the morning, and the incongruous sound of birds chirping interrupted the sounds of barking and howling through my bedroom window. I had woken up in one of those rare moods that compelled me to get up despite aching all over and feeling like I'd never gone to sleep at all. Brushing my teeth in the bathroom, I worked those plastic white bristles in tight circles on my teeth and spat great big globs of white, minty foam into the basin with a great deal of satisfaction. Glancing down at my wristwatch, I saw that I was making great time. I can't explain the compulsion that had come over me when I woke up, but I'd had this sudden passion for making pancakes to celebrate our rescue. I wanted to be the first one downstairs to surprise the other two with a fantastic breakfast.

While I still cringed at the idea of being separated from them, I couldn't help but take every opportunity to celebrate with them, no matter the reason.

I was finally able to open my eye all the way, though it remained visibly injured and mostly red. In the right light, I supposed, it may go unnoticed. Maybe I wouldn't have to explain anything after all.

Having thrown my damp hair up in a bun, I walked briskly out of the steamy bathroom to the kitchen downstairs. But on my way through the foyer, I was stopped by a familiar sound.

Knock, knock, knock.

I stared wide eyed at the heavy front door. It was as though I'd been thrown back into some old dream, as I'd completely forgotten about last night's experience. In fact, as I waited for more sounds, I attempted to sort out my memory of the night before.

My eyes moved to the upstairs landing, hoping and praying that Roden was on his way downstairs. But he wasn't. I heard the knocks again.

I walked toward the large door, coming to stand between the two boarded-up windows, and forced myself to look through the peephole. I closed one eye and tried to focus my vision through the fisheye lens. A haggard-looking figure was slouched to my right, halfway out of my field of vision. I stepped away from the door, shocked at what I saw. *Who is this person? Are they dangerous? Are they infected? Are there more people I couldn't see? Are they innocent victims like ourselves?*

Somewhat stunned, I backed away from the door, planning to head upstairs to find Roden.

"There you are." I heard Roden's deep voice from behind me. He must have beaten me to the kitchen. "I just started some breakfast." I looked back at his chipper demeanor and grinning face.

"I was just looking for you," I began, already a little breathless.

"And I was looking for you," he replied. "What do you think of pancakes?" I stared at the kitchen towel over his shoulder and the spatula in his hand.

"Um, actually...we seem to have a visitor."

"What?"

"There's someone at the front door. He keeps knocking."

"Did you get a good look?" he asked, immediately going up to the door's peephole and peering through.

"No, I—I think it's a man, but I couldn't make out much."

"Damn," he said, pulling away from the door with a blank expression. He turned slightly to his left, deep in thought.

"What's the matter? Who is it?"

His eyes flickered up to meet mine briefly. "It's James."

"James?" My hand instinctively went to my eye at the memory of my last encounter with him.

"I think...I think he was here knocking last night too. I thought I was imagining it. I mean, who in their right mind would stand out there knocking all night?"

"Nobody in their right mind," he muttered pensively.

"What are you going to do?" I asked as I surveyed his troubled features.

"Nothing. He'll go away."

That morning, we made a fantastic breakfast, and I did my best to be in celebratory mode. But I couldn't ignore the knocks, and I struggled to come up with anything to tell August when he asked about them. He had heard them on his way to breakfast, but at least we couldn't hear them in the kitchen.

"Someone's knocking," I acknowledged as I set his plate of pancakes and sliced fruit down on the table. "But it's too dangerous to open the door." He didn't exactly seem satisfied, but the pajamaed five-year-old was quickly distracted by the presence of butter and syrup and milk.

I threw a wary look at Roden as we sat down to eat, but it went unnoticed. He appeared uneasy and deep in thought throughout our celebratory breakfast.

"HEY, IT STOPPED," August said with a smile. He had just returned from the bathroom that was just down the hall from the dining room.

"What stopped?" I asked.

"The knocking," he said matter-of-factly, as though surprised that I hadn't guessed. I stared back at his furrowed brow and crooked smile. "He must have left."

"That's good," Roden said, standing up to gather our plates.

"I'll clean up in here if you want to help him get ready," I offered, joining Roden at the sink. "And then we can all pack."

He agreed just in time for August to leap out of his chair and try to tackle him. "Airplane! Airplane!" the boy chanted as Roden laughed and helped him up onto his back.

"All right, all right," Roden muttered before transforming his voice by covering his mouth with one hand. "Attention, passengers, we are now boarding flight number two-nine-four-seven. Please fasten your seatbelts and prepare for liftoff."

I cleaned the kitchen in peace after that, although the question occurred to me whether there was any point in cleaning up after ourselves anymore. *What will happen to the mansion? How long will the refuge be under quarantine before it's cleaned up? Will Roden ever see his house again?* I paused to watch a stray bubble lift up and float into the air. It slowed and drifted just in front of my face, causing me to grin.

After drying off the last of the dishes, I headed upstairs to help with the packing. I was surprised to find August in his bedroom alone. He was struggling with mismatched socks where he sat on his bed. "Are you all alone in here?" I asked.

He looked up at the sound of my voice but then dropped his gaze to focus on his stubborn sock again. "Yep," he muttered.

"Where's Roden?" I asked, settling down on my knees to help him.

"Heard a noise," he said. "He said you must've left the balcony door open." I removed one of the socks and dug a matching one out of his bag.

"The balcony door? Why would I do that?" By now I was mostly talking to myself, though. "I haven't even gone out there by myself..."

Just then I heard a loud crash. And another. It was coming from down the hallway. I knew then that someone must have broken in again.

In a panic, I immediately pulled August off the bed by his arms. I looked out into the hallway, but there was no one there. The sounds of struggle in another room were accompanied by indistinct voices.

"Follow me," I whispered to the startled child. We ran across the hallway and down two rooms, away from the noise. I closed the bathroom door and locked it, keeping the light off in the process.

Once here, I realized that we may not be safe for very long. Sure, there were many rooms in the house, but if someone happened to try to open this door, he might guess that someone was in here. I opened the cabinet doors.

There were supplies in there but enough space to fit August if I rearranged everything. I set to work, cramming the supplies to one side, letting some of it spill out onto the black-and-white square tiled floor before picking it up again. "Come on, I need you to get in here," I whispered.

"Why?" he asked in a quivering, much-too-loud voice.

"Shhh. It's okay. It's just safer in here, okay? Everything's going to be fine. I just want to be extra careful, okay?"

"What about you?" he asked. There were tears in his eyes as he quickly realized that I couldn't fit in there if I tried.

"I...I don't know," I mumbled at first, uncertain what I should do. Then I realized my mistake, because his crying grew louder. "No, no, no, sweetie. I'm going to be all right. I just don't know what to do yet. But everything's going to be fine, okay? I just need you to do what I say. Can you do that, buddy? Can you stay in here real quiet for me until we get everything safe again?"

He nodded reluctantly before climbing into the cabinet. A small part of me felt cruel for making him climb into that cramped-up space with those tears running down his cheeks. "Okay, sweetie, I have to go try to help Roden, all right?"

"No!"

"Yes. I at least have to see what's going on out there. He might need my help. But you can help us by staying in here and being quiet no matter what. I'm going to leave the door unlocked, so even if someone comes in here, I want you to be silent, and don't open these doors. Can you do that for me?"

He nodded again.

Standing next to the door, I closed my eyes and took a deep breath, pressing my ear against the door one last time. It was quiet. I slowly, silently opened the door, thankful that this particular door didn't squeak like so many of the others. There was no sign of movement in the hallway. I stepped across the hall and pressed my back up against the wall before inching my way down to where the noise had been. I stopped when I heard a voice.

"You're a selfish bastard for hidin' all by yourself in this mansion, ya know that?" I was just inches away from the doorway, but it didn't sound like anyone was about to approach me. I heard a chair move. Then I heard a groan.

Roden must be hurt.

I knew then that I had to get to my gun. I made my way down the hallway to my bedroom where the small black case was hidden at the top shelf of the closet. Roden had placed it there a few days ago in case of an emergency, but I hadn't even imagined that I would take it down from where it was hidden. I winced as I heard a floorboard creak but was relieved when nobody appeared in the hallway.

In the bedroom, I pulled the case off the top shelf and set it on the bed. I opened it, pausing to examine the weapon before touching it. There were two magazines loaded with twenty-two caliber bullets, ten each. Twenty shots. I shoved one full magazine into my denim pocket and cautiously loaded the gun with the other. Making sure that the safety was on, I placed the gun carefully into the waist of my jeans, pulling at my long-sleeved shirt to hide it. I would never typically put a gun there, as I had no intention of shooting myself in the foot or anywhere else, but I knew that I needed the element of surprise on my side when I walked into that room.

I tried to steady my breathing as I walked slowly down the hallway. My palms were clammy, and I felt sweat dampen my temples and the base of my neck. I swallowed. I turned the corner. As if on cue, the old hardwood floor creaked to announce my arrival.

The room was one that I wasn't very familiar with. It was located just next to a second-floor balcony entrance and was the same room in which Roden found the closet full of games that night. When I rounded the corner, Roden was unconscious, sprawled out on the floor. I could barely see the side of his jaw, which was bruised a dark purple. There was a gash on his head, and his wrists were tied together with what looked like the cords from a set of blinds.

James caught sight of me with a momentary look of surprise etched into his brow, which quickly settled into something like amusement. He slowly grinned, pulling a cigarette in his left hand up to cracked lips. "Well, well, well," he spoke in a voice that dripped with condescension. "Look who it is."

I remained in the doorway, doing my best to play the part of the naive and ignorant person he most certainly took me for. He held a shotgun in his other hand but didn't seem to be in a hurry to aim it at me.

"I heard a noise," I said dumbly.

"Don't be afraid, beautiful. Come on in here and have a chat."

I stepped warily forward but kept my distance and moved left toward the other side of the room. I had a closer look at Roden from here but knew better than to get too close. There was a plush chair nearby, so I sat down on the edge of it, training my eyes on James across the room.

James busied himself with smoking, getting caught up in one slow drag after another. He caught me looking at him and cracked another smile. "Found these in a house off Splinterwood," he said. "Been through quite a few houses... none of 'em as safe as this one, though. The lucky bastard." He glared down at Roden again. "Nearly died gettin' a supplies drop, ya know. No balconies. Dangerous as hell out there."

"Then why were you knocking all night?" I interrupted, momentarily forgetting to play stupid.

His eyes glowered as he looked at me. He took another drag before answering. "Thought we were better friends than that. Thought he'd let me in. But he didn't, selfish sonofabitch. He was gonna let me get eaten by wolves." Something in our conversation seemed to reignite his anger, because he crossed the room after that and kicked Roden in the stomach.

Roden groaned on the floor and began to writhe in pain, the blood on his head smearing across the wood, leaving thick, dark stains behind.

"Wake up." James growled. "Your Indian princess is here. You lied to me, you bastard. You told me you was alone in this ol' house." I watched James back away from him, readjusting his shotgun in the process, his heavy black boots leaving a trail of mud. Meanwhile, Roden turned over on his back, revealing a cheekbone that was cut wide open and bleeding onto the torn sleeve of his arm.

"Can't see as I blame him though. If I happened to be in possession of my very own Indian princess, well..." He let out a long whistle before laughing to himself. "That's what I call a recipe for fun."

"Wh—what do you want with us?" I stammered, trying to ignore the lingering gaze that came with his words.

"Oh, I'm takin' over your house, I reckon. You can either stay on here with me," he said, pausing to emphasize his next words, "which I promise to make a most thrillin' experience. Or you can leave by yourself. Into the dark and spooky woods by your lonesome..." He lowered himself into a squatting position, tapping ashes off his cigarette over Roden's body as he spoke. "I trust you to make the obvious decision, Princess. I know you will do it. I do know that."

"What about Roden?"

"Oh, now, Adams is a different story. Ya see, when word got to me that Adams killed a lady friend of mine in this very house, well...that don't sit too well with me. No, see I'm a man of justice at my core. An' the way I see it, Adams here has got to die. Troublin', ain't it? But don't worry your pretty little head anymore. The main thing is that you will not be alone. You can stay on in this house as long as you like for all I care."

My thoughts turned to August, who was certainly alone right now. I looked up to see that James had moved toward the window and was gazing through the blinds. His back was turned toward me. *I could shoot him right now*, I thought. *I have no choice. He's going to kill Roden. There was no reason to go get the gun if I don't have the guts to shoot him. I have to do it. I have to do it now.*

James turned back around to smirk at me again, ending my silent conflict.

"So how did you happen to get caught in his net, anyway?"

"I was lost," I answered. "He gave me shelter."

"Well, I'll be. I can see it now. Isn't that romantic? You were just as helpless as a lamb, weren't you? I'll bet that was somethin'. And I suppose you trusted him, just like that?"

"No, I...I didn't," I answered honestly. "I've had a fear of guns all my life."

"Yer kiddin' me. Well, there's somethin' you need to get straight right now, Beautiful. This man is a murderer. Plain and simple. And in this lawless land we find ourselves in, murderers have got to die. It's the only way to make things right, you hear?"

"But he saved my life."

"Ahh, well see, savin' the life of a beautiful woman and takin' her home with him is about the most selfish thing a man can do, if you ask me. Don't you go fallin' for him just for that. Besides, he won't be around much longer. And you and I will have plenty of time to get acquainted. You see, ownin' a gun doesn't make a man bad. But killin' innocent women who are tryin' to survive...and leavin' your ol' pal out with the wolves... well those are real crimes. And they have got to be prosecuted. It's the only way for justice to prevail in times like these."

I watched his gaze lower to where Roden was. He had regained consciousness again and was glaring up at James from the floor while trying to wipe up his own blood with his tied hands.

"Don't you dare look at me like that, you filthy sonofabitch!" James shouted as he took two steps toward Roden and kicked him twice in the stomach.

"Stop it!" I screamed. And I was going to keep screaming at him. But he abruptly heeded my words and walked toward me instead. Roden coughed and choked on the floor as James stepped over his body, quickly closing the space between us.

James backhanded me across the face, leaving me dizzy and overwhelmed by the sting on my skin. My skin that was still healing from the last break-in. I sat back down in the chair, open-mouthed and blinking back tears.

I looked up in time to see Roden push himself off the floor and lunge at James. But James reacted quickly and shoved his head into the floor. He cocked his gun before aiming it at Roden's head. "I will kill you, you hear me? I will kill you!" The sound of his voice was intense and full of spit.

They were both panting when James shoved Roden back onto the floor and walked away a few paces. James stood looking out the window again, breathing heavily for several seconds. He slowly turned back around. "But first, our little princess here is gonna get me somethin' to eat." He wiped his forehead with his bare and dirty forearm. "No need to rush what you can enjoy instead, right? Eat now, kill later." He cocked his head to one side pensively. "Yeah, yeah, I like that..." he mused, turning a sinister grin on me as he spoke.

CHAPTER SEVENTEEN

I stood in the kitchen in disbelief as to what was happening. I was cooking for James. It was just sandwiches and water, but still. I loathed every second of it.

And I was scared.

Roden was badly hurt and unable to help anyone. August was hidden away in the bathroom, terrified and probably feeling abandoned by now. And I was making a sandwich for a murderer.

I made half of a sandwich to take up to August, as I couldn't stand the thought of his being in there alone and starving. I would find a way to check on him. *And then what?* I still didn't even know if I was capable of either pulling a trigger or killing a man. That was not something I ever wanted to have on my conscience. But he made it clear that he intended to murder Roden, and I could not let that happen. No, come what may, I was going to kill James.

Slipping the paper towel-wrapped sandwich under my shirt, I paused to readjust the pistol that was still wedged in at my side. Then I took a moment to survey the kitchen. *What happened to our happy little home? Was security always such an illusion, or only in Willow's Bend?*

I made my way back upstairs and found that James had opened the closet door and was going through the board games. He turned to look at me as I entered the room. "Ya like games, Beautiful?"

"Not really, no," I lied. I couldn't fathom a context in which answering yes to that question would prove to be a smart move. I set his plate down on an ottoman and stepped away. "I'm going to the restroom."

His gaze grew more serious as he spoke. "Be sure and hurry back. I'd hate to have to hunt you down. But if I have to, I will."

A chill ran down my spine as I turned my back on him and left the room.

I locked the bathroom door behind me and turned the faucet on full blast in case our voices carried. "August," I whispered, before slowly opening the cabinet door of his hiding place. But what I saw was more of a statue than a human boy. He seemed to be literally scared stiff. "Sweetie, are you okay?"

He began to cry, falling forward into my arms, but I quickly tried to correct him. "Shh, no, sweetie. I'm afraid we're not done yet. You've got to stay in here a little longer, okay? I brought you a snack though." He looked down at the sandwich I placed in his hands as though it were the most repulsive thing in the world. "I know it's not fun, but we're going to be just fine. I just need you to be strong a little while longer, okay? Roden's hurt, and he needs my help."

I reluctantly left August in the same position as before, pausing to flush the toilet before turning off the faucet and opening the door. I was only comforted by the thought that so far James had no idea he was in the house.

Stepping into the game room, I had to wave a hand in front of my face to defuse the smoke cloud. James was sitting on the floor with the sandwich in one hand and a deck of cards in the other. He must have just stopped smoking, because there was a smashed cigarette butt next to where he sat. Next to his shotgun was a dirt-smeared package of American Spirit cigarettes.

"You ever play poker before?" he asked.

"No, not really."

"You know how to shuffle and deal, don't you? Why don't you do that while I finish my dinner?" he asked. I looked uncertainly back at him.

"Go on, I trust you." He winked.

I slowly approached him, reaching my hand out as far as I could to pick up the deck without getting any closer than necessary. The air was cold in the room as I shuffled the deck and dealt the hands. Behind me I could hear the slamming of the open balcony door as the wind blew it against the wall again and again.

Looking to my right, I saw that Roden was struggling to sit up against a desk to watch us.

"James," he said, through panting breaths. "We'll let you have the entire first floor. Just leave us alone."

"You won't *let* me do anything, Adams. You're about five minutes away from bein' dead. Now keep your mouth shut or I'll find a way to keep it shut for you. Ya got that?"

I played two grueling games of poker with James while he muttered lyrics to songs I'd never heard before.

"Ya know, things would be a lot more enjoyable if you'd loosen up," he muttered at last, laying his cards down. "The days of corsets and Puritans are long gone, my friend."

"Even so, it sure woulda been nice to have the company of a lady during all my recent trials and tribulations. A life-threatenin' experience like that wakes a man up to the value of certain common liberties, and I've no doubt that the pleasure of your company woulda suited me just fine."

I avoided his gaze, though I could feel his hard, demanding stare across from me.

"You got any idea what it's really like out there?" His question prompted me to look up, just as he lit a new cigarette and took a slow drag. His eyelids fluttered as his head tilted back slightly. He slowly reopened his eyes and leveled an inscrutable gaze at me. When he finally exhaled, he did so with a thick puff of gray smoke and the single word: "Wolves."

I turned my head and coughed.

"Do you have any idea in that pretty Cherokee head of yours what them wolves are really like?" I silently wondered how he knew that I was Cherokee. I was surprised when he stood up and began slowly pacing the length of the room with a vacant look in his eyes. I wasn't sure if he was still addressing me or whether he remembered that Roden was still in the room at all. "They're just as smart as before, you know. Less rational in some ways, maybe, but just as smart. That's why they stick together. Despite their fury for one another, fury for themselves, fury for life and the God who made 'em. You think they want food? You're wrong. All they want is to kill. They crave the ripping, the tearing, the fall of darkness and rise of chaos and violence. The smallest release from the grip that holds 'em....that's all they want. The legions that possess 'em, that drive 'em..."

He suddenly turned to face me as though waking up from a dream. He took another drag, his hand trembling this time. Then he came close, causing me to recoil. He hung his tormented face just inches from mine. And in his face I saw skin transformed by harsh wind and dry, cold air. I saw eyes that forgot what it meant to sleep, bloodshot and strained. When he spoke, it was as though he were possessed by a memory. Or maybe by the very legions he spoke of.

"You ever been hunted? You ever... I knew I was a dead man when I left my cabin. But I had no choice. No...I had no choice. I was outta food, outta cigarettes, drivin' myself crazy... My phone rang. Emily had been murdered at the mansion, they said. At the mansion where there was food and shelter and no one to stand in my way. Except him. And so I knew that's where I had to go. Two miles. I came two miles in the cold and rain. I never been left in so much darkness, so much isolation in all my life. And that's the honest-to-God truth.

"The howls... In here you hear 'em and they're distant, and they're not for you. Maybe they keep you up at night, maybe they scare you a little. Out there? They surrounded me. They taunted me. They tortured me, an' that was the only reason for it. They weren't talkin' to each other. No, Princess. They were talkin' to me.

"An' God only knows how I survived without a bite, without bein' ripped to chunks and shreds. So don't you look at me like I'm the evil one, Princess. You don't know evil so pure, so dark

as what I been through. No, I'm the one who's been to hell
and back. I've only killed wolves. Never killed no innocents.
So you should be kissin' my feet right now. I deserve your
sympathy, not that scum. Lucky you, I'm in just the mood to
give you a chance to redeem yourself. And I think you will.
Once Adams is outta the picture, I think you'll come to your
senses just fine."

I was certain that he was waiting for me to agree with him,
so I looked away instead. His story had taken me by surprise,
it's true. And to some degree, I couldn't help feeling sympathy
for him, for anyone who suffered in Willow's Bend, especially
anyone who suffered alone. But that sympathy would dissipate
like cigarette smoke as soon as Roden was gone. No. I pitied
him, and I would kill him.

When James finally spoke again, he announced that he was
going to the bathroom. "Don't trouble yourself, Beautiful. I'll
find it. Give you some time to think about your future...if you
choose to have one."

When he left the room, I slowly stood up and walked to the
doorway, making sure he was gone.

Then I rushed to untie Roden.

"Where is August?" he whispered while I fumbled with the
cords around his wrists.

"He's in the bathroom," I answered, sheepishly.

"What?" he asked angrily.

"I know, I know. He's under the sink, and he knows to stay
quiet."

"He's a five-year-old child, Charlotte!" The disapproval in
his voice was only emphasized by the drying blood at the side
of his mouth. I couldn't bear to look at it.

"I know. I'm sorry! It's all I could think of to do."

"Look, that's good," he said, looking down at his wrists.
"Just leave it loose and I'll get it off when I need to. Do you
have your gun?"

"Yes."

"Give it to me," he said. "Here, give me that pillow and
we'll hide it under there."

"No way! He'll find it. I'm keeping it."

"Char, listen to me!"

That's when I heard the floor creak. I froze. "Well, well, well, what are we whisperin' about?"

We remained silent.

"And by the way," he continued, taking deliberate steps to the window. "You *are* the only other two people in this house, right?" He slowly turned his head to look at Roden, then me.

"Of course," I answered, doing my best to furrow my brow and appear surprised.

"That's funny," he said, laughing toward the window. "'Cause I coulda sworn I heard a kid cryin' somewhere down the hallway. Now, Beautiful, I know you want to stay on my good side, so do be honest with me."

He took three deliberate steps toward me, the hard soles of his boots thudding loudly with each step. "You've got a child here, don't ya?" He asked the question while looking hard into my eyes.

Instead of answering him, though, I looked at Roden, saying, "He must have heard Ambrose."

"Who?" James asked.

"You know who," Roden answered, curtly.

A wave of recognition passed over James's eyes. He threw back his head and laughed before speaking. "You mean, that ol' myth?" He laughed again. "You really expect me to believe that ol' Willow Mansion myth about the little bastard boy runnin' around this house playin' peek-a-boo through the windows. You've got to be kiddin' me. I know you're smarter than that. Even you, Adams, gotta be smarter than that."

"I saw him last night," I answered honestly. "He came to my room, and then he disappeared. I didn't hear him then, but he looked like he'd been crying."

There was a long, awkward silence as James scrutinized my features. *Is he going to shoot me?* I thought. *Is this the end? Will he kill Roden just to punish me?*

James walked toward the window and collapsed in a chair.

"Well, I'll be. Yer tellin' the truth, Beautiful. I can see it in yer pretty brown eyes." He let out another obnoxiously long whistle before continuing. "Ya gotta love Willow's Bend. I sure do, which is why I have no plans of gettin' rescued. No, sir. This is my home. Always will be, 'til kingdom come.

"Now," he continued. "I do believe I've wasted enough time in the company of this murderer. And, Beautiful, if you can't restrain yerself, then I suggest you'd better go on and tell him goodbye."

He waited. I looked at Roden, but realized I couldn't do it. No, I would kill James many times over rather than say goodbye once to Roden. I couldn't even fake it.

"No," I said. "I'd—I'd rather not say goodbye."

James scrutinized my features. "Suit yerself, Beautiful," he said at last. "Although, that really is pretty harsh. Ah, well, guess you didn't care for 'em much after all. Don't blame you."

He held his shotgun up, cocking it before lowering it again.

I stood up anxiously.

"Beautiful, did you happen to know Miss Emily?"

Emily. The infected girl Roden killed to save my life.

"Briefly," I answered.

"Well, now there was a real treasure. It's a shame that such a charm had to be destroyed by this here dog. She was as friendly as they get and beautiful to boot." As he spoke, I detected a hint of genuine, human sympathy. And it was startling to think that it existed in the heart of someone like James. Confusing, actually. And not at all comforting when I knew I had to kill him.

"Welp, time to get up, Adams. I'd sure hate to taint a room in my fancy new house with your blood all over this... is this what you call a Persian rug? Well, I'll be... I daresay I'm gonna like my new abode. Up, Adams. We're goin' to the balcony." I watched James kick Roden in the side again before he struggled to pull himself to a stand. He could barely get up and seemed to lose his balance more than once, causing me to wonder if he had a concussion.

"Beautiful, I'd like for you to come with us. It's not that I don't trust you, but, well, who knows? Maybe I'll help you get over that fear of yours. You just may even learn a thing or two. Let's go."

As I followed behind, Roden began to turn down the hallway toward the second-floor balcony entrance, but James stopped him.

"I don't think so. Nope, we're gonna do this in style, Adams. Upstairs."

And so the three of us climbed the stairs to the third-floor balcony as my heart beat in wild, rapid succession. I wasn't ready. Perhaps I'd never be ready. My hands were clammy, and the metal at my side had warmed up to my skin.

The blast of cold air from the open balcony door almost took my breath away. It was freezing. Precipitation blew at a ninety-degree angle into my face and neck and sleeves with some kind of mist hovering between sleet and snow. On the third-floor balcony there was very little to shelter us from the piercing wind, and my teeth chattered noisily in spite of myself.

James was directing Roden where to stand when it happened. Roden jabbed him with his elbow in the eye and started throwing punches, having dropped the cords before James could notice. But he was weak and falling over already when James recovered and tackled him. I heard their shoes scraping against the concrete, the groaning and punches being thrown as I moved to get out of their way. But then Roden was coughing and spitting out a bloody tooth where he lay on the concrete's cold, hard surface. It was all over pretty quickly.

I told myself to breathe, but the shock of Roden's struggle only heightened my panic.

"All right! All right!" James began to shout, waving his arms in the air and wiping the blood off his face. I was fairly certain at this point that he was losing his mind at last. "You want to do this the hard way? You want to go grovelin' and bleedin' in front of the girl? Okay, then!" He pulled his gun into position and cocked it, just inches away from Roden's head.

"Wait! Wait, please!" I moved forward and gently pushed the barrel of the gun away, imploring to James. "I need to say goodbye, please."

"You said—"

"I changed my mind."

He surveyed me through the sleet, and for a moment I thought he wouldn't budge. His nose was bleeding from

Roden's punch, and I suppose that must have hurt his pride and reignited his fury. But then he seemed to soften a little. "Fine. But make it quick. And don't ever say I never did you any favors."

"Please," I said, trying to look as innocent as possible. "Give us a minute without that gun pointed. I'm scared of guns, remember? It'll only take a minute, I promise."

To my surprise, James rolled his eyes and took a few steps in the other direction. "Women never can make up their minds, and that is a fact," he mumbled. He had the gun down at his side and his back toward us as he leaned against the rail, shaking his head. I couldn't believe the golden opportunity. At least, if there ever is a such thing as a golden opportunity to kill someone, then this was it.

"Roden," I said, looking down at his crumpled form. His eyes shown with the look of someone who had entirely given up. I was shocked to see how quickly they had lost their former light. "I just want you to know that I will remember what you told me..." Such as shooting three rapid shots in the chest. "And I won't let you down." And once I said that, I made the final decision to do what I had to do, because I realized that I could not let him down.

My voice and my hands were both trembling, and there were genuine tears in my eyes for fear of the consequences, fear of death, and most of all...fear that I'd fail. But I made the decision all the same. "I just want to say, goodbye...James."

I pulled out the gun, scratching my stomach painfully in the process, and turned off the safety before James registered the sound of his own name and turned around to face me.

"Now, Beautiful, I don't think you want to do that..." He began with his hands pleading away from his body. But I saw the gun beginning to move in my direction. "Beautiful—"

"My name," I said as I chambered my first bullet. "Is Atsila." With both hands securely supporting the gun, I slid my finger to the trigger, just as Roden had instructed.

One. Two. Three shots in the chest, each one sending a jolt through my entire body. The third sent James backward over the rail of the balcony like a comically large and ugly limp doll before I heard the thud of his body hit the ground below.

A casing landed on my collar bone and burned my skin before I shook it off. I stood still for a while after that. Maybe I was in shock. Perhaps I was waiting for the ringing in my ears to stop or expecting some awful side effect to follow, such as throwing up or passing out. Maybe I expected him to reappear. Or maybe some part of me sensed what was coming.

I heard their sound before I caught sight of them. I'm not sure why, but I took the few steps to the balcony's rail and scanned the horizon until I saw where the barking was coming from. The ravenous, rabid pack of dogs and wolves ascended the hill, having fully merged the domestic pets with the feral beasts until both were transmogrified into one hulking, blood-spattered nightmare. The pack made a beeline for the body, their ragged and muddied coats converging on one another in the rain, flooding the landscape like a dark and moving Monet painting. I averted my eyes and turned to help Roden, realizing that what I wanted was to get as far away from that scene as possible.

As I helped move Roden's broken and fragile body beneath the eaves, I couldn't erase the images from my mind. It was more than I could bear to see the former pets of adults and children alike diving into that hellish feast below. *Who would have ever thought they were capable of this?* But I had to suppose that they were all wolves now. And it was a quiet voice in the back of my mind that whispered, *Maybe we all are.*

I moved to set the gun down on a window's ledge, feeling the metal leave my cold fingers with a stiffness that wasn't there before. Staring down at my trembling palms, I told myself that I was only shivering because it was cold. But the ringing in my ears gave way to the sounds of the beasts below.

CHAPTER EIGHTEEN

"We'll be waiting," I said into the receiver before hanging the phone back up on its hook.

Now that the CDC had confirmed that the rescue team was on its way, I could finally go search for August.

"August?" I called, opening the bathroom door. I opened the cabinet door, but there was no child in sight. Three heart-pounding seconds later, I jerked the shower curtain open to find him curled up in a petrified ball.

"Th—there was a spider..." he said. He was crying so hard that I could just make out the words. "I'm sorry."

"Darling, don't apologize," I managed to gush out. "It's all over, and we're going to be okay now. I won't leave you alone anymore." I continued to brush his hair back and hug him to my chest as he cried, but I knew we had to move.

We made our way to where Roden was still on the floor of the balcony, his clothes soaked through and jaw shivering. As much as I hated for August to see him this way, I knew I didn't have a choice. At least the rain had rinsed away most of the blood from his face.

I heard the faint sounds of the helicopter in the distance as August and I joined Roden in his corner.

"Char, are you okay?" Roden mumbled once I was crouched up close to him. "Is he okay?"

But August managed to wedge himself beneath Roden's arm before I could answer. With his arms wrapped tightly around Roden's chest and his head burrowed against him, I knew there was no need for me to answer. Roden closed his eyes and put his head down as we waited.

ONCE WE WERE securely in the helicopter, I had a strange mixture of emotions as we eased up and away from Willow Mansion. Naturally, I was glad to be leaving. And perhaps it was also natural to cherish all the memories we made there. But it was something less rational, less concrete that welled up inside me as the view grew smaller and more difficult to keep in sight. I was thinking about Daphne du Maurier's novel *Rebecca*. And I suppose a part of me was waiting to see the house go up in flames. It all seemed so...right. I even imagined that it was one of James's old American Spirits that caused the fire, that it started somewhere in the game room.

As I let go of that last real glimpse of the mansion, I saw the gigantic flames licking its vine-trellised walls until it was completely devoured in smoke and ash. In my memory, I can't see it any other way.

August and I were strapped in next to each other, and he somehow managed to fall asleep leaning into my arms. I examined my hands again as he slept, shocked to find that they were no longer trembling. I had not thrown up or passed out. I had no mental or emotional breakdowns. I couldn't help but wonder if I was not calloused or depraved for not experiencing any of these sensations after ending the life of a human being. A series of moral and spiritual questions made their rounds in my mind that day, but most of them didn't last any longer than that. The fact remained that Roden and August were alive right now. And I could never regret that.

I took a deep breath and leaned my head back.

After a while I grew curious and turned to look at the row behind us. A medic was shining a light in Roden's eyes, and there was already a bandage on his left arm and two on his face. I watched his green eyes move left and right as instructed. They abruptly stopped when they caught my gaze, causing me to smile.

ON THE FOLLOWING DAY, and the day after, and the day after that, I assume that the sun must have risen the way it does every single day. That royal diadem must have been lifted into the air again and again, cresting and crowning the day somewhere around noon and slowly falling away again into the folds of darkness and out of sight.

I would imagine that, somewhere, a mallard was padding its webbed feet across shore, making some feeble but spritely quack as it left the faintest of footprints in the wet, grainy sand. Perhaps a frigid breeze had taken its course across Otter Lake and sent ripples sailing in its wake, splashing the beaver as he traversed in and out of his home. Birds sang their muted winter songs, and squirrels scuttled from limb to limb.

Any and perhaps all of these things were happening over the next few days that passed. At least, I imagined they did. I imagined a lot of things as I lay on a metal bed with stark white sheets in a hideous, pale green hospital gown. After all, there were no windows in this room. At least, the glass covering one side of the room might have been a window, but for me it was opaque.

I was hooked up to a monitor, with something dripping down from one of those bags through a tube into my veins. I was given shots. I gave seven blood samples every day for the first week, not to mention the hair follicles and samples of my skin tissue. I grew used to the company of scientists in long white lab coats and thick glasses as I answered question after question about what I saw, how Danny had acted, what Emily looked like, and about the attack. I was physically examined day after day for any sign of infection, any side effects or clues as to the science of what happened out there. And I was given a stack of magazines to thumb through—all the trashy, celebrity gossip types that numb your mind and make you wonder what the world is coming to.

I was eventually transferred to a standard recovery room, which even had a window overlooking the parking lot. I spent a lot of time watching the curious pigeons watch me from the window ledge and thinking about Roden and August and my family. I was relieved to be in a normal hospital setting, knowing that it was a final step before I'd be released to return home. The sterile smell of harshly washed linens and disinfectants hung thick and pervasive in the air as though trying to fight off the unsterile memories of Willow's Bend.

This place, which I knew to be in many ways life giving and life preserving, a place where infants were welcomed into the world and the clinically dead were brought back to life, was such a harsh contradiction to the woods in which I'd made my home for the last few months. Here, life was dictated and enforced, studied and filed away. Here, life was a policy and a procedure, arduously protected from lawsuits and germs. Out there, it was wild and at times feral and unpleasant but unregulated and liberating all the same. And even in the safety of the hospital, I found myself missing the profound richness of the country air. I closed my eyes and revisited that enchanted watering hole again and again, opening my eyes to feel cleaner after diving into its mysterious and organic depths than I ever did after showering in the tiny bathroom in my recovery room.

A nurse walked in to drop something off, mentioning that it was a gift from another patient. It was a slick-covered, thin copy of Henry Vaughan poems. On the back cover, there was still a sticker that indicated it was purchased from the hospital's gift shop.

I flipped the book open to find a note in Roden's handwriting, next to a dog-eared page marking "The World." His message was short:

Hang in there, my dear, heroic friend. I have it on good authority that they can't keep us in here forever.
Your Fellow Inmate,

— R.A.

I think I read that poem at least twenty times that afternoon, compelled by the belief that Roden himself was somehow enveloped in it, that his very heart and soul and life story were echoed by the length of every verse and the beat of every syllable. As I pulled a piece of paper and pen toward me on one of those rickety eating trays, I attempted to understand the way I felt.

What I felt didn't have entirely to do with Roden. I was caught up in Henry Vaughan too, being drawn into that inevitable intimacy of a poet's world, a writer's work. As I had met with Henry James and Leo Tolstoy and Elizabeth Bishop and so many others, I met with Vaughan again and again with each reading of his poetry, taking in pieces of his soul, letting them teach me and change me and shape me as so many others had and maybe more. In that way I took in pieces of Roden's soul too and found that we were a little bit more of the same person than we had been before. Such is literature's power over me, and perhaps its power over everyone, but it resonated over and in me profoundly until at last it was forced to break forth, cresting the barriers and bursting through the remaining reservations, rushing out like a tidal wave in the form of ink onto a blank page.

OVER THE NEXT YEAR and a half, I somehow gravitated back to school, finishing my degree as though nothing more had occurred in the refuge than what was intended to: healing, self-therapy, and writing. Nobody tried to stop me from returning to a normal life. I had a different roommate, a different apartment, a different job, a different view from a different balcony. Life seemed to keep moving in the way that life does, in spite of all I'd seen and done and heard that should have made it stop. The cicadas still sang in the summer while the fireflies danced and winked flirtatiously around the timber, and the persimmons hung onto their tired branches well into the winter, possessing their secrets like some oracles in the form of forks and spoons and knives.

I made an effort to keep up with August and Roden, feeling the magnetic pull to my past like an ocean's tide, causing me to drift back to these two again and again. August was placed in foster care, which neither Roden nor myself were too happy about. However, the family he was placed with seemed nice when we visited, and he seemed happy enough most of the time. But I think the three of us ached for one another's company, and it was most evident in these all too brief moments of time when we were together.

Roden secured a teaching position at a university a couple hours north of where I lived. It was a more prestigious position than he had even imagined for himself, and we knew that the publicity of Willow's Bend had given him an incredible advantage in the environmental science field.

We made a point to meet up for coffee every now and then, Roden and I. It was strange at first, getting to know this person outside of context, outside of the very things that had brought us together. It was strange to find in myself that I longed for his company despite no longer having any real need for it to survive. However natural it might have been to grow attached to someone I'd been thrown together with in the midst of tragedy or desperation, that veil was torn down in the broad daylight of normal life. It was torn down in the lush settings of parks in the springtime and the constant hum of nondescript chatter in dimly lit cafés. And it was impossible to put back up in the summer heat at August's ball games. And yet, I found that I was still drawn to Roden Adams because he was still Roden Adams, and I was still Charlotte Benson.

When Roden and I met, we talked about adjusting to a new life—as that was the only way either of us could see it now—starting over, rebuilding, and living in a world that was forever changed, though perhaps not by us at all. And maybe not even by Willow's Bend. More likely, it had changed in our absence by the slow and steady corrosion of time, like water on a slope. Of course, this change was much more profoundly marked for Roden than it was for me. My sabbatical had been short compared to his, and he had a lot of adjusting to do now that he'd been routed out of the reclusive life he'd chosen since Sophia's death.

We talked mostly about August in the beginning, in between the visits we paid him together. We talked too of Danny, though we hadn't heard from him since that day at the mansion. But when we spoke of him, we always spoke in the present tense, wondering what he was doing, and not if but *how* he had survived so far. I think that we both chose to assume that he had his reasons for not reaching out, or that he only needed a little more time to heal before we would hear from him. And we did not waver in that certainty.

After that we talked about other things, like my thesis, and the house he was thinking of buying close to the university. But if there were any awkward pauses in the conversation, I don't think either of us noticed. There seemed to be this unwritten agreement that silence was okay, that silence was still a sacred thing here in the air between us.

I distinctly recall one such stretch of silence while we sat in the corner of a café on a Saturday afternoon. I had been staring out the window, watching a spring shower that patted the windows and stained the sidewalk like shadowy fingerprints. Reflective drops slipped down the glass in front of me when Roden began to speak.

"That's amazing," he muttered quietly to himself.

"What is?" I asked, turning away from the glass to face him. All signs of his encounter with James had been erased long ago, and in its place were good health. His dark hair set off his green eyes. He had gone for a clean-shaven look for the sake of his teaching career, yet he had somehow maintained his habit of spending countless hours in the sun. He had been teaching a seminar that morning, so his crisp white sleeves were rolled up to his elbows, the familiar scars still visible on the table as he picked up his coffee cup. I had watched him hastily shove his tie into the pocket of his slacks as he walked into the café, evidently glad to see the work week come to an end.

"You didn't even notice, did you?" he asked, wearing a curious gaze.

"Notice what?" I asked, feeling a vague smile on my lips as I contemplated his perpetual inner conflict between the sharply dressed, well-liked professor and the antisocial shooting instructor with calloused palms and muddy boots.

"The siren," he answered, his eyebrows reflecting his surprise. "That ambulance went by a couple minutes ago, and you didn't even flinch."

"Oh," I said, astonished. I vaguely remembered the ambulance.

He smiled from across the table. "You've come a long way, Charlotte."

I turned back to the window and the *tap-taps* of soothing raindrops as I considered that he was right. That looming sense of danger and tragedy that had haunted me since childhood had evaporated completely. The darkest memories of my childhood now gave way to the abundance of brighter days, to glistening summers with my family, and a true sense of comfort and security. My memory of Gavin only lingered with the fragrant sweetness of first love and a tenderness for the life that he had lived, as brief as it may have been.

"Yeah, I guess I have," I acknowledged at last.

"I'm glad," he replied. His features knitted into an expression of sincerity and affection. "I'm so glad." He reached across the table to where my hand had been playing with a folded paper napkin. He took my hand in his, holding it there for the first time as though it were the hundredth time, and exhaled a deep breath as he turned back to the window and watched the rain fall to the pavement. We fell into that familiar silence once more.

When Roden and I weren't together, I distinctly felt that a part of myself was missing. Not in the same way I felt when Gavin died. No, the missing part was alive and well. It was just much too far away. It was an incessant, pervasive aching, and I often wondered or rather hoped that he felt it too.

I suppose that if there is one good thing about heartache, it makes for good poetry. And I always knew that wherever I went and whatever I did with my life, I'd be writing poetry. I'd be writing verses to depict those subtle, slow, seeping pains of missing someone every day—whether it be for the love of that person or merely the memory of losing them, or even the memory of *almost* losing them. I'd be writing down my fears, stale, aged fears, distorted or even conquered, but still giving off that effluvium of tragedy and harshness. I'd be writing about redemption and resurrection and miracles. I'd be writing about Roden and August and Danny and Gavin.

But when I wasn't writing, such as on those cool early summer evenings when I was compelled to leave the bedroom window open and listen to the wind in the trees and the hum of lawn mowers and locusts and distant voices, I'd lay there with my head against the cool of the pillow and close my eyes. Like that night in the mansion, I'd start willing them both back to me—Roden and August—silently pleading them to come find me, to come knock on my door, to come sit and talk and be.

And I'd think that someday...perhaps someday I'd learn to let go of my dream— the one where the three of us were together again.

But not tonight.

For tonight, I'd dream.

EPILOGUE

It is strange the way some memories live with you long after they should have died away. I awoke from vivid dreams of standing on the bridge with Danny, staring out over the quiet river, watching its serpentine form snake back behind copses of towering trees, the stoic cypresses with their multicolored rings marking off time at the midriff.

And when I awoke, I could never quite remember what was said or done, only that Danny was there and alive. And that wolves were howling in the distance.

Psalm 13:5-6
But I trust in your loving kindness.
My heart rejoices in your salvation.
I will sing to Yahweh,
Because he has been good to me.

ABOUT 'THE AUTHOR

Photo by Jordan Mobley

NATASHA WITTMAN is a poet, former newspaper columnist, and irrepressible writer. As an Oklahoma native, she has a unique passion for the landscapes and people of her home state, which is a driving force for many of the scenes and characters in her writing. The seed of the story for *Wolves and Men* was inspired by a particularly haunting dream. Natasha writes and lives in Edmond, Oklahoma, with her husband Micah and daughter Evelyn, where she enjoys classic literature, good coffee, and family. *Wolves and Men* is her debut novel. You can find out more about Natasha on her blog: steepandsavor.blogspot.com